To DAD
LOVE Grace e BRAD
2022 x

T
PORTCHESTER CASTLE MURDERS

A gripping crime thriller full of twists

PAULINE ROWSON

The Solent Murder Mysteries Book 6

Originally published as
Footsteps on the Shore

JOFFE BOOKS

Revised edition 2022
Joffe Books, London
www.joffebooks.com

First published by Fathom in Great Britain in 2012
as *Footsteps on the Shore*

Cover art by Dee Dee Book Covers

ISBN: 978-1-80405-157-3

This book is dedicated to Jim Gross, Hilary Johnson and Amy Myers for their unstinting support, encouragement and belief in me; to my publisher for making it possible; and to my readers, with many grateful thanks.

CHAPTER ONE

Friday, 13 March

'Where is everyone?' Inspector Andy Horton swept into the CID room at Portsmouth station and addressed the wiry, dark-haired figure leaning back in his chair, chewing gum and tapping a pencil thoughtfully on his chin.

'You're looking at him,' Sergeant Cantelli answered, throwing the pencil down and sitting up.

Horton frowned. 'And DC Walters?'

'Probably in the canteen. Must be all of an hour since he last ate, and you know how faint he gets if he has to go too long without food.' Cantelli smiled, obviously expecting one in return, but Horton wasn't in the mood. Cantelli's expression darkened. 'What's wrong, Andy? You look as though you'd like to commit murder.'

'I would, and of the mindless moron who did this.' He thrust a piece of paper into Cantelli's hand. On it was a drawing of a diagonal cross with a broken circle etched above it.

'What's it mean?' asked Cantelli, puzzled, turning it this way and that to study it.

'No idea, but some idiot thought it a huge joke to scratch it on my Harley.'

Cantelli's head shot up and his dark eyes widened. 'Blimey, no wonder you're in a foul mood. Who would do that?'

'I intend to find out.' Horton waltzed through to his office, wrenching off his leather biker's jacket and slinging it on the coat stand. 'And when I do, I'll string him up by the balls.'

'It's not a Hell's Angel emblem, is it? Harleys and all that,' asked Cantelli, following him.

'A Hell's Angel wouldn't deface a Harley, not even if he hated my guts. He'd scratch that symbol on my face or tattoo it on my private parts.'

'Perhaps it doesn't mean anything and it's just some sicko's idea of fun.'

'Well, I'm not laughing.' Horton's fury was undiminished since first sight of the abomination that morning. On discovering it he'd raced back to the marina office and demanded to view the security CCTV tapes of the car park above the pontoon where he lived on a borrowed yacht, but there were no sightings of the graffiti artist and no car unaccounted for by Eddie in the office. In fact, there were only three cars in the car park after 10 p.m. last night, when Horton had returned to his boat following a long and tedious day dealing with pointless paperwork and Portsmouth's criminal classes, whose sole pleasure in life was making other people's lives as miserable as their own wretched existence. The only bright spot had been yesterday afternoon, when he had viewed a yacht that he hoped would soon become his permanent home.

He simply couldn't believe a boat owner, either a visiting one or an existing berth holder, could have been responsible for the act of vandalism on his Harley, but he got a list of visitors to the marina from Eddie. There was only one, a Peter Medlow on Sunrise. Horton located the yacht, a classic 1950 Hillyard, which made him even more doubtful that its owner could have defaced a Harley Davidson. A man who chose to sail such a revered yacht couldn't spoil an iconic machine. But being a police officer, he knew that no one was above suspicion, not even the Pope, though he doubted he'd be visiting Southsea Marina by boat on a chilly, still March night. Medlow had turned out to be a friendly widower in his early sixties, a retired bank manager with a self-effacing manner. Hardly Horton's graffiti artist.

Cantelli said, 'Maybe someone's jealous of you.'

Horton sat at a desk so overflowing with paperwork that it looked in danger of collapse, and eyed Cantelli incredulously. 'Barney, I live on a borrowed boat, I'm about to get divorced. My estranged wife won't let me see, let alone speak to my daughter, who she's intent on sending away to a boarding school against her wishes, and the only woman I thought I could get close to has put herself beyond my reach by returning to Sweden. How could anyone possibly be jealous of me?'

'Thea Carlsson's still in touch with you though, isn't she?' Cantelli asked, throwing himself into the seat opposite Horton.

Horton shook his head. 'No.' He felt a mixture of sadness and anger that the slender, fair woman he'd rescued from a burning building less than two months ago had turned her back on him. He had hoped something might come of their feelings for one another, but he should have known better. They both carried too much baggage. In a moment of bitter disappointment he had accused her of running away from her pain — her brother's death — but she had calmly replied, 'Isn't that what you've been doing for over thirty years?' She'd been referring to his mother's disappearance when he was ten. She was right; and even though two recent cases had opened up the past for him and given him leads, he'd not pursued them. He hadn't even looked at the missing persons file since returning to duty four weeks ago. He felt a stab of guilt, and then anger that he should be made to feel guilty when his mother had deserted him, not the other way around.

'It could be a threat then,' Cantelli posed, frowning with concern as he once again studied the symbol. 'Some kind of coded warning perhaps?'

Horton had already considered this, along with who would threaten him and why. He had enemies — who didn't in this job? — and although he sincerely hoped that the more dangerous of them were banged up, he wasn't going to bet on it, not with the way the justice system seemed to be operating. But one particular villain had sprung to mind, and one he had never seen. Neither did he know his real identity, only that the head of the Intelligence Directorate, Detective Chief Superintendent Sawyer, called him Zeus because he wielded his thunderbolts to control his family of crooks and kill anyone who stepped a millimetre out of line. And that brought Horton right back to thoughts of his mother, because Sawyer had told him she might once have been associated with Zeus. Sawyer had hoped to enlist Horton's help in running Zeus to ground but Horton had refused, not out of fear for himself but because he knew the Zeuses of this world wouldn't hesitate to get at him by hurting his daughter, and that was a no-brainer as far as he was concerned. But, he reasoned, an international villain like Zeus wouldn't be arsing around scratching symbols on his Harley; the threat would have been much more physical and painful.

Cantelli said, 'Someone at the university might know what that symbol means.'

'It means some brainless lowlife gets his kicks from vandalizing other people's property. And I'm going to find out who it is.' Reaching for his phone, Horton added, 'I shall view every CCTV tape from all the cameras in the area, including those along the seafront and—'

'Inspector Horton!'

Cantelli started and jumped up, while Horton quickly stifled the groan that had automatically sprung to his lips as he stared at the taut, thin figure of the head of CID, Detective Chief Inspector Lorraine Bliss, who was standing in his doorway and looking about as friendly as the Grimpen Mire. She wasn't due back from her secondment at HQ for another fortnight, so what the devil was she doing here now?

He replaced the phone and flashed Cantelli a look. By the sergeant's expression it was clear, though, he was equally surprised by Bliss's sudden reappearance. Maybe this was a short visit, Horton thought hopefully, and she'd quickly return to HQ where she had been examining pay and performance.

Pointedly consulting her watch, she said curtly, 'You're late.'

Horton stared at her hollowed face and sharp green eyes, resenting both her manner and her comment. With an effort he bit his tongue to stem the automatic retort, the desire to remind her of the countless times he'd worked late, come in early or during his off-duty days.

'My office. Now.' She turned on her heel and marched away, leaving him to stare at the light brown ponytail, the narrow backside in the tight black skirt, and the head held so high that he wondered if there was something stuck on the ceiling of the CID operations room.

'What's wrong with her office?' Cantelli said.

'Hopefully it's infected with a plague of locusts,' Horton said with bitterness, rising. 'I take back everything I ever said about Friday the thirteenth being a load of superstitious old bollocks. Get hold of those CCTV tapes for me, Barney. And find DC Walters before the Wicked Witch of the North notices he's missing.'

Horton dived into the corridor, wondering if Bliss's colleagues at HQ had got as sick of her as he was. He'd only worked under her for a brief spell before she'd been spirited away but it had been long enough for them both to recognize that friendship, or even a civil working partnership, was about as likely as world peace. He considered her to be petty, vindictive, bureaucratic, and ambitious to the point that she didn't care which of her subordinates or colleagues she dropped in the shit. She clearly considered him embittered at being overlooked for promotion, insubordinate for daring to disagree with her, and a maverick for not always conforming to a rule book which was already a joke among most police officers, and fast becoming a rather sick and sad one with the majority of the public.

He pushed open her office door prepared for a bollocking and was surprised to find that Bliss wasn't alone. Two pairs of eyes — other than Bliss's critical green ones — swivelled to study him and neither pair was very friendly. He recognized the square-set woman in heavily rimmed glasses as Beverley Attworth, the head of the probation service. The man beside her he didn't know. Dressed in faded, patched jeans and a shapeless brown jumper, he was in his late twenties with shoulder-length black hair framing a pinched unshaven face. 'Sit,' Bliss commanded.

Maybe he should bark, Horton thought, taking the vacant chair the other side of Bliss's immaculately tidy desk beside Beverley Attworth. He gave her a brief smile but didn't get one in return, which was hardly surprising because he didn't think he'd ever seen her smile. Still, he didn't have much to smile about at the moment either, he thought, recalling with suppressed fury that emblem on his Harley.

Bliss said, 'You know Ms Attworth. This is her colleague, Matt Boynton.'

Boynton's fleshy lips gave a nervous twitch which Horton interpreted as a smile, though it could have been wind. Judging by the tension in the room, Horton thought that whatever this was about, it wasn't good.

Abruptly, Bliss announced, 'Luke Felton is missing.'

Felton? Horton quickly searched his brain for some recollection of the name. Fortunately, it came to him instantly. 'The Natalie Raymonds murder in September 1997,' he answered promptly, drawing a stunned look from Bliss. He'd been a sergeant seconded to the vice squad at the time, and Luke Felton had been found in the doorway of a house they'd gone to raid, which had been suspected of being a brothel. Felton had been suffering withdrawal symptoms from heroin and was wanted in connection with the murder of Natalie Raymonds on the coastal path on Hayling Island. Felton had had nothing to do with the brothel, but because he'd been found at the house it had scuppered the raid. DCI Sean Lovell, had been on the Raymonds case, a man Horton had both worked with and respected, and who, he recalled, had died suddenly of a heart attack before Felton had been convicted and sentenced to prison. Horton couldn't remember how many years Felton had got, but surely it was too soon for his release. But Bliss had said 'missing'.

'Don't tell me he's escaped,' Horton groaned.

'He was granted parole in January after serving ten years of his fourteen-year sentence. He was given an automatic conditional release licence on the second of February.'

Horton eyed Bliss incredulously before swinging his gaze to Beverley Attworth. She shifted her large backside and looked both hostile and defensive.

'He'd been a model prisoner,' she said defiantly. 'All his reports were favourable. He was truly repentant for what he'd done and he'd served over two-thirds of his sentence.'

'Oh, that's all right then,' Horton answered flippantly.

'Inspector!'

Bliss could 'Inspector' him all she liked. 'Why weren't we told he was out?'

Attworth answered. 'Luke was assessed as a level one category. He's deemed a low risk to the community. There was no need to place him on the Dangerous Persons Database—'

'Hang on,' Horton protested, his hackles rising even further. 'We are talking about a murderer. I would say he posed a very serious threat to the public.'

Matt Boynton sat forward and brushed his floppy hair off his forehead. 'Luke Felton's been clean since undergoing the prison drug treatment programme. He's completely reformed.'

There's no such animal; once a villain, always a villain, thought Horton. 'He's on the streets where he could easily have access to heroin, or any class A drug, and once hooked he could kill for five pence if he thought it would buy him his next fix.'

But Boynton was shaking his head vigorously. He opened his mouth to reply, only Attworth got there first. 'Luke Felton was being closely monitored—'

'By whom?' Horton scoffed.

Attworth and Boynton exchanged glances. Yeah, by nobody. Tersely Horton said, 'Where's Felton living?'

Boynton answered. 'Crown House. It's a supervised hostel in the city.'

Horton knew it well. It was in an area that was renowned for druggies and dealers; not the best place to house a former drug addict. As if reading his mind, Boynton added, 'I don't for a minute believe Luke's returned to drugs, for the simple reason that two weeks ago he managed to secure a very good job at Kempton Marine.'

Horton quickly covered his surprise. That was his father-in-law's company, where his soon-to-be ex-wife, Catherine, worked as marketing manager and her fat lover, Edward Shawford, as sales manager. Would this investigation bring him into contact with her? He tensed at the thought. He hadn't seen Catherine since January and that had hardly been a joyous occasion. On impulse, and fuelled by anger and disappointment at being denied access to his daughter on Christmas Eve, as Catherine had agreed, he'd gone haring up to Heathrow Airport to meet them on their return from spending Christmas and New Year at Catherine's parents' villa in Cyprus. The memory of how Emma had run into his arms caused a lump in Horton's throat and a stab at his heart. Briskly he pulled himself up and, addressing Beverley Attworth, said, 'When exactly did Felton go missing?'

'He didn't show up for work on Wednesday or Thursday. Kelly Masters, the personnel officer at Kempton's, called Matt this morning, who called me after checking with the hostel that Luke wasn't there. The hostel supervisor, Mr Harmsworth, says he hasn't seen Luke since Tuesday morning when he left for work.'

Horton rapidly ran through the litany of crimes since Felton's disappearance but there had been no incidents involving serious assault. Only the usual pub punch-ups and domestics, unless something had happened on his patch last night, and he hadn't had time to check that.

Boynton quickly added, 'Luke was very excited about his job. He wouldn't abscond or slide back into crime and miss such a chance.'

'Maybe the temptation was too great,' Horton said. 'Perhaps he was offered drugs and couldn't help himself.'

'No.'

There was no shifting Boynton. Horton tried another idea. 'Maybe he met up with a friend, or a girl, and is shacked up with one of them?'

Boynton shook his head. 'He hasn't any girlfriends or friends in the area.'

Horton eyed him sceptically; he didn't believe that for a moment. He said, 'Do Natalie Raymonds' family know that Felton's been released on licence?'

Boynton answered. 'I spoke to Julian Raymonds, her husband. He's remarried.'

No reason why he shouldn't, thought Horton. Perhaps it had helped him to get over the trauma of his wife's death.

Beverley Attworth added, 'Natalie's mother died three years after Natalie was killed. Her father went to live with his son in Australia. Luke's sister, Olivia Danbury, and his brother Ashley Felton, were also contacted about Luke's release — their parents are dead. They both live locally and said they wanted nothing to do with Luke, so I don't think he could have gone there.'

'But you haven't physically checked?'

'Of course not,' she said huffily.

Which meant they would. At a nod from Bliss, Horton rose. Crisply, Bliss said, 'Mr Boynton will provide you with all the information you need about Luke Felton.' Boynton scrambled up and smiled sheepishly at Horton as Bliss continued, 'We keep this from the media, Inspector. I do not want members of the public unduly concerned.'

And they would be if the press got hold of the story and blew it up in their usual scaremongering style. For once Horton wouldn't really blame them if they did. Felton shouldn't have been released in the first place, but now that he had been they'd better find him, and quickly, before he committed another crime. Or perhaps Felton had already killed again and was in hiding, or lying somewhere in a drug-induced stupor.

Horton pushed open the door to the CID room leaving Boynton to trail in after him. Walters had returned from the canteen and Horton swiftly made the introductions, and brought Cantelli and Walters up to speed. Even before he'd finished speaking, he could see that Cantelli recollected the case, which didn't surprise him; what Cantelli didn't remember wasn't usually worth putting on the back of a postage stamp.

Cantelli said, 'The murder of Natalie Raymonds wasn't Felton's first offence. He was convicted of assault and robbery on an elderly woman collecting her pension in August 1995, for which he received a community sentence. He was a middle-class, well-educated young man in his mid-twenties whose parents couldn't believe it of their respectable son until they were told he was a druggie.'

Horton was even more impressed by Cantelli's complete recall and must have shown it, because Cantelli quickly added, 'I wasn't working on either case but Charlotte, my wife,' he explained for Boynton's benefit, 'knew Luke's mother, Sonia. They trained as nurses together and worked on the same ward before Charlotte gave up work completely when Sadie was born. They kept in touch until Sonia Felton died, which wasn't long after Luke was convicted for Natalie's murder.'

Horton turned to Walters. 'Any reports of violent assaults last night?'

'Nothing with Felton's MO on it.'

'Get the case notes on the Natalie Raymonds murder, and apply to see Luke Felton's prison files, including his medical records. Find out who visited him inside and start checking to see if he's contacted any of them. Cantelli and I will talk to the sister and brother.' To Boynton, Horton said, 'Did Felton have any girlfriends before prison?'

'I don't know. I don't think so.'

Again Horton turned to Walters. 'Call the hospitals in the area to see if he's had an accident. I take it you haven't already done that?' Horton tossed at Boynton.

'I didn't even think of it. I suppose it's a possibility.' Boynton looked concerned.

'A remote one, unless he had no ID on him and has got amnesia or is unconscious. Do you have a recent photograph of him?'

'On file.'

'Email it to DC Walters the moment you return to your office. Walters, when you get it, circulate it to all officers.'

Walters nodded. Horton again addressed Boynton. 'If you hear from him, or learn anything about his whereabouts, let us know immediately.'

With a flick of his hair and a sniff, Boynton nodded in agreement before slouching off. Horton glanced down at the paper on Cantelli's desk containing the drawing of the symbol etched on his Harley. That would have to wait. Stuffing it in his pocket he said, 'Let's see what the hostel supervisor can tell us about Luke Felton.'

CHAPTER TWO

Not a great deal, it transpired. Harmsworth had last seen Luke Felton on Tuesday morning at about eight thirty when Luke had been on his way to work. Following the hostel supervisor's eighteen-stone frame up the narrow stairs in the gothic-style Edwardian building, which was as out of place in the middle of the run-down council flats and seedy second-hand shops as a pensioner in a night club, Horton realised that one thing was certain — Harmsworth wouldn't have been a regular visitor to Luke Felton's room on the third floor. Horton doubted he'd even checked to see if Felton had been in his room when Matt Boynton had called him.

'I would have thought Felton would have been under curfew,' Cantelli said.

'This isn't a prison,' Harmsworth wheezed over his shoulder.

More's the pity, thought Horton. 'Do you live on the premises?'

'I've got a flat on the ground floor just behind the office, but officially I only work during the day. I'm not their nursemaid,' he panted defensively. 'They've got a key to the front door and to their own rooms. Luke was one of the better ones though. Polite, friendly, no drink and no drugs as far as I could tell,' he added hastily. 'He was grateful to be free, and swore he'd never do anything to risk being sent back to prison.'

'They all say that,' Cantelli said wearily.

'No, Luke was different,' Harmsworth answered vehemently. 'You could tell he meant it.'

Luke Felton had certainly got his probation officer and this man wrapped around his little finger. They climbed the rest of the stairs in silence, or rather with Harmsworth panting like a rhino in childbirth. At the top he reached for his keys and unlocked the door.

Stepping inside, Horton was immediately struck by how clinically tidy the room was. Luke Felton obviously observed prison routine here. Its furnishings were plain and spartan; along with the wardrobe, there was a three-drawer chest and a single made-up bed. There were no dirty underpants or sweaty socks lying on the grey tiled floor; no clothes hanging out of the cheap melamine wardrobe; no books and no technology, not even a television set. Horton wondered what Felton did with himself in his spare time. This certainly didn't look like the room of a drug addict.

'He should come and keep house for us,' Cantelli exclaimed admiringly.

Harmsworth made to flop on the bed but a look from Horton prevented him. Instead, the fat man took out a handkerchief, mopped his crimson face and propped himself up against the door post, puffing like an old steam engine. 'Luke is very particular,' he gasped.

Yeah, and how would you know, thought Horton, crossing to the wardrobe as Cantelli took the chest of drawers.

'Was Felton friendly with anyone in particular?' Cantelli asked, rifling through the drawers.

Harmsworth considered this for a moment while Horton flicked through the meagre belongings in the wardrobe: a checked shirt, pair of cargoes, trainers and that seemed to be it. No discarded needles or drugs, not even a can of lager.

'He seemed to get on well with Tyler Yarland,' Harmsworth answered. 'Yarland's on bail for car theft and vandalism. Comes from a rough background, parents dumped him into social services care when he was a kid and he's been pushed from pillar to post ever since.'

And there but for the grace of God go I, or could have gone, thought Horton, pulling down the sports bag from the top of the wardrobe. He'd had some scrapes with the law as a kid until a foster father, who had been a policeman, had changed the course of his life for ever. There was nothing in the bag. He glanced at Cantelli, who shook his head to indicate he'd found nothing of any note in the chest of drawers.

'Where's Tyler Yarland now?' Horton asked, as Cantelli lifted the mattress and checked under the bed.

Harmsworth glanced at his watch. 'Probably still in bed. Most of them don't get up until midday. There's not much to get up for.'

'Except to collect their social security giro and buy booze and fags,' Horton quipped.

Harmsworth shrugged his fat shoulders. 'Yarland's room's the third one along the corridor.'

Cantelli slipped out and Horton crossed to the window. They were at the rear of the building, overlooking the small car park. Horton watched a woman of about twenty-five emerge from one of the run-down flats opposite. She was pushing a crying baby, with a child of about Emma's age, eight, trailing miserably behind. Why wasn't the child in school? Classes had begun two hours ago.

He thought of the boarding school that Catherine wanted to send Emma to and recalled with anguish his daughter's sobs on the telephone because she didn't want to go. He'd visited Northover School without Catherine's knowledge two weeks ago, and to his annoyance, had found it excellent. He'd been looking for a reason to hate it and certainly to rescue Emma from its clutches. But it was small, homely and comfortable, and had facilities to die for. It was also select and expensive, and the fact that his father-in-law, Luke Felton's employer, had agreed with Catherine to pay the fees stuck in Horton's craw. It was obvious to him what they were trying to do, and that was to ease him out of his daughter's life. Well, they won't succeed, he thought with furious determination. It was his responsibility and pleasure to make sure his daughter got the best of everything, and that would certainly be a darn sight more than he'd ever had as a child, including love.

His mind flashed back to his own childhood. This was his inheritance: a bleak and barren urban landscape, a tough school, the streets his playground, a succession of children's homes and foster parents, emptiness, longing and anger. Yet there had been love and laughter with his mother before that terrible November day when he had waited for her to come home from work at the casino and she hadn't. And he recalled again a memory that had returned recently while he'd been on the Isle of Wight. She'd turned, laughing, and called to him as they were walking across the golf course at Bembridge. Over the last few weeks, he'd tried to remember more of that day and whether they had been alone or accompanied by a man, but the memory had dissipated leaving him no further clues as to her whereabouts.

Hastily he turned his mind back to Luke Felton. He could take trips down his miserable memory lane in his own time. He wondered how Felton had got into drugs, and why. Was it for the experience? Had it started in a small way and he'd then gotten addicted to harder stuff? Or had he been influenced by the wrong crowd, jeered and goaded into experimenting, and hadn't wanted to lose face? Whatever had happened, it had made him desperate and violent, and an innocent woman had lost her life.

'Does Felton talk about his crime?' he asked, turning back to Harmsworth.

'No, and I didn't ask. That's not my job.'

What is, wondered Horton. As if reading his mind, Harmsworth added defensively, 'I'm here to make sure the place doesn't get trashed.'

'A caretaker then,' Horton said, but his sarcasm was lost on Harmsworth. 'Is anything of Felton's missing? Clothes, mobile phone?'

Harmsworth shrugged his fat shoulders.

'Does Felton have a mobile phone?' If it had GPS then it could pinpoint where he was.

'I've not seen him with one.'

That didn't necessarily mean he didn't have one. 'What was Felton wearing when you last saw him?'

Harmsworth's face screwed up in the effort to recall. 'Green cargoes, trainers, a T-shirt — grey I think — and a navy blue jacket.'

Horton jotted this down and said, 'We're waiting for a recent photograph of Felton from his probation officer, do you have one?'

'On the computer.'

Harmsworth locked the door and handed Horton the key. If Luke returned then he'd have his own key, and if he didn't then Horton didn't want any Tyler, Wayne or Dwayne wandering in and helping themselves to what there was of Luke Felton's meagre possessions.

He followed Harmsworth to his office on the ground floor at the front of the building in time to see the back of a slight, scruffily dressed man with greasy black hair scuttle out of the door. He'd know that shambling shifty figure anywhere: Ronnie Rookley. Through Harmsworth's office window Horton watched Rookley dash across the road and dive into a dirty café opposite.

Turning back, Horton asked Harmsworth if Felton had used the payphone he'd seen in the hall.

'It's been out of order for three weeks. And he hasn't used my office phone.' Harmsworth eased his bulk into the swivel chair behind his desk in the corner of the shabby office and tapped into his computer. A minute later Horton was staring at a printed picture of Luke Felton. He saw a man in his late thirties with fair cropped hair, a square-jawed open face, and blue eyes that held no fear or wariness, but weren't cockily confident either. Horton thought back to the Luke Felton he'd seen in September 1997, and how then he had looked much the same as any other junkie: dirty, dishevelled, unshaven, pale-skinned and spotty, but with blood on his clothes — blood which had turned out to be Natalie Raymonds'.

Cantelli sauntered in. 'Yarland claims he hasn't seen Felton since Monday night and then only in passing. He has no idea why he's missing. I spoke to a couple of others who didn't even seem to know who Felton was, let alone when they last saw him.'

That didn't surprise Horton. In this kind of place, and with these kinds of men, they'd meet a wall of silence. It probably wasn't even worth sending officers to question them.

With instructions to Harmsworth to call them if Luke Felton showed up, Horton gestured to Cantelli to follow him. Stepping out of Crown House by the front entrance, Horton handed Cantelli the photograph of Felton. Then, nodding at the café opposite, he said, 'I'm hungry.'

Cantelli eyed it, horrified. 'We'll get food poisoning.'

'Better stick to coffee and conversation then, though it's more likely to be expletives and grunts. Recognize that disgusting figure?' Horton asked, as they dodged through the traffic and stood outside the café.

The slight man at the counter turned, saw them, started nervously and dived for the door, but Horton reached it first. As he pushed it open Cantelli muttered, 'Thought I could smell manure in Crown House.'

'When did they let you out, Ronnie?' Horton said loudly, blocking the man's exit, and forcing him to slide into a chair at a table close to the door. Cantelli crossed to the big balding man behind the counter, who was eyeing them like a bouncer in a night club looking for a reason to eject them and not much caring how trivial it might be. Breathing could be enough, thought Horton.

'Keep your voice down, can't you?' the small man with the pock-marked skin muttered, glancing over his shoulder.

'Ronnie, we're the only sad bastards in here!' Horton eyed the heavily tattooed man in his mid-fifties, sporting more earrings than a jeweller's window, sitting beside him. He wondered what criminal activity Rookley was plotting this time, because knowing him of old, he wasn't in here for his health.

'There's him.' Rookley jerked his head in the direction of big belly man. Horton studied the hard-featured face behind the counter. Horton didn't know him but maybe Cantelli did.

'Who is he?'

'Jack.'

'Jack who?'

'How the fuck should I know?'

'Because you're a crook, a thief, a liar and used to dealing with the low-life scum of Portsmouth. And you were talking to him about five seconds ago. I could see you through the window.'

'I was ordering a drink.'

Horton eyed the empty table in front of them. 'Didn't realize it was table service,' he said sarcastically. 'So what were you doing at Crown House?'

'I live there.'

'Since when?'

Rookley shifted his scrawny figure. 'October. I'm out on licence. Got a year of my sentence left and I don't want nothing to bugger it up and go back inside.'

'Did you hear that, Sergeant?' Horton boomed, causing Rookley to flinch. 'Ronnie's out on licence and reformed.'

'That just goes to show miracles can happen,' replied Cantelli, placing three chipped mugs on the table, one of which he pushed towards Rookley. Rookley peered at the dark brown liquid as if it were poison. Cantelli said, 'They're out of Earl Grey.' He pulled up a seat to the right of Rookley, blocking his other exit route.

Rookley shot a nervous look at the balding proprietor. Horton thought, if he's that scared of him why come here?

'Luke Felton,' he said abruptly.

'Who?'

'Don't give me that crap. You live in the same building.'

'So what?'

'Where is he?'

Rookley shrugged his narrow shoulders. 'In bed?'

'He's missing.'

Rookley sniffed and relinquished eye contact. 'So?'

'When did you last see him?'

'Dunno.'

But Horton knew Rookley was lying. Rookley's eyes scanned the café and then focused on the window facing the street. Horton saw him stiffen. Following the direction of his gaze, he saw a tall black man lounging against the lamp post on the corner of a narrow street outside the council's housing office; his head was shaking in rhythm to the music that was plugged into his ears, a baseball cap was rammed low over his brow and his hands were thrust deep into the pockets of a large black leather bomber jacket.

Rookley quickly buried his face in the mug and swallowed a mouthful of tea before pulling a face. Horton didn't blame him. It smelt like shit and looked like something that had come from the sewage farm at Bedhampton. Horton valued his throat and stomach too highly to drink the coffee that Cantelli had bought him, and the sergeant hadn't attempted to lift his cracked mug to his lips.

'We were talking about Luke Felton,' pressed Horton.

'I've got to go.' Rookley half rose.

'Sit down,' Horton commanded quietly but firmly. 'Unless you cooperate I will ask questions incredibly loudly before I take you to the station, where I will—'

'OK, you've made your point. I heard something, that's all.'

'Like what?' Horton's patience was wearing a little thin. It was time to squeeze some information out of the runt. The black man had gone.

Rookley licked his lips and dashed another glance at big belly man. 'Not here,' he hissed.

'Just tell me where Luke is,' Horton sighed.

Rookley shifted. 'Can't now, but I might be able to tonight.' Was he bullshitting? Horton thought it highly probable. Rookley just wanted shot of him. As if reading his mind Rookley quickly added, 'I need to ask around a bit.' Horton didn't believe it for one minute. He was stalling.

Why? But Horton said, 'OK, where?'

'Milton Locks. Nine o'clock.'

'Why there?'

'Why not?'

'How do I know you'll be there?'

'Because you know where I'm living and I don't want you sniffing around after me.'

Horton quickly weighed up whether to press him, decided it would be a waste of time and scraped back his chair. 'I'll be there. Just make sure you are, Ronnie.'

Rookley scurried away without looking back. Horton watched big belly man's eyes follow him before they swivelled back to Horton. The hatred in them was unmistakable, but Horton didn't let that worry him. Crossing to him, Horton said, 'When did you last see Luke Felton?'

'Fuck off, copper.'

Horton held his hostile stare a moment longer before obliging.

'Do you know the café owner?' he asked Cantelli when they were outside.

Cantelli shook his head. Big belly man now had a mobile phone pressed to his ear. 'Give me the photograph of Felton and keep your eye on handsome in there.'

Horton slipped across the road as the traffic lights changed and darted down the narrow side street by the housing office. Turning right into a small car park at the rear of the run-down shops and flats he found what he was looking for: a dark saloon car. Inside it was the large black man who'd been lounging against the wall by the housing office. Checking no one was watching him, Horton opened the passenger door and climbed in.

'What the hell were you doing in there, Andy?'

'Looking for him.' Horton thrust the photograph of Luke Felton at Hans Olewbo of the drug squad. 'Have you seen him?'

Olewbo looked cagey.

'When was the last time?' pressed Horton.

After a moment Olewbo said, 'Monday night about seven.'

'What was he doing?'

'Entering Crown House.'

'Front or back entrance?'

'Back. Why?'

'And you didn't see him leave Tuesday morning at eight thirty?'

'A man's got to sleep.'

'You know he used to be into heroin?'

'I haven't seen him dealing or receiving. What's he done?'

Horton told him, and why he'd followed Rookley into the café.

Olewbo cursed. 'Wish someone had told us.'

'I just have. So what's your interest here, Hans? Is it Rookley, Crown House or big belly man in the café? Or maybe all three,' Horton added, when he didn't get an immediate answer.

Hans checked his rear-view mirror. After a moment he said, 'We've got information that someone is bringing in a shed load of crack and circulating it to the kids on the estate. That café could be the pick-up point. Jack Belton, the café proprietor, has a conviction for drug dealing in London. He was released three years ago and has been in Portsmouth for two years and things round here have got a hell of a lot worse in the last eighteen months. We received information which led us to him and set up surveillance on Monday morning, but so far, sod all. What did Rookley tell you?'

'Nothing. Could Luke Felton have gained easy access to drugs?'

Olewbo gave him an incredulous stare. 'They're giving it out like lemon sherbet around here.'

'OK, daft question,' Horton admitted. He opened the car door, knowing he'd get nothing more from Hans. Brightly he said, 'Hope I haven't blown your cover.'

'I'll survive. Now bugger off.'

Horton found Cantelli where he'd left him. 'Handsome's got customers,' Cantelli said, nodding at the café. 'Lads with hoods. They bought Coke. The drink in a can,' he added with a grin to Horton's surprised look. 'Though that might not be the kind of coke they asked for. Rookley's also just left Crown House again.'

Cantelli nodded his head in the direction of the large parish church on the corner of a busy junction where Horton saw Rookley's slight figure.

'Let's see where he's going, Barney, and in such a hurry.'

'Probably cashing his giro.'

Cantelli could be right, but Horton was convinced that Rookley knew a great deal about Luke Felton's vanishing act, and, away from that greasy café and the flapping ears of the proprietor, Horton would get him to tell it, and save himself a late night meeting and endless hours looking for Felton. He said as much to Cantelli as they pulled onto the main road, causing a motorbike to swerve around them and Cantelli to curse after it.

'Rookley might even be meeting Luke Felton to warn him we're looking for him,' Horton added as Cantelli indicated left by the church. He relayed what Olewbo had told him, adding, 'Rookley could have gone to the café to pick up drugs for Felton. If we can nab him for supplying drugs and bring Luke Felton in, that might put a smile on DCI Bliss's face.'

Cantelli threw him a dubious glance, forcing Horton to say, 'I know pigs might fly.'

Through the now steadily falling rain Horton watched Rookley, his collar turned up, shoulders hunched, head towards the prison, which could hardly be his destination, having just got out of one. Before reaching it, though, Rookley turned left into the cemetery as a funeral procession swung into it from the opposite direction.

'No post offices in a cemetery,' Horton said cheerfully.

'Plenty of crypts though, which make excellent hiding places.'

'Perhaps he's visiting the grave of a relative or friend?'

'Doubt he's got any.'

'There's a sister.'

'Poor her.'

Cantelli swung into the cemetery after the funeral cortège.

'Pull over, Barney, I'll tail Rookley on foot. Hang around here in case he doubles back.'

Rookley veered off the central path to his right and Horton followed him at a discreet distance, weaving his way through the lurching weather-beaten headstones. Ahead he saw the funeral cortège draw to a halt and beyond it two gravediggers sheltering from the rain under a tree. He hadn't gone much further when his phone rang. Horton glanced at Rookley, who was some distance ahead and hadn't heard it. Seeing the caller was Cantelli, Horton answered it.

'Sorry, Andy, but we've got a body in Portsmouth Harbour. No ID, and difficult to tell who it is, but Seaton thinks it's a man.'

Horton looked after the retreating figure of Rookley.

'It could be Luke Felton,' Cantelli pressed. 'And Seaton says the tide's coming in fast.'

Horton cursed. Was it Felton? Or was he here, in hiding? Was Rookley meeting him? If it hadn't been for the question of the tide, Horton wouldn't have hesitated; he'd have checked Rookley out first. He dashed an irritated glance at his watch. It was less than two hours to high tide, but depending on exactly where the body was, the water could reach it much sooner.

Watching Rookley disappear around the bend of a path, reluctantly Horton said, 'Tell Seaton we're on our way.'

CHAPTER THREE

Horton stared down at what was left of the corpse lying in the thick slimy mud of the harbour and wasn't surprised that PC Johns, standing guard over it, looked green, or that PC Seaton hadn't been able to say who it was. There wasn't much left of this poor soul to tell anything and Horton wasn't about to go through what remained of the clothes searching for an ID. Dr Clayton, or rather her whistling mortuary attendant, Brian, could have that pleasure.

Hunching his shoulders against the cold penetrating rain sweeping off the sea, and desperately trying to control his heaving stomach, Horton forced himself to study what remained of the blackened flesh that hadn't been eaten by the sea life. There was no hair on the corpse and the rotted clothes were so covered in mud, seaweed, barnacles and sea creatures that Horton couldn't see if they fitted the description Harmsworth had given them. There were also no shoes on the body.

Cantelli cleared his throat. 'Think my breakfast's about to come up.'

Horton was glad he hadn't had any. He'd been too preoccupied with the symbol on his Harley to worry about food. 'Better not let the gallery see you.' He nodded up at the elevated road to their left, which led to the railway station and the ferries to Gosport across the harbour, and to the Isle of Wight beyond the Solent.

'Ghouls,' muttered Cantelli, pulling a handkerchief from his jacket and making a great pretence of blowing his nose. Horton knew it was to disguise the disgusting smell of the bloated body, which rose sickeningly above the smell of the mud. Even Dr Price, drunk or sober, wouldn't have difficulty certifying death this time.

'Would Felton's body look like that if he's only been missing since Tuesday night?' Cantelli voiced the question which had been running through Horton's mind.

Horton shrugged an answer. That was down to Dr Clayton, the pathologist, to tell them, though he hoped Price might have some idea. 'How tall is Felton?' he asked.

Cantelli reached into his pocket and pulled out his notepad. 'Five feet ten inches and of slim build.'

Horton again studied the corpse. 'The height's about the same.' But the body looked large, which, of course, could be the bloating from being in the water. Horton stared out at a grey, turbulent, rain swept harbour; the seagulls cawed and screeched overhead, a black and orange tug boat bucked in the roll of the waves as it headed out against the tide which was rushing in. The water was already in the channel to their right, slapping against one of the historic dockyard's attractions, the ironclad warship HMS Warrior; soon it would be over the causeway and the corpse. They had about thirty-five minutes. It wasn't long.

His eyes flicked back to the shore where officers, including PC Seaton, were helping to keep the growing numbers of tourists and sightseers at bay. Horton thought the rain would have dampened their curiosity, but clearly not. He watched with relief as Dr Price's battered Volvo pulled up and behind it the van containing Phil Taylor and his scene of crime officers. Horton wished the corpse was covered by a tent, but there wasn't time for that, and the best they could do was screen it with their bodies. Price would only be minutes. Taylor and his SOCO team of two, longer.

Seaton had told them on their arrival that a Mr Hackett had made the gruesome discovery just before 11 a.m. He'd been preparing his small fishing boat ready to take out into the Solent when the weather cleared, and, as he had put it, he 'Almost trod on the poor sod.'

Horton turned back to the body, his eyes scanning the area around it, and said, 'He must have been washed up in the early hours of the morning on or around high tide, which was just before one o'clock.' And he could guess why no one had spotted it before Mr Hackett; the colour of the corpse blended almost perfectly with the mud, and anyone seeing the clothes would think it was rags brought up with the tide. But where had the body come from? There were hundreds of places, around the Solent and beyond.

Cantelli pulled out a packet of gum and offered it to PC Johns, who took a piece gratefully while Horton refused. 'Maybe he fell overboard.'

Which meant it was unlikely to be Luke Felton, unless he'd been meeting a drug dealer on a boat. Horton said, 'Call Sergeant Elkins and ask if he's come across any drifting or abandoned boats in the last few days.'

Cantelli stepped back along the causeway, nodding a greeting to Dr Price who drew level with Horton. Price's bloodshot eyes looked warily out to sea before switching their scrutiny to the corpse.

'Well, he's definitely dead,' he declared. 'I can tell that by his colour. It's amazing what you learn at medical school.'

Horton sometimes wondered if Dr Price had ever attended one. Maybe the patients in his practice did too. Even though Horton had never heard of any complaints against Price, he was heartily glad he wasn't registered at his surgery. The rain was dripping off Price's wide-brimmed waterproof hat, the sort of article Horton wished he was wearing. His hair was plastered to his scalp and running off his face. His trousers sodden.

'As to cause of death . . .' Price crouched over the body. He seemed oblivious to the stench, but then perhaps the alcohol Horton could smell on him anaesthetized the doctor to that. 'There are no visible signs and I'm not touching him. I'll leave that to our delightful pathologist.'

'Time of death?' asked Horton hopefully.

'No idea, but judging by the generalized bloating and the fact the body is greenish-black, I'd say it's been in the water for sixty to seventy-five hours, possibly more.'

Horton did some rapid calculations. Seventy-five hours took them back to Tuesday morning when Luke Felton had been seen going to work by Harmsworth, and had, as far as they were aware, been at work all day. They would check. But sixty hours took them to 11 p.m. on Tuesday night, and that meant it could be Felton.

Horton said, 'It is a man then?'

Price shrugged his bony shoulders. 'Difficult to tell. Even if what is left of his clothes wasn't covering his private parts, the fish will probably have taken a fancy to them. Dr Clayton will tell you.' And with a grunt he shambled off slightly unsteadily, waving a hand as he passed Taylor and his two colleagues, Beth Tremaine and the photographer, Jim Clarke.

The sea was getting perilously close. For once Horton was glad of Dr Price's brevity. To Taylor, he said, 'You've got about twenty minutes before the tide hits here.'

'There's not much we can do anyway, except photograph and video the position of the body and take samples from where it lies,' Taylor replied mournfully, frowning at the sea, obviously annoyed with it for having the gall to interfere with his usual thorough procedure.

Cantelli came off the phone. 'Elkins says there are no reports of abandoned or drifting boats anywhere in the Solent. And none of a man overboard or reports of a missing seaman.'

'So if it is foul play he could have been thrown overboard from a boat and left to drown, or been killed or knocked unconscious and then tossed overboard.'

'Or he could have walked into the sea to commit suicide, or fallen from a cliff on the Isle of Wight.'

'Call Walters and ask him to check if anyone's been reported missing in the last seventy-five hours.'

Cantelli threw a worried glance at the advancing tide.

'You can do it ashore,' Horton said, swivelling his gaze to Mr Hackett, who was holding court among his buddies outside the timber hut belonging to the Portsmouth Net Fishermen's Association. 'And talk to Mr Hackett. See if there's anything else we should know about.'

With a look of relief, Cantelli hurried down the causeway while PC Johns looked enviously after him, before turning back to glare at the sea as though by sheer force of will he could hold it back. Others more noble had tried and failed, so Horton didn't hold out much hope of a humble and burly PC succeeding.

As Taylor's team did their stuff under the curious eyes of travellers and onlookers on the elevated road, Horton tossed up whether to tell DCI Bliss about this development and decided not to. It would only send her flapping around like a distressed seagull. He also saw no reason to call in Superintendent Uckfield of the major crime team, not unless it proved to be murder.

He quickly scanned the crowd for journalists, saw none he recognized, but knew they'd be here soon enough; along with photographers and camera crew who would be able to pick out a flea on an elephant's arse if there had been elephants in Portsmouth Harbour. They'd have no problem with something as large as a corpse.

Was it Luke Felton, he wondered, watching a grey naval ship making its stately way out of the harbour. The vessel seemed so close he could almost touch it. It was travelling slowly, but nevertheless Horton eyed its wash with concern. But if the corpse was Luke, then why had Rookley gone to the cemetery? Had he simply been taking a short cut through the graveyard on his way to meeting one of his criminal friends? Or had he seen them following and decided to throw them off the scent by diving into the cemetery? But Horton didn't credit Rookley with that much intelligence. Rookley was a nasty piece of work, with a record of theft and violence that stretched back to childhood, but he'd never been done for drug dealing. Still, there was a first time for everything.

He rammed his hands in his pockets and stamped his wet feet to get them warm, wondering if the unit he'd asked Sergeant Warren to despatch to the cemetery had been successful in finding Rookley. Perhaps they'd not even gone; Warren's diatribe on the shortage of manpower didn't exactly inspire Horton with hope. If Rookley wasn't located, and if he didn't show tonight, then Horton would have him picked up tomorrow.

'There's nothing of any significance here, Inspector.' Taylor's nasal tones broke through Horton's thoughts. The photographer nodded to indicate he'd got the images he needed, which was just as well as the sea, swollen by the naval ship's progress, washed up against the body. Horton addressed PC Johns, 'Tell the undertakers they can remove the body.'

Johns didn't need telling twice. The bedraggled PC hurried back to the shore while Horton stayed to watch the rotting corpse being scraped off the mud and lifted into a body bag before being placed on the trolley and wheeled away. It wasn't a pleasant experience. He examined the area where the corpse had lain. There was nothing but mud. Leaving Taylor and his team to collect further samples, he was relieved and thankful to return to the car where he squelched into the passenger seat and called Dr Gaye Clayton. He got her voice mail, so left a brief message telling her the body was on its way and he'd appreciate an ID as soon as possible.

Horton then called Sergeant Warren. The one unit he had been able to spare to search the cemetery reported no sign of Rookley. 'It's a big place, Inspector. How long do you expect me to keep them there?' Horton could hear the complaint in Warren's dour Scottish tones.

'You can call it off,' Horton said briefly and rang off before having to suffer Warren's phoney gratitude. Seeing that Cantelli was still deep in conversation with Mr Hackett, huddled under the protection of the hut doorway, Horton punched in a number on his mobile phone and a few minutes later had arranged for a survey on the boat he had viewed late yesterday afternoon and was hoping to buy. He then called the owner, Mrs Trotman, to tell her, but there was no reply and no answer machine. He'd try later.

Reaching into his pocket, he unfurled the paper containing the symbol scratched on his Harley and scrutinized it, but it still looked like a series of random squiggles. It had been carved almost certainly by a penknife, which would have taken some time to execute. Was it the act of a mindless moron who got his kicks from vandalizing other people's property — a drunken yob, maybe, staggering home? But there were no pubs or clubs en route to or from the marina, except the restaurant at the marina itself, and Horton could hardly see its upmarket clientele doing something so destructive and malicious. Still, it might be worth asking the owner about his customers last night. Though when he'd be able to do so was another matter entirely, and the marina CCTV hadn't picked up anything. He doubted the CCTV cameras on the seafront would either, even if he did have the time to view them, which seemed increasingly unlikely as the day was unfolding. And that brought him back to the body.

If it wasn't Luke Felton, then who was it and how had he died? Were they looking at a suspicious death, suicide or an accident? Was there a family somewhere who would need to be given the bad news?

Cantelli climbed into the car. 'Hackett didn't have anything to add to what we already know from Seaton, and Walters says no one's reported a missing person in the last seventy-five hours, or in fact over the last four days. He also says that neither Luke Felton nor anyone fitting his description has been taken to the local hospitals. I've got the addresses of Luke's brother, Ashley Felton, and his sister, Olivia Danbury. Do you want to call on them now? Ashley Felton lives not far away in Old Portsmouth, the sister on the slopes of Portsdown Hill.'

That was to the north of the city, where Kempton Marine was based: Luke Felton's employer, and Catherine's. Would she be there now, Horton wondered with a quickening heartbeat? Would he get the chance to talk to her? Perhaps even persuade her to let him see Emma, this weekend or next?

'Let's check what time Luke Felton left work first,' he said, stretching the seatbelt across him. 'Someone at Kempton's might be able to tell us more about Felton's movements.' He caught Cantelli's wary glance. 'It's OK,' he added. 'I promise to be on my best behaviour.'

Clearly Cantelli didn't believe that, and as they headed out of the city towards Kempton Marine, Horton wondered if it was a promise he'd be able to keep himself.

CHAPTER FOUR

Neither Catherine's car nor that of her fat lover, Edward Shawford, were in the car park. Horton wasn't sure whether to feel disappointed or relieved. His father-in-law's Mercedes was in its customary managing director's space, but Horton decided not to announce himself to Toby Kempton; he didn't think he'd be greeted as the all-conquering hero, more like someone who had escaped from a leper colony.

It had been a year since he'd been inside the building and then it had been under very different circumstances. He'd stormed in here angry and hurt that Catherine had thrown him out after she'd chosen to believe an accusation of rape by a girl he'd been detailed to get close to while working undercover on a special investigation. He'd started drinking heavily and in April, Catherine had refused to let him see his daughter. In July the case against him had been dropped, and slowly, with Cantelli's help, he'd begun to put his life back together again. In August, when he'd returned to work after his suspension, he'd cleared his name, but by then the damage had been done both to his promotion chances and his marriage. His life, and Catherine's, had been changed, but here nothing had, except the receptionist — Cantelli threw him a concerned glance, sensing his tension, as he asked for the personnel officer, Kelly Masters.

Four minutes later they stepped into her small, modern office and Horton was once again facing the large dark-haired woman in her late twenties who he'd tried many times to avoid kissing at the office Christmas parties.

'Andy, how lovely to see you,' she said with a smile, leaning forward to embrace him.

'We're here about Luke Felton,' he said abruptly, stalling her. He didn't want her false sympathy, which he knew of old would be tinged with a kind of malicious glee at another person's misfortune. And neither did he wish to encourage her sexual advances. On the way here he'd warned Cantelli about Kelly Masters' reputation as a man-eater. Not that he had any concerns about Cantelli falling into her clutches. He was strictly a one-woman man, and who wouldn't be, thought Horton, considering Charlotte Cantelli.

Kelly's dark brown eyes flickered with anger at the rebuff and her mouth tightened, but she forced a smile from her lips and managed a concerned frown before switching her charms on Cantelli, who gave her his bewildered idiot look.

Getting the message, with an irritable scowl she waved them into seats across a low table, letting her short skirt ride up her pale tree-trunk legs. Horton wondered what Luke Felton had made of her, or rather what Kelly had made of him. Luke wouldn't have been much of a challenge though. Deprived of sex for ten years, he would have shagged any female in sight, though Horton didn't know the latter was Felton's sexual preference. But he did know Kelly Masters, and as long as it was male and breathing it could have been any colour of the rainbow, size, shape or age, married or not. She didn't discriminate.

Curtly, he said, 'What kind of work did Luke Felton do here?'

'Why do you want to know that?' she snapped, abandoning the charm offensive. 'It's got nothing to do with him disappearing.'

Horton eyed her steadily and said nothing.

She flushed under the harshness of his gaze and said tautly, 'He just came to work and then went home.'

‘Doing what?’ asked Cantelli in a friendlier tone.

She switched her gaze to the sergeant, and relaxed slightly. ‘Designing our new web site and providing computer support for the factory. We should have had someone years ago, but you know how it is with budgets and getting the right person.’

‘So Luke Felton came cheap,’ Horton taunted, knowing he should ease off but not seeming able to, or caring. Being so close to Catherine and the fact that he might see her was making him edgy. That, and thoughts of what Kelly and others here must know about his marital break-up, and what Catherine might have said about him, were eating away at him like rats at rotting flesh.

Her dark eyes flashed daggers at him. ‘Luke is engaged on a project basis. I offered him a fee for three months’ work, payable at the end of each month, and with an option to renew, or the offer of a permanent job, depending how he got on.’

‘And how did he get on?’ asked Cantelli lightly. Horton could hear his colleague silently urging him to back down.

‘Very well. I can’t understand why he hasn’t shown up for work.’

‘I can. Drugs.’

She switched her hostile gaze to Horton. ‘I don’t believe that.’

‘Why not?’

‘Because he said he was clean. Oh, you can scoff, but I believe him. He works hard and keeps himself to himself, which is more than I can say for some of the staff, including the sales and marketing team.’

That was nasty, but then he had provoked it.

Hastily, Cantelli jumped in. ‘How do the staff feel about him working here?’

‘They don’t know his background. He isn’t going to broadcast it and neither am I.’

Horton reckoned she underestimated the jungle grapevine. Everybody probably knew.

Cantelli continued. 'How did he get the job? Did you advertise it?'

Horton thought she looked uneasy as she answered. 'Yes, but the applicants weren't suitable. They were either too highly qualified or not qualified enough. Then I happened to mention it to Matt and he said—'

'Matt Boynton? You know him?' Horton sharply interrupted.

'Is that any of your business?' she said coolly.

'It is when a man convicted for murder is missing.'

She eyed him malevolently. 'If you really must know, Matt and I were at university together.' Then, directing her remarks to Cantelli, she continued. 'I saw Matt when I was out one night and we happened to get talking about work. Matt said he knew someone who would be ideal for the project. I was interviewing at the time and I said send him along, not really thinking he'd be any good. But he was perfect.'

'Weren't you worried about employing someone with a violent record?'

'Matt assured me that Luke was reformed and Luke didn't seem capable of violence, let alone committing murder.'

'But he did, and he went to prison for it,' Cantelli said.

'But he's served his time and learnt his lesson.'

Horton wasn't convinced of the latter and Felton certainly hadn't served his full term. He wondered if Catherine's father was aware of Felton's record. He asked her.

'Toby leaves me to engage the right people. It's my job,' she replied haughtily.

Which meant no. Horton said, 'You'd better tell him before someone else does.'

She opened her mouth to reply but Cantelli got there first.

'When was the last time you saw him, Miss Masters?'

'Tuesday evening. He left here just after six.'

Horton studied her carefully. She could be lying. Perhaps Luke Felton had spent the evening with her, or the night, and now she was too concerned to admit it.

Cantelli again. 'Did he contact you after that, to tell you he wasn't coming into work perhaps?'

'I didn't even know he hadn't been in until this morning. I was at a conference in London on Wednesday and Thursday. When I discovered this morning that he hadn't been into work and hadn't reported sick I called the number he gave me. The man I spoke to, a Mr Harmsworth, said he didn't know where Luke was, so I called Matt. Perhaps he's had an accident.'

Walters had already ruled that out, locally at least. Horton said, 'Did Luke talk to you about his time in prison?'

'No.'

That was clearly a lie. Her eyes darted away from him. Horton reckoned she'd had a nice little post-coital chat with Luke about that, and probably a lot more.

Cantelli said, 'Did he speak of his friends or family?'

'No,' she answered with a note of exasperation. 'He worked.' She was beginning to look frazzled.

'Was there any member of staff he talked to or seemed close to?'

'I've already said. He worked alone.'

That didn't stop him communicating with someone, thought Horton. With a glance at Cantelli, he said, 'We need to talk to the staff.' Cantelli put away his notebook.

'Is that really necessary?' she said in alarm. 'They won't be able to help you.'

Horton knew the reason for her trepidation. She'd come in for some criticism over her decision to engage an ex-convict. Well, that was her lookout.

Cantelli slipped out of the office, aiming a silent plea at Horton, urging him to go easy. Kelly Masters watched him go with fear and a fidget.

'Did Luke speak to any customers on the telephone?' Horton asked.

'He had no need to.'

'But you weren't with him in his office. So you don't know that for sure.'

'I do because there's no telephone at his work station,' she cried triumphantly.

'What about email? I take it he would have had access to that and the Internet.'

She squirmed. 'Well, yes.'

Horton rose. 'Show me where Luke worked.'

With ill grace she hauled herself up and led him along the corridor to a small office on the right. There was no one in it, but beyond the glass partitioning Horton could see Cantelli talking to a group of people in a large open-plan office. Catherine wasn't among them, but then she had her own office on the other side of the reception area. And was she in there now? he wondered. Had she returned?

With a churning gut, he pushed thoughts of her away and turned his attention to the desk in front of him. On it was a computer monitor and little else. He opened the desk drawers — only some paper and pens.

'Did Luke have a laptop or mobile phone?'

'Not that I know of,' she said sulkily.

'No one is to touch this computer. I'll send someone to collect it. I'll also need access to any passwords.' They needed to check which sites Felton had visited and who he'd communicated with. He didn't think that was Ronnie Rookley. He doubted Rookley even knew how to switch on a computer. But Felton could have been involved in something that had led to his body being washed up in the harbour — if it was him.

She was looking worried, as well she might. Toby Kempton wasn't going to be pleased if his company name appeared in the press along with that of a convicted criminal. Catherine, as marketing manager, would have the media on her back, and bloody good luck to her, he thought, not without a touch of malicious satisfaction. He knew that Bliss's instructions to contain this story were about as likely to be fulfilled as a politician hiding an affair, because although Kelly Masters, Toby Kempton and Catherine wouldn't blab, he wouldn't put it past one of the employees Cantelli was talking to wanting to get his or her name in the newspapers.

By the time Horton returned to reception Cantelli was talking to the receptionist, a woman in her forties with straight dark hair in a short bob and a worried frown on her studious face. Cantelli broke off his conversation and headed towards Horton.

'Andrea confirms that Luke Felton left here just after six o'clock on Tuesday night. She was just leaving herself and seems to have been the last person to have seen him.'

And that put it within the scope of Dr Price's most recent estimate of the time of death for the body in the harbour, though Horton would wait for Gaye Clayton's more precise prognosis before jumping to any conclusions. And before saying anything to Kelly Masters about it.

'Luke was on foot,' Cantelli was saying. 'Andrea assumed he caught the bus. No one admits to knowing anything about Felton. They say they hardly spoke to him, he stayed in his room, eyes glued to his computer, fingers fixed on the keyboard. A typical geek who was a bit stuck up, talked posh and looked down his nose at everyone is the general view. No one mentioned him being released from prison, or the murder, so I said nothing about it, but I don't think it'll be long before word gets around.'

'We'll need to—' but Horton didn't get any further as the door to the right of reception burst open and a tall, silver haired man in his late fifties charged out with an expression like a constipated bulldog.

'What the devil is going on, Horton? What right do you have barging in here questioning my staff without my permission?'

Horton held the hot angry glare of Toby Kempton, noting that he was no longer good old Andy. An employee had obviously already run hot-foot to the boss.

'I have every right, Toby,' Horton stressed, feeling a small stab of victory as his father-in-law's complexion darkened. 'A potentially dangerous man, convicted of a brutal murder while under the influence of heroin, and out on conditional licence, has gone missing. And not only did you employ him but this was also the last place he was seen.'

'Rubbish. This has nothing to do with me or my business.'

'He worked here, Toby. He had access to the Internet where he could have made contact with someone who could have supplied him with drugs. He could have assaulted or killed someone—'

'Could have is not good enough. I could have won the lottery. I will not have you storming in here accusing my staff of harbouring a criminal, upsetting and unsettling them. When you have evidence then you can return. And only if I give my permission.'

Horton stepped forward. He could feel his temper rising; with an effort he tried to draw on the years of control he'd learnt in the children's homes to contain it. Briskly he said, 'No one has accused your staff of anything. Luke Felton worked here. Luke Felton is missing. We need to find him, and if you, or anyone else, prevents us from doing our job then you will be charged with hindering us in our enquiries.' Kempton looked as though he was about to burst a blood vessel, but Horton didn't give a toss about that. 'Someone will collect the computer Luke was working on and I suggest you cooperate.'

'You can suggest all you damn well like, but unless you have a warrant you are not taking a thing out of this factory.'

'Then we'll get a warrant. But if you believe you can switch computers and give us one that Felton wasn't working on, I have a note of the serial number. And if you think you can wipe it clean then let me tell you, our Hi-tech unit can trace everything Felton has looked at and everyone he has communicated with since he started here.'

'Get out.' Kempton stormed to the entrance and wrenched open the door, just as Catherine was walking towards it. Horton noted her surprise while quickly taking in her smart trousers and jacket. Her blonde hair was longer than when he'd last seen her just after Christmas, and she was looking good — slim and younger than her thirty-five years. He rapidly examined his feelings and found only bitterness.

'What's going on?' she asked, hurrying towards them looking worried. 'Is Emma all right?'

'You should know,' Horton couldn't help quipping, 'she's in your charge.'

'Dad?'

'Inspector Horton is leaving.'

Horton turned to Toby Kempton and said evenly, 'I suggest you talk to Kelly Masters. I'm sure she's discreet, but you never can tell what she might let slip when pressed.' He knew that was below the belt and he had no evidence to suggest Toby Kempton had slept with Kelly Masters, but sod it, it was worth a try. He held Kempton's fuming eyes long enough to see a flicker of unease in them, which sent a warm glow to his cold heart before he swept through the door. He felt Catherine staring after him. He wanted to say something to her but he was too tense and besides, there wasn't any point. He didn't know what to say that hadn't already been shouted, snarled or hurled. And this wasn't the time or place to discuss the only thing they now had in common: Emma. By the time Cantelli had zapped open the car door, both Toby Kempton and Catherine had disappeared from view.

'That went well,' Cantelli said with heavy irony as he started the car.

Horton didn't reply. His gut was still churning. Kempton had always been an egocentric, pompous prick at the best of times and had obviously taken his daughter's side in the breakup of their marriage, which Horton had to grudgingly admit was only natural. He couldn't help wondering, though, exactly what Catherine had told her father about him; he'd probably been made out to be Saddam Hussein, Stalin, Mussolini and Hitler all rolled into one.

But there was one thing for sure. Whatever Kempton said, did or felt about him there was no way on this earth his father-in-law was going to pay Emma's school fees and take the place that was rightfully his. And if he had to blackmail, bully and threaten him to prevent it then he would. He needed to act soon, because he had a terrible feeling that between them Catherine and Toby were going to poison Emma against him so much that he would never get to see his lovely daughter again. That thought chilled him to the bone and beyond. It simply wasn't an option.

'Lunch?' Cantelli said hopefully.

Not without effort Horton pulled himself together. He glanced at the clock on the dashboard; it was almost two thirty and an age since breakfast, which he hadn't eaten because of that damn etching on his Harley and DCI Bliss's sudden return to duty. He still didn't know why she had returned from her secondment earlier than planned. It didn't matter now. She was back and there was nothing he could do about it. He found he had no appetite though, the bloated body in the harbour and Toby Kempton had put paid to that.

'Turn right,' he instructed Cantelli. 'We'll see if Olivia Danbury's in.'

Cantelli threw him a pleading look.

'Perhaps she'll give us a cup of tea,' Horton added, punching in Mrs Trotman's telephone number with a feeling of desperation. He had to get the yacht he'd viewed yesterday as quickly as possible so that he had somewhere for Emma to stay. And yet, even then he could almost hear the family court judge crying incredulously, 'A yacht! You intend letting a child sleep on board a yacht!'

'It's solids I need, not liquid,' Cantelli grumbled, as Horton listened to the phone ringing.

Getting no answer, he hung up, saying, 'Then let's hope Mrs Danbury gives you a biscuit.'

CHAPTER FIVE

Olivia Danbury didn't even offer them a smile, let alone any refreshments. Horton reckoned the skinny blonde woman in her mid-thirties didn't have much to smile about, unless you counted the large detached modern house set behind electronic gates in landscaped gardens, the sweeping driveway, tennis courts and panoramic views over the harbour across to the Isle of Wight. A deep frown crossed her suntanned face as Cantelli made the introductions. Horton mentally compared her to the picture Harmsworth had given them of Luke Felton and thought she was younger than her brother, but apart from the colour of the hostile blue eyes, there was no similarity between them.

'How many times do I have to say it?' she declared angrily. 'I have not seen Luke and I don't want to see him, ever.'

Reluctantly, she had let them in but kept them standing in a black-and-white tiled hall with an elaborate marble staircase and wrought-iron balustrade that wouldn't have looked out of place in a Hollywood movie. Horton wondered who Cantelli was imagining gliding down the staircase given his love of old movies.

He said, 'Has Luke been in touch since he was released on licence?'

'No.'

'What about while he was in prison?' The gaze she bestowed on Horton was about as friendly as the one Rookley's mate in the café had given him.

'No. Now is that it? Because I've got to go out.'

Horton doubted that. She just wanted shot of them. He said, 'Has your brother, Ashley, been in contact with Luke since his release?'

'No.'

He didn't know if that was the truth. They'd speak to Ashley Felton anyway.

Cantelli held out his business card. 'Will you contact us if Luke attempts to get in touch?'

Horton thought she couldn't have shown her disgust more if Cantelli had been holding a pile of dog shit. The sergeant's hand remained resolutely outstretched until, with an explosive sigh, strong enough to turn a windmill, she snatched the card from him. Horton reckoned she'd tear it into tiny shreds and drop it into a bin with her nicely manicured fingers as soon as their backs were turned. Still, he could understand her anger, which perhaps disguised her shame and emotional turmoil. It wasn't nice having a convicted killer in the family. He saw no need to tell her about the body in the harbour, not when they didn't know if it was Luke Felton.

Gently he said, 'We understand your distress and anger, Mrs Danbury. We'll do our best to find Luke and, because he's broken the conditions of his licence, he'll be sent back to prison.'

'And long may he rot there.'

Horton held her hostile glare, but the lady was not for breaking her eye contact. There was no hint of compassion. If Luke was dead then he didn't think Olivia Danbury would shed any tears for him.

There didn't seem much point in hanging around. Horton thanked her, and in the car Cantelli said, 'Seeing as we didn't get a biscuit, can we grab a burger? My stomach's rattling like a snake in a cage. There's a mobile café along the top of the hill.'

Horton nodded.

'Could she be hiding her brother in that mansion?' Cantelli said, indicating right on to the hill road.

'I don't see why she should,' Horton replied, thinking the house was big enough to hide a whole regiment. 'If Luke Felton did visit her then how did he get there? He doesn't have a car and her house is hardly on a bus route.' People who lived in places like the Danburys didn't need buses.

'Someone could have given him a lift.'

That was possible, although judging by Olivia Danbury's reaction, Horton guessed that visiting his sister was the last thing Luke Felton would have wanted to do. And if Olivia Danbury was lying then he thought her a damn good actress. Besides, why should she lie? Unless Luke had committed a crime and she was shielding him. But that looked about as likely as the Queen harbouring a known villain.

As Cantelli pulled into the car park and dashed across to the burger stand, Horton wondered what Olivia Danbury's husband did for a living. Whatever it was, it was clearly lucrative. He also wondered if they had children. There had been no signs of any. And, he thought, there would be no sleeping aboard yachts for the likes of them, not unless it was the floating gin palace kind of boat; the type that resembled a small ferry. He wasn't envious; not of that. Just of anyone who could be with their child.

He watched the rain sweep in from the sea across the city and called Dr Clayton. Expecting her voice mail, he was pleased when she answered. He asked if she'd got anything from the body to help identify it.

'Not a thing,' she answered in an annoyingly bright tone. 'Brian's removed what was left of the clothing and sent it off to the lab. It appears to be some kind of T-shirt, original colour beige, or white; a light colour certainly.'

'Grey?' asked Horton, thinking about Harmsworth's description of Luke's clothing, which Cantelli had confirmed with the receptionist and other staff.

'Could be. There was no manufacturer's label. The small amount of trouser material we managed to salvage is cotton, possibly dark grey or green — again no label.' This was sounding more like Luke Felton every minute.

'There was no jewellery on the corpse,' Dr Clayton added. 'I'll check for tattoos, scarring and birth marks when I conduct the autopsy but the condition of the body might make that difficult.'

And that reminded Horton they needed Luke Felton's medical records urgently. Cantelli slipped back into the car, bringing with him a blast of damp chill wind and the smell of fried onions. Horton took his burger.

He said, 'Dr Price said the corpse had probably been dead between sixty and seventy-five hours. Is his assumption anywhere near correct?' He took a bite of his burger.

'Putrefaction is usually slower in water than in air and even slower in cold water, which is what the sea is this time of year: exceedingly cold,' she said. 'If he fell in, or was pushed, he wouldn't have lasted longer than ten minutes. His body would have sunk until the putrefactive gases pushed it to the surface and allowed it to float. Generally, at this time of year, in the sea, that could take anywhere between three to five days, and putrefaction is, as you saw, well advanced.'

Horton stared at his hamburger with a distinct lack of appetite. He wished he hadn't asked. It couldn't be Luke Felton then.

'But it's possible,' Gaye Clayton continued, making him wonder if he'd have to reconsider, 'that instead of sinking, his body got wedged under water where it was attacked by fish, sea lice and other fauna. And in that case the time of death could certainly be considerably more recent. Once removed from the water putrefactive changes advance considerably, which could be what has happened here. The body could have become dislodged and then been washed up.'

Horton pushed his half-eaten burger back in the bag. He had no idea how long the body had been in the harbour, but surely not that long, because someone would have discovered it before Mr Hackett. They had no option but to question all the boat owners in the harbour to establish who had last been on that part of the causeway before Mr Hackett. 'Any idea how he died?' Horton asked hopefully.

'Not yet. I've scheduled a full autopsy first thing tomorrow morning.'

'Can't you do it sooner?'

'No, busy afternoon.'

Horton would have to be content with that. 'It is a man then?'

'Yes. Though there's not much left of his external organs.'

Horton suppressed a shudder. 'Can you give me any indication of his age?'

'Not yet I can't.'

Frustrated at the delay and lack of information, Horton rang off and relayed to Cantelli what Dr Clayton had said as they headed down into Portsmouth. By the time they drew up outside Ashley Felton's apartment the rain had stopped and a watery sun was breaking through.

There was no answer to Cantelli's persistent finger on the bell. Horton gazed up at the art deco building on the Old Portsmouth waterfront and envied Ashley Felton his spectacular views over the busy entrance to the harbour. Of course Luke Felton could be hiding inside, but somehow Horton doubted it, although it didn't escape his attention that this wasn't far from where their body had washed up this morning. He said as much to Cantelli, adding, 'Ashley Felton could have pushed his brother over the edge of the quay on an incoming tide. The currents are exceptionally strong here.' He stared across the narrow harbour towards the shores of the town of Gosport opposite.

'Wouldn't someone have seen that?'

'Not in the dark. Or perhaps they did but they don't want to get involved.'

'But why would Ashley Felton want to do that?' Cantelli eyed him incredulously.

'To preserve the family name or out of anger, shame . . .'

'Are you serious?'

'No.' Horton gave a brief smile as the Wightlink ferry glided slowly out of the harbour. He turned back to the car.

'Do you want me at your meeting with Rookley tonight?' asked Cantelli, swinging the car round and heading back to the station.

'Thanks, but no. I can handle him, if he turns up, and I'm not banking on it.' But what he did hope was that Walters would have unearthed some information on Luke Felton that could help them find him, and quickly, or identify him as the body in the harbour.

Walters greeted them in CID with the news that the prison had emailed a list of Felton's prison listeners, volunteers who were there to help Luke and other inmates through their sentence.

'There were three,' Walters said, 'and I've spoken to each of them on the phone. They claim they haven't seen or spoken to Luke. They all live on the Isle of Wight where Felton served his sentence.'

Horton thought they could be lying, and Luke could be hitched up with one of them. He'd ask the local police to call on them to make sure. He said, 'What did they tell you about Luke?'

'Said he was reserved and not that interested in seeing them. The last one visited him over a year ago. I'm still waiting for his medical notes to come through.'

'Chase them up. And find out who else was released from prison around the same time as Felton and if he formed special relationships with any inmates. He might be hiding out with an ex-con.'

Horton turned but Walters hailed him. 'The case notes on the Natalie Raymonds murder have been sent over.' He tapped the top of a box file on his desk with a podgy finger.

'Is that it?'

'It's all they've sent.'

Horton picked up the box and headed for his office, where he cleared a space among the paper on his desk. He checked his voice mail. Phil Taylor had left a message to say he was emailing over the photographs of the body in the harbour and would follow it up with hard copies and the video shortly. Horton quickly ran through his emails, most of which seemed to be from Bliss asking him to file some inconsequential report or other. Ignoring these he found the photographs Taylor had mentioned. The sight of the body almost made the couple of mouthfuls of his burger come back up, but there was nothing more they could tell him that he didn't already know. Which was precious little.

He turned his attention to the Natalie Raymonds file. He doubted it would throw any light on where Felton might be but he didn't like working in the dark. He read that Detective Superintendent Duncan Chawley had been in charge of the investigation. Horton hadn't really known him because Chawley had been stationed at Havant CID for most of his career. On the occasions Horton had met him he recalled a clever, confident man with a dry wit and a reputation for getting results. Bliss would have liked him. Maybe she'd even worked with him at Havant before transferring to Portsmouth on her promotion to DCI, although calculating Chawley's age Horton doubted it. Chawley had been in his mid-fifties at the time of the Luke Felton case.

Horton read that Natalie Raymonds had been born Natalie Mather in 1970. She had been twenty-seven when she was killed on Friday 19 September 1997 and from her photograph, she'd been a stunner: a brown-eyed brunette with shoulder length hair and a wide smile that looked as though she had loved life. She had married Julian Raymonds in October 1996.

He dug deeper into the file until he located Julian Raymonds' statement. Raymonds had met Natalie when she had been working for a corporate hospitality company during Cowes Week in August 1996. It had been a whirlwind romance as well as a short marriage. Raymonds, a yacht broker, had been selling expensive yachts and had taken a group of customers and prospective customers to Cowes. At the time of his wife's murder, he had been at the Southampton Boat Show.

During the night of Friday 19 September, and throughout the 20th, Raymonds had tried several times to contact his wife at home and on her mobile phone and had grown increasingly worried when he got no answer. At 7.30 p.m. on the twentieth he had returned home to find no sign of his wife and had officially reported her missing. It was dark by then and too early in the investigation to conduct a search, but there had been no need to mount one because the following day her body had been found by a man walking his two Golden Retrievers in the undergrowth of a small copse close to the shore of Langstone Harbour and just off the Hayling Coastal Path.

The pathologist's report stated that Natalie had been killed sometime between 3 p.m. and 10 p.m. on 19 September. Quickly, checking Raymonds' statement, Horton saw he had been staying at a small hotel near the docks in Southampton, even though he could easily have travelled to Southampton, some thirty miles away, each day. But Raymonds said the evenings were spent entertaining customers and prospective customers, or more likely boozing, thought Horton. And possibly playing the field, though he had no reason to believe that, just his suspicious mind.

Raymonds had been on the stand all day, every day, and there must have been several witnesses to that, namely clients and other boat show exhibitors. Horton wondered if that had been checked, before pulling himself up; he wasn't reinvestigating the Natalie Raymonds murder, only trying to find her killer: Luke Felton. Raymonds said that Natalie regularly ran along the coastal path, which wasn't far from where they lived.

Horton read that Natalie had been wearing white running shoes, black track suit bottoms, with a short tight V-neck white T-shirt. A black bum bag — empty — was found beside her body, along with a small bottle of water. Her husband later confirmed the bag usually contained Natalie's mobile telephone and occasionally money. Felton's prints had been found on the bottle, and his DNA from his hairs on her body. He was already on record for drug offences, theft and an assault on a pensioner in 1995. The matching of his prints instigated a search for him. His parents claimed not to have seen him since Wednesday night, and Felton was picked up in Southsea on Monday 22 September at 11.15 p.m. suffering withdrawal symptoms from heroin and with blood on his clothes. Natalie's as it turned out. The testimony of a witness, a Peter Bailey, who came forward to say that he'd seen Luke Felton at the northern end of the coastal path at about 4 p.m. on 19 September heading south, clinched it.

Pretty conclusive then, thought Horton, digging out the photographs of Natalie Raymonds' body and spreading them out on his desk; she was lying on her back, fully clothed. There was some deterioration in the body due to the weather, the length of time it had been exposed and the action of animal and bird life, but he could still see where her face had been bludgeoned. Horton again consulted the pathologist's report; according to the pathologist, Natalie had been strangled with something soft and made of silk — a tie was the most likely option — before being struck three times with a rock.

Horton sat back, tapping his pen thoughtfully against his chin. Several aspects of the case bothered him. For a start, Natalie Raymonds had been a fit young woman, so why didn't she run away from drug-crazed Felton? Maybe he had surprised her as she ran past him; he'd grabbed her, quickly lassoed the tie around her neck and pulled it tight until she died. But still Horton wondered if she might have been able to defend herself against Felton, at least enough to get away.

Secondly, what had Luke Felton been doing on the coastal path? It was hardly the usual haunt of drug addicts. He had been living with his parents in Portsmouth, so how had he got to Hayling Island, twelve miles away by road? There was no mention of him owning a car. And he couldn't have travelled by the small passenger ferry to the south of the island because the witness had seen him at the northern end. Horton considered this with a frown. Walking two miles to where Natalie's body was found was hardly the act of a drug-crazed addict, unless he went to meet a drug dealer. Still, it was an odd place for a rendezvous. Horton didn't remember anything about Natalie Raymonds being on drugs or dealing in them and the pathologist would have picked it up if she'd been an addict.

And thirdly, why did Luke Felton strangle Natalie with a tie and not his bare hands? No tie had been found on Felton, and he'd been wearing a T-shirt when he was picked up.

Natalie's mobile phone hadn't been found either, but then Horton knew Luke Felton could have sold that to buy more drugs. In 1997 mobile phones weren't as commonplace as now and most mobile phone users were on a contract.

Horton looked for the record of Natalie's calls, but couldn't find them in the file. So he began to search for Luke Felton's statement. He hadn't got far when his door swung open and Bliss stormed in with a face like a cat's behind. Now what! he thought with exasperation. Friday the thirteenth was certainly living up to its reputation.

'Mr Kempton has made an official complaint against your offensive and bullying behaviour,' Bliss launched angrily.

Horton might have known. 'Now hold on—'

'No, you hold on, Inspector. I will not tolerate inappropriate behaviour in my CID team. You have allowed your personal affairs to interfere with your job and that is completely unacceptable, not to mention wholly unprofessional.'

Ah, so Kempton was playing dirty, and so was Bliss by the sounds of it. Well, two could play at that game, but in order to succeed, Horton knew he had to be smarter than he'd been this morning.

'Well, Inspector? I'm waiting for an answer.'

Crisply, Horton said, 'Luke Felton had access to the Internet and email. We need to check his computer to see if he made contact—'

'That is not what I meant,' she raged, flinging her hands on his desk and leaning across it to stare at him. Horton didn't budge an inch or bat an eyelid. 'What are you going to do about Mr Kempton?'

'Get a warrant as he insists.' Horton contrived to look bewildered, which seemed to really get up her nose.

Straightening up she said tautly, 'Are you being deliberately obtuse and insubordinate? You owe him an apology for barging in and interviewing his staff without his permission.'

Technically she was correct, but he wasn't going to let a small matter like that get in his way. And he had a feeling that Kempton would have stalled him.

Bliss was clearly waiting for a response. Eyeing her steadily he said, 'Luke Felton is missing. His sister claims she hasn't seen or heard from him and his last known movements are leaving Kempton's at just after six o'clock on Tuesday night. He might even be dead, though we have no positive ID on the body found in the harbour yet.'

'Body? What body?' she screeched.

Horton gave a silent groan. He might have known he'd pay the price for not calling her. Swiftly he gave her the facts, watching her grim expression.

'Good of you to tell me,' she sneered, eyeing him contemptuously. 'From now on, Inspector Horton, you will inform me the moment you have any news of Felton and the body in the harbour. And you will also apologize to Mr Kempton. Is that clear?'

He nodded curtly. She turned and marched out. A few seconds later a tap came at his door and Horton beckoned Cantelli in.

'I gather DCI Bliss is not best pleased with our efforts today,' he said, sitting opposite Horton.

'Mine, not yours. I can handle it.'

'Not sure I caught the bit where you told her about Rookley?'

Horton shrugged a response. He knew if he had done so, Bliss would have insisted that uniform accompany him and that he bring Rookley in.

Cantelli continued. 'The warrant for Felton's computer should be with us first thing tomorrow. Matt Boynton says Luke didn't have a mobile phone and I've checked with the phone company, who confirm that the payphone at Crown House has been out of order for three weeks and they've had no request to repair it. I've also done a quick search on the Internet for that symbol.'

'And?' For a moment Horton had forgotten all about that.

'It doesn't look good, Andy. The nearest resemblance I could find is the pagan symbol of death.'

Horton glanced at the sergeant in surprise.

Hastily Cantelli added, 'I've only checked it on a couple of web sites. I could be wrong.' Horton sincerely hoped so.

'You should ask someone in the Scientific Services Department to look into it for you,' Cantelli pressed.

'I will,' Horton replied, drawing a sceptical look from Cantelli before he left.

If the symbol was a death threat, then why not kill him last night when the perpetrator had the chance? A lighted match would have done it, and almost had not very long ago. He'd just managed to leap off his beloved boat Nutmeg before it had gone up in flames. He shuddered at the memory. Since then, he'd been living on a yacht belonging to a friend of Sergeant Elkins of the Marine Unit. But the friend was returning from abroad at the end of April, which reminded Horton about the yacht he was hoping to buy and had viewed yesterday. The owner might be at home now. He made to call her when another thought occurred to him, one that sent cold shivers up and down his spine; obviously his graffiti artist didn't want him dead — not yet anyway. He wanted first to torment him, like a cat playing with a mouse. Perhaps whoever was responsible was saying, 'See what I can do to something you cherish. Next time I'll hurt something you really love.' Horton's heart leapt into his throat. Emma. If that was so then he had to find this maniac urgently. But how?

The trilling of his mobile phone sliced through his thoughts. Horton saw it flash up as an anonymous caller. It might be Rookley, or someone else with information about Luke.

'Yes?' he answered it eagerly.

'Willow Bank, Shore Road, Portchester,' a foreign accent announced abruptly.

Horton started in surprise. He didn't recognize the voice but he recognized the address. It was the home of Mrs Trotman, the woman he'd been trying to get hold of all day to tell her about the survey he'd arranged on her boat. 'Is there a problem?' he asked, puzzled, wondering if perhaps she'd changed her mind about selling it to him.

'The lady who lives there is dead.'

Horton stared at his phone. This was a joke, it had to be, and a dreadfully sick one. Harshly, he said, 'I don't think this is—'

'Your business?' interjected the caller with hostility, misinterpreting what Horton had been about to say. 'Find her killer.' The line went dead, leaving an 'or else' vibrating in the air.

Horton punched in Mrs Trotman's number, drumming his fingers impatiently on the desk, recalling the gentle, dark-haired, attractive woman in her mid-thirties. No answer. Shit. Lifting his coat from the stand he hurried into the CID office. 'Cantelli, you're with me. Walters, send a car to Willow Bank, Shore Road, Portchester. Someone's just reported a murder, and I hope to God he's wrong.'

CHAPTER SIX

Horton stared with disbelief at the body lying on the grass of the windswept garden and felt a deep weariness settle over him. Two corpses in one day were enough to sadden and sicken any copper, but the body in the mud — horrific though it was — was far less upsetting than this. This death he took personally and with complete bewilderment; who on earth could have wanted the slender woman with the lean face and sad, deep brown eyes dead?

Yesterday he'd smiled and spoken to Venetia Trotman, now she was lying with the right-hand side of what was left of her barely recognizable and battered face pressed against the wet grass. Her right arm was crumpled under her body, her left arm outstretched, slim fingers clenched. She was wearing the same clothes he'd seen her dressed in yesterday: a navy blue cardigan over a white jumper, navy blue trousers, socks and blue deck shoes. But no coat. Yesterday, when he had left her just after five thirty, she had been wearing a red and blue sailing jacket.

She was facing her home; a substantial brick and tiled period house that Horton knew by its design had to be at least two hundred years old. Had she been returning there from the boat, which was moored at the bottom of a concrete slipway at the end of this extensive garden, when her assailant had attacked her? He couldn't see the boat from where he was standing because the house and garden were on a raised bank above the shore, which was screened by a tangle of trees and bushes. Or had she gone into the garden from the house to investigate a noise, or someone suspicious lurking in the shrubbery, and surprised her attacker? But why no coat? Perhaps she'd been in too much of a hurry to investigate the disturbance to put it on, though it had been a cold night. And depending on her time of death, she would also have got wet. It had started raining at about 5 a.m. He'd laid on his bunk, after yet another fitful night's sleep, listening to it hitting the deck.

Dr Clayton and SOCO might be able to tell them more, or rather tell Superintendent Uckfield because this was definitely murder, unlike the body in the harbour, which could be suicide or an accidental death. Horton had already rung the head of the major crime team. Soon Uckfield and the great useless hulk, DI Dennings, would be clodhopping all over the place. Horton had asked for a tent and arc lights, as the day was drawing in and in less than an hour it would be sunset. Cantelli had called Dr Price who was on his way.

'This place must be the best-kept secret this side of the Solent,' Cantelli said, as Horton stepped aside to let two officers cordon off the area around the body. Another two were sealing off the road to the house: a narrow, winding no through lane with no other dwellings situated along its stretch of roughly a mile. The only neighbours were rabbits in the surrounding fields to the north and west, and ghosts that haunted the ruins of the Roman fort of nearby Portchester Castle to the east, which faced on to Paulsgrove Lake, a wide expanse of sea feeding into Portsmouth Harbour.

'I didn't know it existed until yesterday,' Horton admitted, glad to turn away from the body and falling into step beside Cantelli, with a heavy heart, as they headed towards the house.

'I'm amazed property developers haven't been banging on their door, it's just ripe for marina flats and houses,'

Cantelli said. 'The Trotmans could have sold this land for a fortune.'

'Perhaps they valued their privacy.' And the price of that privacy might just have cost Venetia Trotman her life, thought Horton.

'Did she have any relatives?'

'I only spoke to her about the boat.'

'And you call yourself a detective.'

Horton gave a brief smile, knowing that sometimes humour helped to handle the brutality of a situation. 'If I'd known she was going to be murdered I'd have asked,' he replied, thinking sometimes this job was shit. No, correction, most times it was. But the thought of getting the scum who had bashed her head in, and making a strong enough case against him that not even the CPS or a jury could drive a truck through, sustained him. Except for two things, he considered dejectedly: it wouldn't be his case, and just as with Luke Felton, the bastard would either get a lenient sentence or be let out on licence to do it again . . . and again. Could Luke Felton have done this? he wondered with a jolt. Not if he was the body in the harbour. And Horton could see no reason why Luke Felton would have been here. But then there was no reason why he had been on the Hayling Coastal Path either, not unless he had known Natalie Raymonds. Maybe he had known Venetia Trotman.

Horton gazed up at the house. There were two windows either side of the rear door and two above them with a small, narrow window squeezed in between on the first floor, above the door. The red brickwork was old, the house beautifully proportioned and maintained. He could sense what Cantelli was thinking; the next of kin could be in for a substantial inheritance, unless the place was mortgaged to the hilt. Perhaps that was the real reason Venetia Trotman had been selling her late husband's boat — she needed the money to pay the mortgage and household bills, perhaps even her husband's debts.

Stretching his fingers into latex gloves, he eyed the sturdy oak door. 'No sign of a break-in.' It would take some considerable effort to break into this. He tentatively tried the handle and the door opened to his touch, which wasn't surprising if she'd rushed out to investigate intruders, though such a thing was brave and foolish.

They stepped inside a small utility room as it began to rain again. The space also clearly doubled as a cloakroom. But there was no sign of the red and blue sailing jacket, only a green waxed jacket and a Burberry raincoat, along with a pair of sturdy walking shoes and green wellington boots; Hunters, he noted. There was also a small empty hook beside the door, which looked as though its function was to hold keys.

Horton examined the rear of the door. Heavy bolts were fixed top and bottom and there was a strong lock on it, with the key still in it. He'd also noted the alarm, which had obviously been deactivated because there was no wailing noise as they entered. But had her killer disabled it? Or perhaps Venetia Trotman had never set it.

Yesterday she had met him at the side of the house and shown him straight down to the boat, waiting on the shore while he'd looked it over. She hadn't asked him for any form of identification, and he hadn't volunteered it. But then why should she ask when she had been expecting him? He'd answered an advertisement placed in the window of a newsagent's shop in the nearby village of Portchester offering a boat for sale. Maybe her killer had done the same and, finding her alone and vulnerable, had returned to rob and kill her. That was a far more likely scenario than laying this at Luke Felton's door. But who was the anonymous caller? He'd obviously found Horton's card on the victim's body.

Forensic would analyse the voice and try to pinpoint the accent, but discovering who it belonged to was about as likely as discovering a destitute banker. And Horton knew that even if they were able to trace where the call had been made, he doubted if it would tell them who had made it. He didn't think it was her killer, because he would hardly have gone to the trouble to report the death. Horton hadn't seen anyone while he was here yesterday and there had been no vehicles parked. A car could have been in the garage though.

He bent down to remove his shoes. Doing the same, Cantelli said, 'No children's coats or shoes and no men's either. How long did you say her husband had been dead?'

'She said three months.'

'Time enough, I guess.'

For some, Horton thought, interpreting the meaning behind Cantelli's solemn tone. The sergeant's father had died of a heart attack shortly before Christmas, and Horton knew that for many, like Cantelli, no time would ever be enough.

He pushed open a door to his right and stepped into a spacious modern kitchen with gleaming white cabinets, a tan-coloured tiled floor, and a large modern range. Cantelli shivered. Horton placed his hand on the radiator. 'Stone cold.' It felt as though the house had been shut up for a long time.

'There's a central heating clock here,' Cantelli said, peering at a device under a wall-mounted gas boiler. 'It's not set on a timer. Perhaps she switched the heating off on the first of March. Spring and all that, according to the Met Office,' he added, opening cupboards. 'Don't think Charlotte would agree with that. Spring to her begins on the first of May at the earliest. She was incredibly tidy, your Mrs Trotman. I don't think a child has ever graced this house, leastways not like any of my five.'

Horton agreed. There were no kitchen implements on display, no letters propped up on the work surface and no pin board with reminders and important telephone numbers on it. He found the dishwasher empty. Ditto the washing machine. He sniffed. 'Disinfectant and furniture polish. Someone's done a thorough cleaning job.'

'Not your average toerag burglar then,' Cantelli replied, opening the fridge. 'Perhaps Mrs Trotman was very house proud. She didn't eat much. No milk, butter or eggs, just some cheese and a yoghurt. And there's hardly anything in the food cupboards. Judging by this,' he added, waving his arm around the clinically neat kitchen, 'it looks as though she was obsessed with cleanliness.'

Perhaps she was, thought Horton, heading for the hall, which was also spotlessly clean. No muddy footprints on the pale blue carpet, or dirty fingerprints, or worse, smeared on the cream-painted walls. But why so little food? Maybe she'd intended going shopping that day.

Beyond the front door was a half-glazed porch. Horton looked for the red and blue sailing jacket hanging there but didn't see it, which meant it had to be on the yacht or upstairs.

Cantelli took the room to the left while Horton entered the one on his right, clearly the sitting room. Everything seemed to be in place. The television set was the latest model and the russet-coloured leather furniture was modern and of good quality, placed on an immaculately kept parquet floor with a large tiger-skin rug underneath an ancient low coffee table devoid of magazines and containing only an empty earthenware bowl. The Adam style fireplace boasted a wood-burning stove of the instant gas variety, and a gilt-edged mirror above it, but that was the only item on the pale-painted walls apart from some uplighters. There were no bookshelves, no photographs, no letters and no dust.

Heavy red curtains draped the ancient windows, which gave on to a front garden and a tall hedge, with evergreen trees hiding the house from the narrow lane beyond. It didn't look to Horton as though anyone had ever sat in the room, let alone lived in it, and for a moment he found himself wondering how it might have looked when first built and furnished by the original occupant, who might have been attached to the castle close by. Although no connoisseur of period design, staring around him he couldn't help feeling as though the heart had been ripped out of this house.

Entering, Cantelli said, 'The dining room's untouched, just a table and six chairs and a cupboard with some glasses, crockery and cutlery inside it in pristine condition. No booze.'

Horton was getting a bad feeling about this place, but defining exactly how bad and in what way he couldn't say, apart from the fact it was too clean, too perfect and too impersonal. But there was more than that. As they headed up the stairs, making sure not to touch the banister, Cantelli expressed part of what Horton felt.

'It's like something out of an estate agent's brochure.'

Yes, cold and clinical. And yet the woman he'd met hadn't struck him that way. She had been friendly, if a little nervous and shy. And did this house fit with what he'd seen of her? No. It was wrong. But then he didn't know her, so who was he to say. It was just a feeling.

The bedrooms at the rear of the house were in the same immaculate and clinical condition as the downstairs rooms. He opened the fitted wardrobes either side of the small iron fireplaces — empty — and turned over the counterpanes in both rooms, frowning with puzzlement before entering the bathroom wedged between the two rooms. There were no toiletries, only fluffy white towels on a stone-cold towel rail matching the gleaming white bathroom suite. None of the rooms showed any sign that anyone had ever visited. The bed linen was as fresh as if it were new. There was also no hint of any next of kin.

Cantelli hailed him. As Horton entered what was clearly the master bedroom, he saw here at least there were signs of life. The contents of a couple of drawers from the chest had been upended on the bed and the fitted wardrobe door was standing open. Horton studied the clothes without touching them. There were a couple of pairs of trousers, a dress, three skirts, a selection of tops, jumpers and underwear; all were top quality and some designer label. He hadn't been married to Catherine for twelve years without learning that much. Peering into the wardrobe he said, 'No suitcases or boxes, and only two pairs of shoes. I thought women had at least thirty.'

Cantelli gave a brief smile. 'My house is overflowing with them. There's nothing in the rest of the drawers,' he added, after gingerly opening them and peering inside. 'And no jewellery. So was she attacked and robbed?'

'Looks that way, and by professionals who knew exactly what they were after.' The advertisement card in the newsagent's window again sprang to mind.

Cantelli, nodding his head towards a door that opened off the bedroom, said, 'The en suite's gleaming so bright you'd think it had just auditioned for a television commercial.'

'Just like the bathroom then. I can't see her killer bleaching and polishing the place before making his getaway.' There was also no sign of any of her late husband's clothes or belongings, or even a photograph of him. Was it a case of out of sight, out of mind? Had she been glad to get him out of her life? Or perhaps she was so upset she couldn't bear to be reminded of him. On the other hand, he thought, hearing a van approaching, perhaps she simply didn't like clutter.

Peering out of the front window, through the rain, he watched the SOCO van swing into the driveway. They were certainly keeping Taylor and Dr Price busy. And this would be another autopsy for Dr Clayton, and a more urgent one than the body found in the harbour.

He glanced at the three perfume bottles on the dressing table — again the expensive variety — and called to mind with sorrow the soft floral scent of the quietly spoken lady. Her make-up was here too, and yet he couldn't recall Venetia Trotman as being 'made-up'. There was also not one single photograph of her. He said as much to Cantelli as they headed down the stairs, adding, 'There's not a book in the house either, and nothing personal that tells us what Venetia Trotman was like.'

'The shoes and boots in the cloakroom suggest she must have liked walking, as well as cleaning.'

'And perhaps gardening,' Horton added, stepping outside and surveying the neat and tidy landscape, which was shrouded in rain. 'As well as sailing,' he added. 'Let's check the boat out before Uckfield arrives.'

Horton didn't think they would find any revealing papers on it, unless they had been placed there since his visit yesterday, but they might find her jacket. He also wanted another look at the yacht, despite knowing now that it could never be his. He didn't much care for it reminding him of the gentle Venetia Trotman's brutal ending. And, besides, it would take time to get the next of kin's permission to purchase it, and they might even wish to keep the yacht themselves. No, he thought, heading across the garden, best to begin his search again.

He chewed over what he and Cantelli had discovered in the house, which was precious little, and it dawned on him why the place had made him feel so uncomfortable. It reminded him too much of the children's homes he'd been consigned to as a boy. Not that they had been as tastefully and luxuriously decorated as Venetia Trotman's house — on the contrary, they'd been shabby — but even with the central heating full on they'd still been cold and empty, because they had lacked a special kind of love. And that was how Venetia Trotman's house had felt to him. There was pride there, yes, but love, no.

In the gathering dark he located the ramshackle gate wedged in among the bushes, which led to a steep slipway and down to the shore. It was low tide and the yacht would be resting on the mud. A stiff March wind was blowing directly off the shore, bringing with it the angry rain, which ran off Horton's cropped hair and dripped down the upturned collar of his sailing jacket. His shoes and feet were soaked for the second time that morning and the rain had again seeped through his trousers.

Cantelli sniffed and rammed his hands deep in his pockets. 'Think I've had enough sea air and rain for one day.'

Horton was beginning to think so too. With a forceful tug the gate gave way. Horton stepped onto the bank and drew up with a start.

With a puzzled frown, Cantelli said, 'I thought you said there was a boat?'

'There was, yesterday.' Now as Horton peered at the concrete slipway there was nothing, not even a single rope. Just a big empty space, the wind and rain, and the dark mud of the harbour beyond.

CHAPTER SEVEN

'So where is it?' Superintendent Uckfield demanded, feet splayed, camel coat flapping open in the wind, staring across the dark harbour — like bloody Nelson without the eye patch and arm in a sling, thought Horton. He refrained from replying that if he knew that, he would have said. He was used to Uckfield's short temper.

Thankfully it had stopped raining in the time that had elapsed between their discovery of the empty mooring and the superintendent's arrival, but for how long Horton didn't know. The air was cold and damp, like him. Cantelli had taken refuge in the victim's house, where he was showing DC Marsden what they'd discovered; that shouldn't take him long, and Horton doubted Cantelli would thaw out inside that refrigerator.

Before Uckfield's arrival, Horton had asked Sergeant Elkins to start a search for the missing yacht. Not that there was much they could do in the dark except ask the marina managers along the coast if it had turned up there, which Horton doubted.

He'd quickly briefed Uckfield about his visit to the place yesterday, the anonymous telephone call and his and Cantelli's quick search of the house, along with what he knew of Venetia Trotman and her dead husband, which was hardly anything at all.

DI Dennings had listened with a baffled frown on his pugilistic face. Horton had finished by putting forward his theory that her killer could also have seen the postcard in the newsagent's window and reconnoitred the house earlier by posing as a prospective buyer, returning late last night to rob it. But if so, he was a remarkably tidy burglar.

Horton said, 'If the yacht had broken its mooring in the early hours of the morning and drifted out with the tide, someone would have seen it by now and reported it.' He knew that officers in the busy commercial ferry port and the naval dockyard to the south-east wouldn't have let a drifting yacht within yards of their shores without investigating it. 'The same applies if her killer cast it loose.'

'It could be the work of the boat thieves,' suggested Dennings, glancing at Uckfield. 'There's been a spate of them over the last month.'

He's looking for a brownie point, thought Horton, coldly eyeing Dennings' fifteen stone of muscle. He thought Dennings slow, dull and devious, an ugly bastard with muscles and no brains. What Dennings thought of him he didn't even bother to consider, but knew it wouldn't be complimentary. He wasn't about to lose sleep over that. Last year he'd spent hours with Dennings on surveillance while working in Specialist Investigations and the man had come out smelling of roses, with a promotion and a place on the major crime team to boot, while he'd been suspended over that false rape allegation. But that was the past, he quickly told himself, knowing that the ghosts of his past never tired of haunting him, and they seemed to be going to town today.

Tersely, he said, 'It doesn't fit the pattern of the other boat thefts.' I've done my homework too. 'They've all been modern motor boats, like yours, Steve,' Horton directed at Uckfield. Yes, Dennings, he's my old buddy, not yours, even though Uckfield had betrayed him by appointing Dennings to his team when the job had been promised to Horton. 'This is a classic wooden yacht, not at all flash.'

'Still valuable in the right market, though,' growled Uckfield. Unfortunately, he was right.

Dennings smirked. 'There's a huge black market for boats and outboard motors in Eastern Europe. The victim could have seen or heard the thieves stealing the boat, rushed out to stop them and got killed for her pains.'

But Horton shook his head. 'You can't see the boat from the house and I doubt she would have heard the engine being started.' The latter was a possibility, but Horton would rather have his teeth pulled than admit it.

Uckfield turned away from the shore and as the three of them headed towards the tent now covering the body, he said, 'She could have been on the boat when the thieves arrived.'

Horton wondered if she might have been. High tide had been at 12.49 a.m. Here, on the upper reaches of Portsmouth Harbour, it meant anyone could have access to the slipway, by boat, two hours either side of high tide, giving them a window of between 11 p.m. and 3 a.m. He doubted if Venetia Trotman would have been preparing to go sailing then, but she could have been on the boat for some other reason, though what, he couldn't imagine. And maybe she had left her sailing jacket there in her haste to escape the boat thieves, who had run after her and silenced her. He put forward his theory.

'We need to find that boat,' Uckfield snapped, pulling a toothpick from his coat pocket and working it into his mouth.

'There's four ways it could have gone,' said Horton. 'Horsea Marina to the east, Fareham Creek to the west, Gosport Marina across the channel, or south out through Portsmouth Harbour, and if it went that way then it could be anywhere. It might even be in France or the Channel Islands by now. Sergeant Elkins will need help to find it and we need to ask the harbour masters, Customs and the Royal Navy Fishery Protection Squadron if they've seen it.'

'See to that, Dennings,' Uckfield commanded, drawing up at the tent. 'What's it called?'

'Shorena.'

Dennings said, 'Her killer, or killers, could have come by vehicle knowing the boat was moored here. They robbed her, killed her, and one of them stole the boat, whilst the other drove away with the loot.'

It was feasible, especially given the advertisement for the boat in the newsagent's window. Horton had seen no vehicle tyre tracks, but that was hardly surprising given the tarmacked road, though SOCO might find traces. Unfortunately, because the lane was so remote, there weren't any nosy neighbours to ask. And if the thieves had come by boat, late at night, no one would have seen them. He said as much.

Uckfield nodded and turned to Dennings. 'Ask Trueman to mobilize the incident suite. I want him working on Venetia Trotman's background. And I want a team inside the house and combing this garden. Marsden can oversee that.' Addressing Horton crisply, Uckfield said, 'Make sure Trueman gets a copy of that anonymous telephone call. We'll get the experts to analyse it. And write your report up as soon as you get back to the station, and let Trueman have it.'

Horton tensed as he saw Dennings' smug smile, but he wasn't going to give him the satisfaction of seeing he was annoyed at being excluded, and angry at Uckfield's curt dismissal. OK, so the Venetia Trotman murder wasn't his case, but there was no need for Uckfield to dismiss him as though he was a PC.

'Not wanted on voyage,' Cantelli said, obviously reading the situation and Horton's expression as he zapped open the car. 'It's a film starring the great Fabia Drake, about—'

'Not now,' Horton said testily. Cantelli could wax lyrical on old movies for hours and Horton wasn't in the mood.

Undeterred, Cantelli continued, 'That film's been running through my mind ever since we went inside the house. I guess it's because the victim lived by the sea. It's a British comedy about a jewel theft on board an ocean voyage. Jewels — Venetia Trotman — sea.'

'I get the connection. Did Marsden express an opinion about the house? He's meant to be bright,' Horton added caustically. Jake Marsden was Uckfield's fast track graduate whizz-kid, destined for dizzy heights.

'He thought it looked like theft. But unless we can get someone to tell us what was in that bedroom to begin with, we're not going to know there was any jewellery to steal, are we? She could have sold it. And I thought of that, not Marsden.'

'Then you get a gold star.'

'I'd sooner go home.'

Horton didn't blame him. It had not been the best of days. And he had that runt Rookley to face yet. Still, he might give him a lead on Luke Felton. And if Uckfield hadn't been in such a hurry to dismiss him, then Horton would have told him about a possible link with the missing prisoner, though he thought the chances of this being laid at Felton's door were remote. Still, a lead was a lead . . . His mind veered back to Venetia Trotman. 'I suppose she could have sold the jewellery to pay her bills after her husband died.'

'Well, she didn't use the money for her central heating, that house is as cold as a Siberian winter. My toes might have dropped off for all I know. I stopped having any feeling in them long ago. If her husband left her penniless then why not sell up and move into a smaller place?'

'Perhaps she was in the process of doing that, though she didn't mention it.' But there was no reason why she should. Just because there wasn't a 'For Sale' board outside the house didn't mean it wasn't on the market. They could check the estate agents, and also find out who had handled her late husband's probate. It's not your case, he told himself sternly. Uckfield had made that quite clear. And to be fair, he knew that Sergeant Trueman would probably already be on to it without any prompting from Uckfield or Neanderthal Man. But there were several things bothering Horton.

He said, 'Did anything strike you about her clothes, Barney?'

'Not enough of them,' Cantelli replied promptly. 'In my experience women have wardrobes full of the stuff. Charlotte even bags things up, labels them and sticks them in the loft. I guess the victim could have done that, we didn't check.'

'Marsden's team will.'

'But somehow, I can't see it. It was as if she'd had a good clear-out, and not only of her husband's clothes. So maybe she was selling up, and has somewhere else to live, which is why she was also selling the boat.'

Horton agreed it was possible. Whatever the situation with Venetia Trotman, he hoped Uckfield would get to the bottom of it and find her killer, and so too did the anonymous caller, whoever and wherever he was.

Cantelli dropped him off at the station, again offering to accompany him to his meeting with Rookley, which Horton again declined. 'No point in us both getting colder and wetter,' he said.

There was no sign of Walters in the CID office, so he'd probably gone home. There was also, thankfully, no sign of Bliss. He wasn't going to complain about that. As he reached his office his phone rang. It was the front desk. 'There's a Mr Neil Danbury here to see you, sir.'

Horton was surprised and hopeful. Danbury must have information on his brother-in-law, Luke Felton; why else would he have taken the trouble to call in, uninvited?

'Show him into an interview room. I'll be down in a moment.'

Horton removed his jacket and swiftly checked his desk for messages. There wasn't one from Walters, which meant he must have drawn a blank on obtaining any further information on Luke Felton. Horton headed downstairs wondering what Neil Danbury could tell him, and hoping that whatever it was it would be significant.

He pushed open the door, but his lips could barely form a smile, let alone manage a greeting, before the well-built man in his mid-forties leapt up, fury contorting his swarthy face and blazing from behind his modern, heavily rimmed spectacles.

'What gives you the right to force your way into my house and accuse my wife of harbouring a criminal?' Danbury roared. 'She has nothing whatsoever to do with that scum of a brother.'

Horton stifled a sigh. He might have known that Friday the thirteenth hadn't finished with him yet. He noted the immaculate dark suit, crisp white shirt and yellow tie, along with the expensive gold watch.

Wearily he said, 'I understand your—'

'No, you don't,' Danbury roared. 'Luke's a killer, a violent, nasty piece of work. Why they let him out, God alone knows. I don't trust him not to kill again. He might already have done so again for all we know.'

Was he referring to Venetia Trotman? If so, the news had got out quickly, but then Horton knew it only took a couple of occupants in the houses opposite the entrance to Shore Road, which had been cordoned off, to alert the media.

'No woman is safe while he's on the loose,' Danbury continued to rage. 'Including my wife.'

Now Horton saw the reason for Danbury's anger. Fear was provoking it. 'You think he might attack his own sister?' he asked, concerned.

'God knows what he'd do for drugs.'

'The prison authorities say he's clean.'

'But he's not in prison,' sneered Danbury.

Quite. Horton couldn't fault that.

Angrily, Danbury said, 'Find him. And when you do, lock him up and throw away the bloody key. And don't bother my wife again. I won't have her worried and upset.' And with that Danbury swept out.

Horton decided he needed sustenance. Uckfield would have to wait until tomorrow for his report and his mobile phone.

As he ate his lasagne and chips in the canteen, he wondered if Trueman had located Venetia Trotman's next of kin.

He also wondered if SOCO had found anything around her body. It was probably too early for the search teams to have discovered much, but Dr Price must have given Uckfield an estimated time of death. And that reminded him of his rotting corpse in the harbour.

Quickly pushing away the image before it could ruin his appetite, he stabbed another chip and reached for his mobile. He might not be involved in the Venetia Trotman investigation but there was no rule preventing him from speaking to Sergeant Elkins.

'We've checked with all the marinas, including those on the Isle of Wight, and there's no sign of Shorena,' Elkins said. 'It's too dark to search for her now but I've put out an alert across all coastal waters around the UK. Not much more we can do tonight. I was just knocking off — unless you've got any other ideas, Andy?'

'None that spring to mind.'

It couldn't simply disappear, Horton thought, ringing off with frustration. But then perhaps it could if it had been scuttled, and he didn't think diving the Solent to try and locate it was a viable option.

He put his tray where the canteen staff wouldn't scold him and returned to his office, where he collected the file on Natalie Raymonds for further reading later on the boat, and headed for Milton Locks.

It was 8.52 p.m. and still raining when he pulled up outside the pub at the end of the road leading to the lock. Leaving the Harley in the car park he hurried down a narrow track away from the comforting lights of the pub and the street lights towards what was left of the disused lock, cursing Rookley for choosing such an exposed rendezvous and himself for being stupid enough to agree to it. When he could go no further, except into the mud of the harbour, Horton reached for his pencil torch and shone it over the sign by the side of the lock while trying, without success, to avoid the slanting rain that drove into his face. He read that the lock was the last remains of the Arundel to Portsmouth

Canal, abandoned in 1832 and recently given a makeover in the name of the environment. He surveyed the area but the intense darkness of the black expanse of Langstone Harbour in front of him seemed to swallow up the meagre light from his torch, and he could see nothing the other side of the lock except a tangle of bushes.

The sound of the wind and rain, plus the faint hum of traffic on the dual carriageway to the north, filled the air. He glanced impatiently at his watch. It was three minutes past nine and no sign of Rookley, but that wasn't surprising. He could be in the pub taking Dutch courage. Perhaps he should join him. After a day like today he thought he could do with a drink, only he didn't drink, and hadn't since August.

His fingers curled around the paper in his pocket bearing the symbol that had been etched on his Harley, recalling Cantelli's words. Did it mean death? Was he in danger? More worrying, could Emma be in danger? Cantelli could be wrong about the interpretation of the symbol, and probably was, but he was right about one thing; he needed to consult an expert. The sound of a car drawing up caught his attention. Rookley? But Rookley didn't own a car. It occurred to Horton too late that Rookley might not be alone, and he could be a sitting target out here, which was no doubt why Rookley had suggested this place and time.

He quickly scanned the dark horizon for a vantage point where he could take cover and yet still see Rookley approach. There was only one and it was behind the bushes on the opposite side of the lock. Horton hurried across to it. The pub door opened, bringing with it a snatch of music and the sound of voices calling goodbye and returning cries. Foolishly he turned in its direction, and just at the same time a small voice whispered 'Danger' and he sensed a shape looming out of the undergrowth. He swung round, but too late. A searing pain shot across his shoulders as a heavy blow struck him. He struggled for balance, lost it and was flying through the air with the ground rushing up towards him. Next, he was spitting mud and water from his mouth with a pain in his shoulder and the throb of a motorbike in his ear. It sounded remarkably like a Harley.

With a grimace he hauled himself up. His leathers were filthy, but he was alive and no broken bones. Whoever had attacked him hadn't finished the job. Thank God. Had that bastard Rookley shoved him in the mud? If so, he'd have his bollocks on a skewer. But from the brief glimpse he'd caught of the figure it had seemed taller and bulkier than Rookley. There was no point pondering it now; his priority was to get out of the lock, hope that his Harley was still where he'd left it, and get back to his yacht.

Fifteen weary minutes later he drew up at the marina and squelched his way down to the pontoon and the yacht, thankful his Harley hadn't been stolen and with eager thoughts of a hot shower, a change of clothes and the chance to bathe his grazed and bloody face. But as he climbed on board, he froze. There was something pinned to the hatch. Who the blazes was leaving him notes? Then surprise gave way to a cold grip of fear as he found himself staring at the same symbol that had been etched on his Harley, only this time executed in a thick black pen on paper. Rapidly, through the sheeting rain, he scanned the marina and the car park, but there was no one in sight.

He ripped off the drawing, noted that the lock on the hatch was still intact, and descended into the cabin where, flicking on the light, he studied the symbol: a cross and a funny-shaped circle above it. What the devil did it mean? Who had left it? It certainly wasn't Ronnie Rookley. Then it occurred to him that maybe the attack had nothing to do with Rookley either. And that meant someone was following him. He hadn't seen anyone, so whoever it was, he was very good.

The hairs pricked at the back of his neck. He didn't like the thought of being stalked and he didn't like not knowing what his stalker wanted. If the symbol meant death, then why not knife him instead of hitting him across the shoulders?

He strained his ears, listening for the slightest movement outside that would tell him his persecutor was back, but only the wind whistling through the halyards and the rain drumming on the coach roof answered him. His assailant, the graffiti artist, had gone — for now. But the question that troubled Horton was, when would he return and what would he do next?

CHAPTER EIGHT

Saturday, 14 March

'What happened to you?' Walters quickly shoved his Daily Mirror in his desk drawer and eyed Horton's cut and bruised face with surprise.

Dumping his jacket and helmet in his office before re-emerging almost immediately, Horton saw Cantelli's frown of concern. 'I'll tell you both over breakfast.' He hoped he could do so before DCI Bliss put in an appearance, though it was the weekend and that usually meant the senior management team would be conspicuous by their absence. Except for Uckfield, who had a major crime to solve — his car was already in the car park, along with Dennings' car.

During the night Horton had done a great deal of thinking about his stalker, none of it resulting in anything productive, except to give him an even worse headache than he'd had after the attack. Early this morning he'd once again viewed the CCTV tapes that Eddie in the marina office kept, but there was no sign of any furtive figure in the marina car park or on the pontoons, and no new visitors. Eddie also confirmed that the visiting yachtsman who had been present when Horton's Harley had been defaced had sailed on to waters new. And no one else had arrived. So who the devil was Horton dealing with? The invisible man? It seemed so. But one thing was clear; he needed to discover what the symbol meant, as Cantelli had urged.

He bought breakfast for them all, earning himself a brownie point with Walters, and grabbed a table at the window overlooking the station car park. From here he could watch for Bliss's arrival in case she decided to stick her beaky nose in.

Cantelli said, 'So what happened? You look as though you've done two rounds with Joe Calzaghe.'

Horton felt as if he had, though the pain in his neck and head was getting better the more he moved it; either that or the strong painkillers he'd swallowed earlier had kicked in. He gave a succinct account of the previous night, leaving out the bit about the note pinned to his yacht and his growing suspicion that his assailant was out for some kind of twisted revenge. He might confess that to Cantelli later, out of the earshot of Walters.

Cantelli asked, 'Do you think Rookley assaulted you?'

'No.' Horton hadn't seen his assailant but he'd got the sense of a bulkier man. Plus, he couldn't see a squirt like Rookley having the strength, or the height, to strike him across the shoulders. He added, 'But Rookley might have seen who did.' And that could give him a lead on his persecutor.

'Could it have been Luke Felton?' posed Walters with his mouth full of bacon.

'Why should he want to push me in the lock?'

'Maybe he went there to meet Rookley for drugs and thought you were there to arrest him.'

Horton considered Walters' suggestion. Rookley might have told Luke about their rendezvous in order to get Luke off his back and get into Horton's good books, but Rookley would then have risked being done for dealing. On the other hand, Rookley might have known that was where Luke would be and set him up, only Luke realized it, hence the attack. That didn't explain the note, but it made him feel better about the attack; perhaps that wasn't his stalker after all.

Horton pushed his empty plate away and scraped back his chair. 'We'll ask him. Let's disturb his beauty sleep.' And after that they'd see if Ashley Felton was at home.

As Cantelli drove through the city streets, Horton checked the wing mirror to his left to see if anyone was following him. He couldn't see anything suspicious and he could swear no one had followed him to the station that morning.

'I've been thinking,' Cantelli said. 'Why would Luke risk losing that job, which by all accounts was the best thing since electricity was invented? Was it invented or discovered? I was never any good at science at school.'

'Because he couldn't stay off the drugs.'

Cantelli eyed him. Horton knew that look. 'Go on, cough it up.'

'Well, perhaps the job wasn't that great. We've only got the word of the bearded wonder and that nymphomaniac personnel officer that it was. What if after Luke arrived at Kempton's he was disappointed to find the job wasn't all it had been cracked up to be? He begins to think I'm being paid peanuts, I'm stuck in a room with no telephone, no contact with any of the staff, chained to a keyboard, this is worse than prison, so sod it.' Horton made to speak but Cantelli forestalled him, 'I haven't finished yet.'

'Remind me to buy you breakfast more often, it seems to have done your grey cells a power of good.'

'It's the bacon sandwich.' Cantelli smiled. 'Always does the trick. Felton expected more. He was better than the job demanded and maybe someone recognized this: a supplier of Kempton Marine, or a visiting rep. Or perhaps Felton talked to someone about the job over a pint after work and this someone offered him a better deal, more money, higher status.'

'Crooked?'

'Not necessarily. Felton could have been headhunted for a legitimate position.'

'Then why not tell his probation officer? Why just walk out and risk returning to prison?'

'Because he hadn't told this person he'd been to prison or that he was out on licence.'

Horton thought about it for a moment. 'Bit stupid that.'

'True. But perhaps Luke saw it as a fresh start in London or Newcastle, say, or some other large city where he could disappear, and thought, yeah, why not, a chance to make real money and begin again, assuming a new name and identity. No questions, no stigma, no probation officers, just a whiz kid on a computer.'

Horton considered this as Cantelli eased the car through the back streets towards Crown House. After a moment he said, 'It's possible. In fact, it's a good idea. I want a list of every visitor to Kempton Marine for the last two weeks. They've got a visitors' book in reception. We had to sign in, so see who else has. Make sure you get a copy of the entries when we go for Felton's computer. We need to check if any of them have spoken to Felton.'

'Just one further thought,' Cantelli added, as he swung into the car park at the rear of Crown House. 'Felton could have seen a position advertised on the Internet. He contacted the organization by email, they asked him to call them and when they heard what he had to say they interviewed him and snapped him up.'

'The computer unit will tell us which sites he visited and who he emailed.' Horton paused as he climbed out of the car and quickly scanned the area. Only two cars passed them; one with an elderly man driving and the other a woman in her twenties, neither likely to be his stalker. 'You might have been rubbish at science but you're a damn good sergeant.'

'And I hope to stay that,' Cantelli answered, as they made their way to the front entrance.

They found Harmsworth in his office. He showed no reaction to Horton's cut and bruised face, but then that was hardly surprising given his clientele at Crown House.

'Have you found Luke Felton?' he said, looking up from his shabby and shambolic desk.

'We want a word with Ronnie Rookley.'

'You'll be lucky. He's not been back since after your visit yesterday.'

Horton considered this, first puzzled, then annoyed. Clearly, Rookley had done a runner. And he'd probably warned the rest of the dealers that the police were sniffing around. Horton didn't think he was going to be flavour of the month with the drug squad.

'We'd like a look at his room.'

'Be my guest.' Harmsworth reached into his pocket and pulled out a set of keys. 'First door on your left at the top of the second floor.'

Cantelli didn't bother to knock. There was no need if Rookley wasn't there, and he'd probably not have bothered even if he had been. He tried the door first before inserting the key and crashing in, shouting, 'Wakey, wakey, rise and shine.' Then he stepped back, almost colliding with Horton. 'My God, this place stinks! Has something died in here and crawled under the bed?'

'Well, it's not Rookley,' Horton answered, swiftly crossing to the empty unmade bed and peering under it. He wished he hadn't. The smell was vile. Rookley must have forgotten where the toilet was. The room was littered with beer cans, foil containers of leftover curry and fast food which appeared to have things crawling in it. 'He could be hiding in the wardrobe,' Horton added, straightening up.

'Nope,' Cantelli replied, holding his nose between the thumb and forefinger of one hand while opening the creaking door with the other. 'Though something unidentifiable might be.' He took a chance and peered inside again. 'Just filthy clothes.'

Horton gazed around at the discarded newspapers, fag packets, beer cans and whisky bottles among the soiled underpants, socks and clothes. What a contrast to Luke Felton's pristine room and Venetia Trotman's immaculate period house, which reminded him that he still needed to give his mobile phone to Trueman so he could take a recording of the anonymous call. He couldn't see any needles or drugs but he wanted this room searched. And he pitied the poor plods who'd have to do it.

'Lock it up, Barney, before we throw up.'

Horton knew they could ask the occupants of Crown House if they'd seen Rookley or knew where he was, ditto Luke Felton, but they'd probably get better results talking to a brick wall.

They left Harmsworth with instructions that he call them the moment Rookley showed up. Outside Horton looked for Hans Olewbo, but there was no sign of his car or the black man, and neither could he see signs of anyone else from the drug squad. That didn't mean they weren't there though.

In the car, he said, 'When you get the chance, check out Rookley's background and see if he could have gone to ground anywhere.'

'He might have gone to his sister's, although, if my memory is correct, she can't stand the sight of him.'

'Not many can. Circulate a picture of his ugly mug to all units and get a unit to check with the bus drivers for any sightings of the scumbag catching a bus to Milton Locks last night. He shouldn't have been difficult to spot with those shifty eyes, greasy hair and earrings. I can't see him walking five miles across town, so you'd better get another unit checking with the taxi drivers in case Rookley was flush after dealing.'

Cantelli nodded. 'I'll also get someone to ask in the pub near the locks for any sightings of him or your assailant.'

Now was the time to tell Cantelli about that note left on his yacht, but Horton didn't. Instead, recalling that Barney's wife had worked with Luke Felton's mother, Sonia, he said, 'Does Charlotte remember anything about Luke Felton?'

'I haven't asked her. Do you want me to?'

'Might be helpful. I'd like to know more about him and his background, other than what's on his file.'

'It might not be necessary if Dr Clayton confirms it's Luke's body she has in the mortuary. Maybe Rookley sold

Luke drugs. Luke took them, staggered into the sea and drowned, and that's why Rookley's scarpered. He's scared of being accused of manslaughter.'

It was possible. Hopefully later this morning they'd have more information on their body, though Horton wondered if the autopsy would be delayed because the one on Venetia Trotman would take priority.

He rubbed at a cut on the side of his face and squinted with tired eyes through the windscreen at a bright blue sky that at last had a hint of spring about it. If he discounted the graffiti artist as his assailant, along with Rookley and Luke Felton, then who else knew about his rendezvous with Rookley at the locks? There was the café proprietor, Jack Belton; he could easily have overheard their conversation. Or perhaps someone had been hiding at the back of the café. Then again Rookley could have confided in someone when he'd returned briefly to Crown House after their meeting in the café. Or perhaps Rookley had met and told this person in the cemetery. And that meant the gravediggers might have seen him. Horton reached for his mobile phone, quickly explaining his thoughts to Cantelli while punching in Walters' number and waiting for him to answer.

'What kept you?'

'I was on the phone to the council parks department to find out if Rookley had any relatives buried in the cemetery like you asked, only there's no one there until Monday.'

Which meant the gravediggers wouldn't be working until then. Horton cursed. Then he recalled the funeral procession. Perhaps one of the mourners had seen Rookley with someone. But if the parks department was closed until Monday, they wouldn't be able to discover who was being buried without asking all the undertakers in the area, and Horton simply didn't have the resources for that. He told Walters to get hold of any CCTV tapes in the area of the cemetery; they might get the chance to view them later to see which direction Rookley had gone after leaving the graveyard, and if he had left with anyone.

As he rang off Cantelli pulled up outside Ashley Felton's waterfront apartment and a few minutes later a man in his early forties, wearing striped pyjama bottoms and a navy sweatshirt, and looking as though he was suffering from the mother of all hangovers, showed them into an apartment with wide windows overlooking the harbour. He punched the remote control and silenced the huge plasma television that took up the opposite wall. Horton thought, with such a spectacular view across the busy harbour who'd want to watch TV?

'Neil told me Luke's missing,' Ashley Felton said with a worried frown. 'It said on the news a body was found yesterday in the harbour.' He gestured at the television, which was showing a local news programme. 'Is it . . . ? Are you here to tell me it's Luke?'

Horton could see that he was genuinely concerned, which was more than his sister and brother-in-law had been.

'We don't have an ID yet, sir,' he said gently.

'Then you want me to identify him.' Ashley Felton's pallid face bleached. He ran a trembling hand over his unshaven chin.

'No. It's been in the water too long for that.'

'God!' He let out a breath and sank onto the sofa, reaching for a packet of cigarettes from the glass-topped table. Horton wished he wouldn't light up; the room already stank of cigarettes and the remains of a cooked breakfast, which littered the dining table in front of the window.

Felton offered the packet across. They both refused. He'd given no indication he'd noticed Horton's battered face, but then the man had a great deal on his mind. Horton quickly appraised him. He had the same square-jawed features as his brother, only Ashley's face was more heavily lined, and his blue eyes bloodshot.

Unzipping his sailing jacket, Horton signalled to Cantelli to start the questioning. With his pencil poised over his notebook, Cantelli said, 'When did you last see Luke, sir?'

Felton lit up with shaking hands and inhaled deeply. Letting the smoke trickle from his nose he said, 'Luke's a fool. You know he had a good job and the chance to make something of himself at last. But then that's Luke for you, determined to screw up his life and anyone else's. I tried to help him, but once he was convicted of that girl's murder, I knew that I couldn't do anything more for him. His conviction killed my parents. They blamed themselves, though they shouldn't have done, but then you do when you have kids, don't you? Even though you know that sometimes there's nothing on earth you can do to prevent them making terrible mistakes. Have you got children?'

'Four girls and one boy,' answered Cantelli.

Ashley Felton looked shocked before he said with feeling, 'Then you'll know exactly what I mean. I've only got one. She's twelve going on eighteen. I see her once a month. I'm divorced.' His eyes swivelled to Horton, who was fully aware that Felton hadn't answered Cantelli's question. So too was Felton.

He drew heavily on his cigarette and said, 'Olivia's furious and upset that Luke's been let out, and I don't expect Natalie Raymonds' family are ecstatic about it.'

Horton said, 'Your brother-in-law didn't seem too pleased either, Mr Felton.'

'Neil is very protective of Olivia. He saw how much Luke's crime affected her. Did you know Luke was arrested for the murder the week before Olivia's wedding? No, well you can imagine what that did to her and my parents.'

Horton thought it certainly explained Olivia's attitude and Danbury's hostility.

Sniffing noisily, Ashley Felton added, 'We're all worried about the media picking up on it. None of us want it raked up again.'

Horton said, 'We're not about to broadcast it, Mr Felton, but we can't stop other people talking to the press.'

'No.' Ashley shifted restlessly in his seat. 'I'm not so worried for myself, I work in London. But Olivia and Neil are well known and respected in the local community, and you know how some people like to stir it up and revel in others' misfortune.'

Horton did. When mud was thrown, it stuck no matter how hard you tried to clean it off with denials and even proof; sometimes it simply wasn't enough. It certainly hadn't been for Catherine. His eyes flicked up to the television screen where he saw the stout figure of Uckfield talking solemnly to several reporters outside the police station, obviously briefing them about the murder. Horton wondered if he had fresh evidence.

Cantelli said, 'What do you do for a living, sir?'

'I run a recruitment company in London.'

And clearly one that hadn't found Luke a job. Out of curiosity Horton asked, 'What does Mr Danbury do?'

'He's an accountant. He took over my father's practice when he died in 2001.' Felton stubbed out his cigarette. 'Sorry, you wanted to know when I last saw Luke. It was the Friday before last, March the sixth. I'd only just arrived home from London when Luke showed up here.'

'What time was this?' asked Cantelli.

'About eight thirty. I was later than usual because there'd been an accident on the A3.'

'How did Luke know where to find you?' asked Horton, recalling what Walters had said about Luke Felton not having any prison visitors. He didn't know how long Ashley Felton had lived here but knew that in 1997 this building had belonged to the ferry company. It had only recently been converted into private flats. Perhaps Ashley Felton had written to his brother.

Ashley looked taken aback at the question. Sniffing and reaching again for his cigarettes, he said, 'My ex-wife could have told him, I suppose. She lives not far from here. I bought this apartment so that I could be close to my daughter.'

Lucky you, thought Horton.

'Or I guess Luke could have found my details through the directory of company directors. I know Olivia didn't tell him. Luke told me about his job, but said he wasn't getting paid until the end of the month and he needed some money until then. He wanted to move out of the place he was living and get a room for himself nearer to work.'

'Did you believe him?' asked Horton.

Felton studied the writing on the packet of cigarettes for a moment. When his eyes came up Horton could see the guilt.

'No. Luke had lied too many times in the past for me to trust him. I told him to ask Kempton's to sub him some money until the end of the month. He said they wouldn't give him enough.'

For what? wondered Horton. Not just a room, he was betting.

'How did he react when you refused him?'

'He went very quiet and left.'

'Was that normal behaviour?'

'No.' Ashley Felton looked uneasy. 'Luke used to fly off the handle at the slightest thing, especially if he didn't get his own way. I was amazed when he didn't scream and shout at me. After he left, I began to wonder if he really had changed in prison and if he was telling the truth about needing the money for a room. Now he's missing I don't know what to think. I feel guilty and responsible, especially if it turns out he's that body in the harbour.' He shook another cigarette from the packet his trembling hands had been fidgeting with. 'And what's worse, a part of me hopes it isn't Luke while there's another part that hopes it is. My God, isn't that awful?' He ran a hand over his face and jumped up. 'To think he might have gone away depressed because I didn't trust him. He told me he had reformed and I just scoffed at him. I thought he wanted money for drugs.'

Horton needed to check if Kelly Masters had arranged an advance on Luke's wages. He said, 'His probation officer says Luke was clean.'

Ashley looked distraught. 'That makes me feel worse.' He lit his cigarette and crossed to the window. Cantelli raised his eyebrows at Horton, who after a moment said, 'Where did Luke go to school?'

Ashley spun round, clearly baffled by the question. 'St Martin's in Southsea. Why?'

'Did he have any special friends? Someone he might have gone to for help or money?'

'I see. I don't know. Not that I remember. Luke was clever. Or I should say is. I shouldn't talk of him in the past, but to me, that Luke doesn't exist. He was accepted for Oxford, you know, reading History. He did a year before he dropped out. By then he was taking drugs. My parents were devastated. Luke didn't seem to care. It was downhill after that.'

Cantelli said nothing about Charlotte having worked with Ashley's mother.

Horton thought he'd sneak in a question or two about Natalie Raymonds. 'Did Luke ever mention Natalie Raymonds to you?'

He sensed Cantelli's surprise.

Ashley said, 'No. I'm sure he didn't know her.'

'Did you or your sister know Natalie, or her husband, Julian Raymonds?'

But Ashley was shaking his head.

That seemed to be that. Horton rose and Cantelli followed suit. Putting his notebook away, Cantelli said, 'If you hear from Luke again, please let us know. Perhaps we could have your telephone number, so we can contact you the moment we have any news.'

Ashley reached for his suit jacket, which was draped over the back of one of the dining chairs, and fishing out a business card he handed it to Cantelli. Eyeing Horton nervously he said, 'This woman who's been found dead at Portchester . . .' His eyes flicked to the television screen but Uckfield was no longer on it. 'Could it . . . no, forget it.'

Horton knew exactly what he was thinking: the same as he and Neil Danbury had thought. He asked, 'Did Luke ever mention a Venetia Trotman?'

'Is that her name? No.' He showed them to the door. 'You'll let me know the moment you identify the body found in the harbour?'

Horton promised they would. Outside Cantelli said, 'Why the question about Natalie Raymonds?'

'Just curious.'

Cantelli rolled his eyes and sighed. 'I hate it when you say that.'

'I just want to know what Luke Felton was doing on that coastal path in 1997.'

'If and when we find him, we'll ask him.'

'And I guess he still won't remember.'

'Then you'll probably have to learn to live with this huge gap in your knowledge.' Cantelli unlocked the car.

Horton smiled. 'It won't be the only one.'

'Ashley Felton seems to be in a bit of a state. If you ask me, I'd say he's on the verge of a mental breakdown.'

Yes, and caused by what? Guilt over his rejection of his brother? Business worries? Or perhaps he had health or marital problems? Horton knew all about the latter. With a glance at his watch, he thought it was time enough for Dr Clayton to have something on their body from the harbour. He told Cantelli to head for the mortuary.

CHAPTER NINE

'What happened to you?' Dr Clayton asked, echoing Walters' words earlier that morning.

'I fell in a lock.'

'Fell?' she cried incredulously, 'From your boat! I don't believe it.'

'It's a long story.'

'And one I haven't got time to hear at the moment because you, or I should say the criminal classes, seem to be keeping me busy — that is, if your body in the harbour was killed, and I don't know that yet. But this poor lady certainly was. You can tell me about your adventure over a drink one day.'

Horton thought that was something worth looking forward to; and not so much the body on the mortuary slab in front of him. As his eyes fell on Venetia Trotman, he tried not to think of her alive on Thursday evening, but he didn't succeed. His anger was just as raw as on first seeing her lying battered on the grass. Brian, the mortuary attendant, hadn't undressed her and neither had she been cleaned. 'Do you have an estimated time of the death?' he asked.

'For her or your unknown man?' asked Gaye.

'Both, but start with Venetia Trotman.'

'I didn't think you were on her case. You weren't at the scene last night.'

'I'm not, but go on.'

Shrugging, she said, 'Last night I put her death some time between one and four on Friday morning.'

Cantelli said, 'A strange time to be in her garden, and fully clothed.'

'Agreed, unless she was suffering from some kind of mental illness. She could have been confused and wandered out there.'

'I don't think so,' Horton said firmly, causing Gaye to raise her eyebrows.

'Why so sure?'

'I met her.'

'Ah.'

Obviously, Uckfield hadn't told Dr Clayton that, but then there was no need for him to have done so. Dr Clayton's estimated time of death coincided with the high tide. Given that, and the fact that the victim's sailing jacket was missing, along with the yacht, it seemed highly probable that she had been on board. Had she been intending to sail it? Had she stowed some of her clothes on the boat ready for travelling — the clothes that were missing from the house?

He said, 'What about cause of death?'

'I'll reserve judgement on that until I've conducted the autopsy. Now, your unknown man,' Gaye said briskly, moving off.

Horton gave Venetia Trotman's corpse a final glance before following Gaye's petite green-gowned figure across the mortuary to a room just beyond it where she slid open the drawer. He stared down at the blackened, sea-life chewed corpse, trying not to breathe for fear of what the smell would do to the breakfast he'd eaten earlier. It hadn't been a pretty sight first time around and it certainly hadn't improved with age. Even Cantelli stopped chewing his gum.

Gaye said, 'The questions are, was the victim alive or dead when he entered the water, and is the cause of death drowning? Well, I found no evidence of water and sea debris in the stomach and only a small amount of the microscopic algae called diatoms in his throat, which indicates he was already dead when he entered the water. As we don't yet know who the victim is we have no evidence of the circumstances arising before his death, therefore no idea what he was doing in, on or near the water. However, because he was wearing clothes and he was dead when entering the water, you can rule out homicide by drowning, and suicide.'

Horton knew that suicides usually piled their clothes up and left them on the shore. He'd already mentally discounted that anyway. And Cantelli's theory that a drugged Luke Felton could have walked into the sea and drowned was now also out.

Gaye Clayton was saying, 'There are no bullets embedded in what is left of the body or any bullet entry or exit wounds, but there are signs of a considerable trauma to his skull.'

Cantelli said, 'He was bludgeoned to death.'

'Not necessarily. The trauma could have come from his body being dashed against an object under or on the water.'

'But something must have killed him if he was dead when he hit the water.'

'Quite. There are a wide range of injuries on his body, consistent with floating in the water, but one more prominent than the others — where, as I thought earlier, he could have become lodged up against something, hence the rapid putrefaction. Have you seen enough?'

'Plenty.'

She slid the drawer shut. Cantelli let out a slow breath and resumed chewing.

Gaye said, 'There was also severe coronary artery atherosclerosis, so it's possible he could have suffered a fatal cardiac arrest with a collapse dead into the water.'

And surely Luke Felton was too young for that, thought Horton, though a cocaine overdose could certainly cause a heart attack. Or if this wasn't Felton then it could have been a natural death. Perhaps the man was out walking by the sea, suffered a heart attack and fell into the water.

Horton said, 'Any indication of where this might have happened?'

'None at all,' she replied brightly. 'Everything's been sent to the lab for analysis, including clothes — what is left of them — skin, organs, fragments of sea life, grit, gravel, sand and anything else I could find in and on him. You might get more from that. There's not a lot more I can tell you at present.'

'What about fingerprints?' asked Cantelli.

'Not enough skin left to lift any complete ones. We'll have to rely on DNA. It's being run through the database, but I doubt you'll get an answer, if there's a match of course, until sometime next week.'

Horton felt irritated by the delay. 'Isn't there anything you can tell us about the identity of the victim?' he asked, exasperated.

She eyed him keenly. 'You sound a tad desperate, Inspector.' He opened his mouth to reply but she held up her hand to silence him. 'I know; it's a matter of life and death. OK, here's what I've got. Got your notebook ready, Sergeant?'

Cantelli waved it at her with a grin and plucked the pencil from behind his right ear.

She began. 'He was five feet eleven inches tall, size nine shoe, aged mid to late forties, dead for at least two weeks, maybe more. What's wrong, Inspector? Have I disappointed you?'

She had. Clearly this was not Luke Felton. Two weeks ago, Luke had been alive and kicking around Crown House. The body was also the wrong age, the wrong height and probably the wrong shoe size. And once again that raised the question of whether Luke had anything to do with Venetia Trotman's death.

'I did have someone in mind,' he said, glancing at Cantelli, who gave a resigned shrug. They'd have to wait to see if they got a DNA match and if the lab came up with anything from the samples Dr Clayton had sent them.

Gaye crossed to the mortuary. 'Are you staying for the autopsy on Venetia Trotman?'

Horton declined. Although he was eager to know how Venetia Trotman had died, he wasn't keen enough to witness Dr Clayton's ritualistic disembowelment, and neither was Cantelli.

'It doesn't answer where Luke Felton is, or Rookley,' Horton said glumly, as they drove back to the station. 'We'll have to circulate Felton's photograph and put out an all-ports alert for him.' And he'd need to tell Uckfield that Luke Felton could be in the frame for Venetia Trotman's murder. They desperately needed to track his movements since Tuesday evening.

Cantelli broke the news over the phone to Ashley Felton, who said he'd let his brother-in-law know. Then, armed with a warrant, Cantelli took himself off to Kempton's to collect Luke's computer, informing Toby Kempton he was on his way. Horton had decided not to accompany him. Not because he was concerned about Toby Kempton's threats — his father-in-law's bullying wasn't going to prevent him from speaking to Kempton's employees again — but he had an itch to see where Natalie had been killed. He didn't mention it to Cantelli, who would only roll his eyes at him again and shake his head. First though, Horton called Sergeant Warren and asked if PC Seaton was on duty. He was, and as luck would have it was in the station. A few minutes later there was a tap on Horton's door and he beckoned Seaton in.

'Take Luke Felton's photograph to the bus station, Seaton, and ask if any drivers on the route past Kempton's in both directions, towards Portchester or Portsmouth, remember seeing Luke Felton on Tuesday evening after work.'

Seaton looked pleased at being given the task. Horton knew he was keen to get into CID and he would be just as eager to take him, if he was ever granted more manpower, which seemed about as likely as him being given the freedom of the city. Collecting his helmet and leather jacket, he detoured to the main incident suite on his way out of the station and was puzzled to find a dejected major crime team and a room silent of ringing phones, bustling with about as much activity as a slug.

'Has your pen run out?' he asked Trueman with surprise, eyeing the crime board. On it were the photographs of the battered body of Venetia Trotman, her name, details of where she was found, when, and the estimated time of death. And nothing else.

'No, our information,' Trueman replied. 'You look a bit worse for wear, Inspector.'

'I'll survive. Didn't you find anything in the house?' He didn't mind telling Trueman what had happened at the lock but he wasn't going to mention it while others were present, especially Dennings. He didn't trust the bastard not to blab it to Bliss and get him into trouble. Thankfully she still hadn't put in an appearance.

'There's not a ruddy thing in it to tell us who she is,' Uckfield grouched, stomping across to the crime board and glaring at it. 'No photographs, no personal papers, no next of kin, and Trueman can't trace her anywhere.' Uckfield spun round and redirected his angry stare towards the stoical sergeant, as if it was his fault.

Trueman didn't take it personally. 'There's no register of birth, or marriage. She has no credit card or bank account. No tax record and no national insurance number. She simply doesn't exist.'

'Not any more she doesn't,' Horton said, intrigued.

Uckfield threw himself down on a chair with an explosive sigh and spread out his short fat legs. 'It seems she didn't in the first place, except for the fact we have a body and you saw and spoke to her when she was alive. The phones are silent even after my TV appeal, which makes me think the buggers have cut us off. We're waiting on Dr Clayton for fingerprints, dental records and DNA. Taylor confirms the victim was killed where she was found. There are some faint shoe prints around the body and the area leading from the boat, and we might get some traces left by our killer on the victim's clothes or skin, but might is no bloody good to me.'

'What about her late husband?' Horton asked, baffled.

Uckfield threw an exasperated glance at Trueman.

'The house is registered to Joseph Trotman, who purchased it in March 1997. There's no mortgage on it. All the utility bills are in his name and have always been paid in cash.'

Did that explain why the central heating had been switched off, Horton wondered, because Venetia Trotman had run out of cash and was afraid she wouldn't be able to pay the bill when it arrived? Perhaps she had sold the jewellery, as he and Cantelli had discussed, and had been using the money to live.

Trueman was saying, 'The late Joseph Trotman also had no credit card or bank account. No tax or national insurance records. But that's not all. Neither his birth nor his death have been registered.'

Horton was mystified. 'She told me he died three months ago.'

'Well, she was telling you porky pies,' bellowed Uckfield.

Evenly Trueman continued. 'I'm checking with the post office to see what mail's been delivered and I've asked the phone company for a complete record of calls.'

Horton considered what he'd learnt. 'It's clear she must have destroyed all the papers in the house, which gave their real names.'

'I think we managed to work that out ourselves,' Uckfield said sarcastically, drawing a smug glint from Dennings.

Horton ignored them both. 'There are two reasons why she'd do that. One, because either one or both of them are wanted for a crime and needed to conceal their identity. Or two, they were on the run from someone criminal and powerful, who's finally caught up with them. Or perhaps who first caught up with Joseph Trotman and killed him and Venetia was trying to escape this person the night she was killed.' Which made Horton recall his anonymous caller; did the man with the foreign accent know or suspect who that killer might be? But if he did, then why not stick around and help them? The answer had to be because he was a criminal himself.

Uckfield sniffed and scratched the inside of his left thigh. 'You met her. What was she like?'

You should have asked me last night instead of sending me away like PC Plod, Horton refrained from saying. Instead, he considered his encounter with the victim, as he had done several times since finding her body, but this time in light of what he now knew. Was there something he'd missed? A hint as to Venetia Trotman's true identity in what she'd said and done? He couldn't see it.

Aloud he said, 'She was softly spoken, no accent, reserved. She seemed a little nervous but that could have been her natural manner. She met me at the front of the house coming from the rear of the building, as though she'd been waiting for me.' He paused as an idea struck him.

'Go on, or is this a new party game and we have to guess what happened next?' grumbled Uckfield.

'Perhaps her killer was already in the house.' And could that have been Luke Felton? Horton wondered. But how could Luke have known Venetia Trotman? Then a thought occurred to him. Could Felton have met someone in prison who had told him about the Trotmans?

Horton continued. 'Her visitor could have arrived unexpectedly. She couldn't cancel my appointment because I hadn't then given her my mobile number, so she had to go through with it. But she didn't want me in the house. Whoever was inside could have been a criminal, or possibly someone on the run, and it explains why the place was wiped clean.'

Surely Luke Felton, stoned or not, wouldn't have bothered to wipe the house of his prints. Then Horton recalled Felton's room at Crown House, neat, tidy and clean to the point of clinical obsession. But why would Luke Felton risk losing his job, go on the run and kill a woman? The answer could be drugs. But that didn't explain why he had been missing since Tuesday and Venetia killed in the early hours of Friday morning.

Swiftly his mind ran over the things he'd learnt about Luke Felton since yesterday. Having been refused money by his brother, Luke Felton had been on his way to his sister's house on Tuesday evening after leaving work when he remembered someone had told him about the Trotmans. He diverted to Willow Bank, and found Venetia alone. He threatened her with exposure over her secret, whatever it was, unless she gave him money. He bought drugs, and then when he needed more, he returned to Willow Bank late Thursday night, but Venetia refused him money. She tried to run away from him. He killed her. That didn't explain the caller with the foreign accent, but nevertheless Horton relayed his ideas to Uckfield, watching his expression change from incredulity to hope and then indignation.

'Why didn't I know about this Luke Felton before?' he thundered.

'Because until an hour ago I thought we might have his body in the mortuary.'

Uckfield grunted. 'Can Felton sail a yacht?'

'I can check with his brother. No sign of Shorena, I take it.'

A sullen-looking Dennings answered. 'No, and it's not registered with the harbour master.'

Horton knew that, unlike a car, there was no legal requirement for registration, or any kind of documentation, tracking the ownership of a boat, although the sensible and responsible boat owner always kept records. Dennings was eyeing Horton malevolently. Horton knew what he was thinking — why involve him when it wasn't his case? And perhaps Uckfield wouldn't be doing so, apart from having Luke Felton in the frame and the fact that Horton was the only person who'd met the victim. That, and the lack of information on the victim, had changed Uckfield's mind.

Uckfield hauled himself up. 'Right. We start work on Luke Felton.'

But Horton halted him. 'That's just one theory.'

'You've got more?' Uckfield replied, rolling his eyes.

'Perhaps Joseph Trotman's not dead at all, but living under another name somewhere, and she was about to join him. Maybe she needed the money quickly for them to get away, but when I didn't buy the boat there and then she decided to cut loose and leave, which was why she was dressed in outdoor clothes at that time of night. But as she was making her escape, she was attacked and killed by whoever it is who is after them.' Uckfield eyed him doubtfully and made to reply, but Horton continued. 'Or perhaps she killed her husband and was frightened of being found out, so she was running away.' There was a short silence before Horton added, 'Or she could have been a squatter and just posing as Joseph's wife, and the real Venetia Trotman was already dead.'

'Bloody hell, I think your imagination's on overtime. Must be something to do with that bang on the head.'

Horton guessed his last idea was a bit on the wild side. 'What about the GPs in the area? Were either of the Trotmans registered as patients?'

Grudgingly Dennings answered. 'We can't get on to that until Monday because the surgeries are closed over the weekend.'

'Hard bloody luck if you're sick,' growled Uckfield, transferring his scratch to his armpit.

Horton said, 'What did the shop owner say about the advertisement for the boat?'

Uckfield nodded at Marsden.

'She placed it a week before she was killed,' Marsden answered brightly, sitting up — like a Springer spaniel about to be tossed a bone, thought Horton. 'He's no idea who responded to it. If anyone did, they would simply have seen it in the window, jotted down the details and called her direct, like you did, sir.'

And the card hadn't given her name or address, just a telephone number.

Marsden added, 'The newsagent can't remember seeing her before she showed up with the advertisement, and he didn't deliver newspapers to the house. I've sent the card to Forensic, but I'm not sure they'll get anything from it other than the shopkeeper's fingerprints, which were taken today, though there might be traces of the victim's on it. I've requested copies of the CCTV tapes from the shopping precinct in case we can identify anyone who is looking at the advertisements in the shop window, other than Inspector Horton, but they've only got the last few days.'

It was better than nothing.

Addressing Trueman, Uckfield said, 'Liaise with DC Walters and get all you can on Luke Felton. See if you can unearth any connection between Felton and the Trotmans. Talking of unearthing, let's not ignore Inspector Horton's other theories. Dennings, you can organize the search of the garden to see if Venetia Trotman buried her husband there and was intending to sail off into the sunset with their life savings. Get the scanning equipment in. Oversee the operation personally. I don't want anything missed.'

Horton could see that Dennings didn't look too happy about being pushed outside for the day, and prayed for rain and gale force winds. He called Ashley Felton's mobile number. It was answered almost immediately, as though he was expecting a call. Horton asked if Luke was an experienced sailor.

There was a short pause before Felton answered. 'Yes. A very good one. You think he could have stolen a boat?'

It was a logical conclusion given his question. 'Do you?'

He heard Ashley take a deep breath. 'I suppose it's possible, but he hasn't taken mine, it's still at the Town Camber. I'm on it now.'

Horton thanked him, promised to keep him updated and rang off. He relayed the information to Trueman and then took his leave for Hayling Island, and the place where Natalie Raymonds had met her death.

CHAPTER TEN

Horton stared across the ebbing tide in Langstone Harbour to the opposite shore of Portsmouth. The weather had clouded over after a promising start. Now the sky was a patchwork of dark scudding clouds which threatened rain, whilst the wind was bringing with it the smell of mud and salt and the cry of the seagulls. He'd left his Harley at the end of Julian Raymonds' road, a cul-de-sac that culminated in a field, which he'd walked across to reach the shore. Climbing down onto the shingle beach he headed south until he came to the rear of the Raymonds' house. There didn't seem to be any signs of life inside. He'd been tempted to call there, but had decided against it. He didn't want to upset Julian Raymonds any more than was necessary, and he couldn't see how Raymonds could tell them where Luke Felton might be.

There was an old wooden pontoon at the bottom of the property but most of it had fallen into the sea. Horton could see buoys in the harbour and a handful of boats moored to them, but not Shorena it seemed, according to Elkins. If Luke Felton was Venetia Trotman's killer, then it was possible he'd taken her yacht out through Portsmouth Harbour in the early hours of Friday morning. This meant he couldn't have been pilled up, or he wouldn't have got far without having an accident.

Horton again eyed Raymonds' house. He could see no rear entrance from it leading onto the shore, though there could have been one in 1997 when Natalie Raymonds had begun her fateful run that September day.

Turning his gaze across the harbour he saw the tops of the yacht masts in his marina and where the channel turned in to enter the lock at Milton. His mind flitted to his attacker and then away again, there didn't seem any point in speculating on who it might or might not have been, but he made a mental note to get a record of recently released criminals to see if any names on the list might have a personal vendetta against him.

He thought about the body found in the harbour. Should he make a media appeal about it? But what could he say? They had no photograph to show, and if someone had seen that rotting corpse before Mr Hackett then they would have said. No one the officers had questioned around the harbour had noticed it. He could put out a general description based on what Dr Clayton had given them, in case it prompted any memories, though something so vague was bound to pull in the loonies and the desperate. Still, it might prompt a lead. He'd do it when he returned to the station.

He headed back the way he'd come until once again he climbed up onto the path that skirted the field. It was rapidly crumbling into the sea, with withered dead oaks leaning drunkenly over on to the shingle. Continuing northwards for half a mile he came to a small copse of trees, bushes and brambles. At this time of year, he could see right through them to the sea beyond, but in September the foliage would have been dense enough to hide Natalie's body until the dogs had sniffed it out two days after she'd been killed.

The pathologist's report had put Natalie's death some time between 3 p.m. and 10 p.m. on 19 September. The witness had seen Luke at the northern end of the coastal path at about 4 p.m. It would have taken Luke about forty minutes to reach the copse, which would put his arrival here at about 4.40 p.m., when it was still daylight. The weather had been good, and it was a popular footpath, so the chances of someone seeing Natalie Raymonds running along it would have been quite high, Horton thought. But no one had seen her, or at least no one had come forward.

He turned and stared back the way he had come. The footpath on the edge of the field was an unofficial one and off the main coastal path. It wouldn't have been used by many people, and perhaps Natalie had gone out running after sunset. Would Luke have been waiting in the copse for her for that length of time? If so, that meant he knew she would run this way. Or perhaps he'd arranged to meet her. Why else would he hang around here? But then Natalie could have been killed just as Luke arrived. Perhaps he'd staggered here after shooting up and she'd stumbled on him. Agitated and high on heroin, he'd strangled her. But he was back to those niggling questions. Why here? And why kill her with a tie?

The first few spots of rain began to fall. There was nothing more to be gained by staying here. As he made his way back to the Harley his phone rang. It was Cantelli reporting that he'd taken the computer used by Felton to the computer crime unit to be dissected.

'Any trouble with Toby Kempton?' asked Horton, sheltering as best he could from the rain under a tree.

'He huffed and he puffed but he didn't blow the house down. I've also got copies of the pages from the visitors' book. Mr Kempton said his secretary will give us the telephone numbers and addresses of the visitors on Monday. We can't start on the list until then anyway because no one will be at work today, but I could run the vehicle registrations through the database.'

'Wait until Monday when someone in the major crime team can help with the calls.' Horton quickly relayed the progress on the Venetia Trotman investigation, which didn't take long, because there was so little to report. He told Cantelli about Uckfield now favouring Felton for Venetia Trotman's murder and why — because it was all he had.

Cantelli said, 'Kelly Masters was at Kempton's. She claimed she had a lot of paperwork to catch up with but I think Toby Kempton ordered her there when he knew we were coming. I asked her if Luke had requested a sub on his wages. She said not.'

'You believe her?'

There was a short silence while Cantelli considered this. 'She sounded surprised at the question, but I don't see why she should lie.'

And neither did Horton, which meant that Luke Felton had lied to his brother, Ashley.

Cantelli continued. 'Walters says that Rookley's sister claims she hasn't heard from him for twenty years and doesn't want to for another twenty. She also says they haven't had any relatives buried in the cemetery for donkey's years. Oh, and Luke's prison medical file will be with us on Monday, unless Superintendent Uckfield can persuade the prison authorities to send it over quicker.'

So, Sunday was stalemate day. The shops might be open, the loonies and muggers might be out, but no one they needed to talk to would be working. Trueman would quietly and methodically dig away — metaphorically speaking — at gaining information on Felton and the Trotmans, while Dennings would physically dig away at Willow Bank, where hopefully he would be up to his knees in mud and soaking wet. But, knowing Dennings of old, he was probably inside the house supping tea, leaving the other poor plods outside. Dennings, like Uckfield, was of the view that there was no point in having rank and not using it.

Both Walters and Cantelli were meant to be off duty tomorrow and Horton could see no reason why they still shouldn't be. He, on the other hand, wanted to be around in case Trueman discovered anything pertinent on Luke Felton or Venetia Trotman, and he had one or two things he wanted to follow up, such as talking to ex-Detective Superintendent Chawley about the Natalie Raymonds case, and viewing the

CCTV tapes from the seafront in the hope he might spot his graffiti artist.

He headed back to the station, checking for anyone following him and wondering if he should move his boat on the high tide in case his stalker returned and wanted to do more than just draw pictures. The earliest he could do so would be around 11 p.m., but this weather might prevent him. And that would mean another sleepless night with half an eye and ear cocked for any sign of his nocturnal visitor.

Reaching his office, without incident or spotting his persecutor, he checked his messages. PC Seaton had left a note before going off duty to say that he'd drawn a blank with the bus drivers for sightings of Luke on the bus routes on Tuesday night. That didn't necessarily mean he hadn't caught a bus, only that none of the drivers had observed him. And Felton could have reached Portchester on foot or hitched a lift.

Horton drafted a press statement about the body on the harbour and emailed it to someone in communications to issue it to the media, which would probably be done on Monday.

As he made his way to the third floor and the drug squad offices, he hoped that Hans Olewbo might be able to tell him more about Rookley's whereabouts, but the drug squad, it appeared, was closed for the weekend. Fetching sandwiches from the canteen, Horton took them to the incident room. Uckfield was in his office on the phone.

'Anything new?' Horton asked Trueman, fetching a beaker of water from the cooler.

'Nobody's dug any bodies up yet, if that's what you mean,' Trueman answered. 'But it's early days. I've got the results from the few fingerprints taken at the house, which could be the victim's, but I can't check if they match yet because we're still waiting on Dr Clayton.'

Stretching across his mobile phone Horton said, 'Take a recording of my anonymous caller, Dave, and see what

Forensic get on it.' He should have remembered earlier but it had got overlooked with everything else happening. He was very keen to trace the foreigner, though he judged it was going to be impossible from that one call. Remembering the manner of the call and the man's disappearance from the scene, Horton thought again that there must be a connection with the victim, or her late husband. Unless he happened to be a delivery driver, or someone calling to cut the trees or clean the windows, or something similar, which was possible, although the tone had conveyed urgency and menace. He said as much to Trueman, who nodded wisely and said they were already looking into that.

'I've also got a list of Felton's fellow inmates,' Trueman said, 'the ones who shared a cell with him, and those released over the last six months, but it's going to take some time checking if they have any connection with the Trotmans because we don't have any photographs of Joseph Trotman, and we don't know his real name. It's a bit like pissing in the wind.'

Horton agreed. To make any headway they needed to find out who the Trotmans really were, and he wasn't sure they were going to do that unless Uckfield got a breakthrough from his media appeal.

'Do you recall anything about the Natalie Raymonds murder?' he asked, biting into his sandwich.

Trueman didn't even blink at the change of subject, but then Horton hadn't expected him to. He said, 'I wasn't involved in it, but I remember Detective Superintendent Chawley was heading it. He was a clever copper, sharp as a razor, and popular too. It was a good result and quick, one of those cases that was over before it began. Wish I could say the same for this one.'

'Could you get me his address? I'd like to see what he remembers about Luke Felton.'

'Sure.'

Horton crossed to study the photographs on the crime board. There were several now of the garden, the house and the lane approaching it, and some of where the boat had been moored. Trueman had also managed to find photographs of a similar make of yacht to the Trotmans'. A thought flashed through Horton's mind, but before he could express it Uckfield's office door crashed open and the big man emerged, pulling on his camel coat.

'Dr Clayton's finished the autopsy on Venetia Trotman and she's gone all coy, insists on seeing me. Says she's got something interesting to show me. I told her I've seen a corpse before but she clammed up, won't tell me on the telephone what she's found. I reckon she fancies me.'

In your dreams, thought Horton.

'You can chaperone me in case she wants my body.'

'For medical science you mean?' muttered Horton, looking at the remaining sandwich in its packet — he doubted he'd have much appetite for it after another visit to the mortuary. 'Present for you, Dave,' he tossed it to Trueman, who caught it, examined it and said, 'Thanks.'

In the car, Horton asked if anyone had seen the yacht, Shorena, going through Portsmouth Harbour.

Uckfield shook his head. 'The damn thing's vanished.'

'Perhaps it's had a change of identity,' Horton said, voicing the idea that had occurred to him while studying the pictures on the crime board.

Uckfield threw him a glance. 'You mean while we've been fannying around asking about Shorena the bugger's renamed her. Isn't it bad luck to change a boat's name?'

Horton nodded.

'Good,' Uckfield replied fervently. 'I hope our killer gets swept overboard in a ruddy great storm, and gets hypothermia, concussion and his bits chewed off by the sea life before the lifeboat rescues him. How would he have had time to change the name?'

'Easy. He came prepared with a sticker already made up and simply stuck it over the yacht's existing name.'

'A planned job then?' Uckfield asked, indicating off the motorway. 'Would Felton have the brains for it?'

Yes, thought Horton, recalling that Ashley Felton had said his brother had won a place at Oxford. 'It could still be boat thieves who've done it a hundred times before, only this time Venetia Trotman disturbed them.'

'I'll get a picture of a similar yacht circulated, and coppers walking the pontoons, checking every bleeding yacht of that type, and its owner.'

'It could be in France or the Channel Islands by now.'

'Then I'll alert the authorities and the police there.'

They passed the rest of the short journey in silence. Horton wanted to ask whether Uckfield was still keen to get Dennings off his team but didn't. If he was, then he would have mentioned it.

They found Dr Clayton in her office looking tired. But then, Horton thought, who wouldn't be after two thorough autopsies.

She began by confirming the time of death. 'Between one thirty a.m. and four thirty a.m. on Friday. There was no salt residue on her clothes but there was grass and mud, which is what you would expect to find. I've sent her clothes and shoes to the lab along with samples from her skin and hair. I understand you're having problems confirming her identity, Superintendent, a bit like your body in the harbour, Inspector Horton.' She flashed him a brief smile before turning her gaze back to Uckfield.

'Brian will let you have copies of her fingerprints and dental records before you leave and he'll email them to Sergeant Trueman. All I can tell you for now is that your victim was a petite woman, five foot two and small boned. She's probably in her mid to late thirties, has never had children or a pregnancy that went to full term, and isn't a virgin. There are no distinguishing marks or tattoos on her and neither has she had any surgery or suffered broken bones. In fact, she was remarkably healthy. Good muscle tone, particularly in the legs.'

'A runner?' Horton asked, interested, as his mind flashed to Natalie Raymonds. Not that that was relevant, except for the possible link of Luke Felton. But Venetia Trotman could hardly have been out jogging in the early hours of the morning wearing her clothes.

Gaye said, 'Possibly. She certainly liked to keep fit.'

Uckfield removed his finger from his nose. 'I can't see her belonging to a gym.'

'She could have been a dancer.'

'Or a walker.' Horton recalled the walking shoes in her house. Perhaps she had kept fit by going for long walks along the shore.

Moodily, Uckfield said, 'OK, we've had the edited highlights, now tell us how she died?'

Gaye rose and beckoned them to follow her to the icy cold room just off the mortuary, where she slid open the drawer. Horton steeled himself once again to study the body.

Pointing, Gaye said, 'You can see the lacerations where she was bludgeoned across the head, face and neck.' She pointed to the discoloured and cut skin. 'Those wounds were inflicted by a heavy round metal object. I'm getting the traces of it analysed. But although the trauma to the face and head could have killed her, they didn't. They were inflicted after she was dead.'

'To make us think that was the cause of death?' asked Horton.

'Perhaps, but it was a clumsy attempt to do so. It wasn't a frenzied attack, it was calculated.'

'How do you know that?' asked Horton sharply.

'Because she was stabbed in the neck.'

Horton looked up in surprise. 'Isn't that unusual?' He'd only come across a neck stabbing once in his career and that was when he'd been a constable in uniform on patrol on a hot summer night in the city centre, when soaring temperatures and alcohol had led to searing passions, jealousy and death.

'It is.' Gaye closed the drawer. 'As you well know, stab wounds to the chest and back are far more common than those to the neck. But stab wounds to the neck can cause rapid death, as in this case, which could be why it was the method used. The weapon severed the vagus nerve and caused severe internal haemorrhage, hence no bleeding externally, except from the other lacerations inflicted with the yet unidentified blunt instrument after death, and they were minimal.'

'Would the killer have blood on him as a result of bludgeoning her?'

'Only splashes, because she was already dead. The stabbing was inflicted by an extremely sharp serrated knife about four inches long and two inches wide. And your killer also seems to have known exactly where to strike and how far to penetrate to kill almost instantly.'

Horton glanced at Uckfield. Did this mean their killer had killed before, and in the same manner? But Luke Felton hadn't used a knife; he'd strangled Natalie Raymonds and then bludgeoned her, which accounted for the blood on his clothes. 'Any idea what kind of knife?'

Gaye thought for a moment. 'It could be a small, sharp vegetable knife, but as the victim's yacht is also missing then it's just as likely it could be a sailing knife taken from the boat, the kind you use for slicing rope in an emergency.'

Uckfield rounded on Horton. 'Did you see one on board?'

'Not that I remember, but I was hardly taking an inventory.'

Uckfield scowled. Gloomily he said, 'It's probably at the bottom of the sea.'

'You never know, Dennings might find it in the garden.'

Uckfield snorted. To Dr Clayton he said, 'Any chance of getting a decent photograph of her?'

Gaye walked towards the benches on the far side of the room. 'I'll pull something together with the aid of the computer and Inspector Horton's description and email it across to you. But I haven't finished yet.'

Horton caught the edge of excitement in her voice and felt a tremor of anticipation. Uckfield halted.

Gaye continued. 'The victim was discovered with her right hand tightly clenched, which was the result of a cadaveric spasm. It's highly unusual and confirms my findings that she died almost the moment the weapon was plunged into her neck. When we unlocked her hand, it wasn't empty.'

Horton felt his pulse quicken. Uckfield eyed her keenly.

She reached across the bench for a small plastic evidence bag. 'This was in it.'

Uckfield took the bag and Horton found himself staring at a small flat key. It clearly wasn't a house key: the wrong size, shape and style. So where did it belong? And why had it been in her hand when she was killed?

He said, 'It looks like a key to a locker or small storage box.'

'Great!' exploded Uckfield. 'Now all we have to do is examine every ruddy locker and box in the country.'

Horton said, 'It's got a number on it. A locksmith could help us pinpoint what type it is and where it came from. That'll be a start at least.'

Uckfield reached for his phone. He was already heading for the door. Over his shoulder he shouted, 'Dr Clayton, I need that photograph. Now!' The door slammed behind him.

Horton addressed Gaye. 'Any other ideas?'

'Not at the moment, but you'll be the first to know if I get any.'

'It's not my case,' he said.

She waggled a finger in her ear and frowned. 'Sorry, didn't hear that. Think I've gone deaf.'

He smiled at her. 'I'd get a doctor to look at that if I was you.'

'I would, if I could find one I trust.'

You and me both, thought Horton, although Dr Clayton was an exception. Only problem was she dealt in dead bodies, not live ones. He gave her a detailed description of the victim before joining Uckfield in the car.

'The key could be to a storage device where she kept her jewellery, which could have been on her boat,' Horton said, as Uckfield swung the car in the direction of the station. 'I didn't see one when I was on board, and I looked in all the boat's lockers, but she could have taken it down there that night, which would be why she was on the boat. She heard a noise, made to get away, didn't bother with her coat but made sure to take the key, which means the box contained something that was very valuable to her.'

'And she put it on the boat because she was planning to escape whoever was after her, who could be Luke Felton,' finished Uckfield. He swore at a motorbike, which overtook him with a roar and swerved in perilously close, causing him to brake.

It wasn't a Harley but it was nevertheless a powerful machine. Instantly Horton recalled the one he'd heard speeding away after his incident in the lock, and with a jolt remembered the same thing happening to Cantelli when they'd been following Rookley to the cemetery. Quickly, Horton tried to read the licence plate before it sped off but it was smeared with mud and unreadable. Coincidence? Perhaps.

He said, 'If Felton didn't kill her, it's possible she was planning to start a new life with someone she thought was a friend, who in fact was her killer. He then steals the boat and makes off with whatever is in that locker. And without the key, I guess he'd just break it open.' Then he paused, adding after a moment, 'Or perhaps her secret was on the verge of being exposed. She could already have been threatened by whoever might have been in the house when I was there. He leaves her for a while—'

'Why?'

Horton didn't answer but continued with his theory. 'She seizes the opportunity to leave that night on the high tide, but her killer returns before she can do so.' He warmed to his idea. 'Perhaps he left her earlier knowing that she'd try to get away with whatever it is that's valuable and in that locker. He waits, returns and then kills her, getting the loot and making his escape on the yacht.'

'Why not simply check the locker was on board after he'd killed her, take the loot and scarper?' demanded Uckfield, as he swung into the station car park.

'Because he needed the yacht to get away. He arrived by boat so he had to leave by one. Luke Felton might have known from an inmate about this loot, whatever it is. He can handle a boat, so maybe he took a small motorboat to get to Willow Bank. His brother, Ashley, has a yacht, but I can't see him aiding and abetting his brother in killing Venetia Trotman. But Felton could be in league with someone he met in prison, someone who knew the Trotmans.'

Uckfield silenced the car engine but neither man made any attempt to alight. Horton continued. 'Let's say Felton and his accomplice arrive by sea on the rising tide and in a tender with an outboard motor. The accomplice, who knows Venetia Trotman, claims to be helping her, but when she realizes his real intentions, she runs away. He kills her while Felton stickers over the yacht's existing name with another he's brought with him. The accomplice jumps on board Shorena, knowing the locker of valuables is there. Towing the tender, they set off for the Solent, going through the harbour under a different name in case they're spotted. When they're certain they're safe they turn their attention to the locker only to find they don't have the key. But that doesn't matter. They smash it open, remove the contents and then abandon the yacht, or better still scuttle it obliterating any prints and evidence, getting away on the tender they've been towing. They return to the shore and into a waiting car.' Then Horton had another thought. 'They might not even have bothered to change the name, taking the risk they wouldn't be seen, and even if they were it would be too late then because they'd already have cleared out the yacht and scuttled it. If they did it in the Solent, then we might never find it.'

'Shit! I hate these guys,' Uckfield expelled.

It didn't explain why Luke had been missing since Tuesday but he knew that Uckfield wouldn't let that stand in his way. And, as he'd already speculated, Luke Felton might have been in Venetia's house, or perhaps even shacked up with this accomplice. Horton opened the car door and turned towards his Harley.

Surprised, Uckfield said, 'Where are you going?'

'Home. This isn't my case. But I'll let you know if I find Luke Felton.'

'Thanks a bloody bunch,' Horton heard Uckfield growl after him.

CHAPTER ELEVEN

Sunday, 15 March

The night passed without incident and without much sleep for Horton, who rubbed a fist against his eyes as he viewed the CCTV tapes from the seafront. All he saw were courting couples performing sexual aerobics in the back of their cars, and speeding drivers who clearly thought they were participating in the Southsea Grand Prix, but no motorbikes. And neither had he heard any last night. This was a waste of time. Yawning, he stabbed off the screen and once again let his eyes travel over the list of recently released criminals Trueman had got from the Isle of Wight prison. He didn't know any of them. He'd have to request a list of those released from all prisons in England, but when he would get it, he had no idea. Meanwhile he'd need to keep alert for his graffiti artist.

Sitting back, he again considered the fact that this Zeus — or someone connected with him — wanted by the Intelligence Directorate might be after him. And that brought him back to thoughts of his mother. Had she been involved with Zeus? He'd already discovered that she had mixed with some doubtful characters and criminal types, but that didn't mean she was crooked.

He stared at his computer for a moment longer before jerking forward in his seat and calling up her missing persons file. And there she was: Jennifer Horton. His heart lurched, as it always did, at the sight of her fair youthful face, and he felt the usual numbing pain of anguish and loneliness. It was a torment to look at her, but one he knew he could no longer ignore or avoid. He had to know what had happened to her, even if the truth was what he had always been led to believe: that she had deliberately abandoned him.

His eyes flicked to the name of the police officer who had briefly investigated her disappearance and who had compiled the missing persons report: PC Adrian Stanley. How old would he be now? Fifty? Sixty? Maybe he was dead. And even if he wasn't, how much of the investigation would he remember? It was a long time ago and Jennifer Horton had been just one of many missing people. But he should find out.

Before he could change his mind, he quickly typed an email asking Trueman to find out where PC Stanley was living. Trueman wouldn't ask why he wanted the information and neither would he divulge who had requested it. He pressed send and then let out the breath he'd been holding before picking up his phone and punching in Hans Olewbo's extension. He'd decide what to do about PC Stanley if and when Trueman located him, he thought, listening to Olewbo's extension ringing. He was about to give up, thinking Olewbo must be out or off duty, when it was answered.

'You know Rookley's gone missing,' Horton said, without preamble. 'Any idea where he might be?'

'No, and if I was you, Andy, I'd think about joining him. You're not Superintendent Oliver's favourite cop.'

'I don't seem to be anyone's.'

'It's gone all quiet around Crown House and Belton's shut up shop.'

'Or the health people have closed him down. When did the café proprietor go walkabout?'

'Yesterday. Oliver thinks the route's been closed.'

'That's hardly my fault.'

'Try telling Oliver that.'

'I need to see the surveillance tapes and photographs for Crown House,' Horton said. He hoped they might show if Rookley or Felton had met anyone outside the premises during the last week.

'Then you'll need clearance from Oliver.'

And that meant involving Bliss, who was sure to take Oliver's side that it was his fault the operation had been compromised. He thought about bypassing Bliss and going straight to Uckfield, who could command access to the files by citing Felton's possible involvement in the Venetia Trotman murder case. However, that would not only take time, it would also sideline him from the investigation.

'Can't you let me have access without Oliver knowing?'

After a short pause, Hans sighed heavily. 'I'll see what I can do.'

As Horton rang off a hesitant knock sounded on his door and he beckoned Seaton in. The young PC was in civvies.

'I'm off duty, sir,' Seaton quickly explained. 'But this morning I thought I'd go back to where Luke might have caught the bus on Tuesday evening when he left work.' He flushed, looking a little uneasy.

Seaton was probably wondering if he'd take the rise out of him for not having a life outside work, like Horton himself. But then Horton had been — and still was — keen, despite all the crap he had to deal with, and he didn't mean from the scum.

Waving Seaton into the seat across his desk, Horton said, 'Go on.'

'As you know, sir, I got no joy from the bus drivers yesterday. We know Luke didn't return to Crown House in Portsmouth, so maybe he didn't go to Portsmouth at all but went in the opposite direction, towards Horsea Marina and Portchester. Perhaps he was meeting someone for a drink, which means he could have called into a pub or café at the marina.' Seaton's colour deepened as he went on, 'I visited them and showed his photograph around.'

And Horton guessed that Seaton had told them he was from CID. So what? Horton didn't care if he'd told them he was the Chief Constable if it got a result.

'Nobody recognized Luke. Then at the traffic lights by Paulsgrove Lake, not far from Kempton's, I wondered if anyone living in the houses opposite might have seen Luke.'

'And had they?' Horton asked eagerly, sitting forward, already knowing the answer by Seaton's expression.

'Yes.' Seaton opened his notebook, trying, but not succeeding, to hide his excitement. 'Mr John Sunnington lives in number twenty-six. He was driving home from work on Tuesday evening and almost went into the back of a car, which pulled over sharply without any indication or warning right in front of him and into the bus lay-by to pick someone up. Mr Sunnington sounded his horn, gave the driver a black look and probably a V-sign, before indicating right and turning into a side road behind his house where his garage is. The man that was picked up was Luke Felton. Mr Sunnington described him to me before I showed him the photograph.'

'Time?'

'Just before six thirty.'

Which fitted with when the receptionist had said Luke had left Kempton's. Luke must have started walking in the direction of Portchester and decided to catch the bus the rest of the way, or perhaps had just been passing the bus stop when this car pulled over. 'Did Mr Sunnington get the registration?' Horton didn't dare hope.

'He did.' Seaton again consulted his notebook, but Horton knew it was for effect. 'It was a red BMW. Mr Sunnington didn't get all the registration number but he got most of it. It was a personalized number plate, ES 368.'

Horton started. 'Are you sure?'

'Yes. Why? You know who it is?' Seaton asked, surprised.

Oh, yes, he knew all right. It was Edward Shawford, sales manager at Kempton's, and his wife's lover.

Horton scraped back his chair. 'Are you doing anything special, Seaton?' he asked, grabbing his sailing jacket.

'Well, no, sir,' Seaton said, puzzled.

'You've got a car?'

'Yes.'

'Good, then let's go and interview the owner of the vehicle.'

Horton knew Shawford lived in a flat in Wickham, a village ten miles to the north-west of Portsmouth. Shawford was divorced and had no children, so unless he was with Catherine, Horton hoped they'd find him in. He thought it advisable to have a witness to their interview, otherwise Shawford was bound to go bellyaching to Bliss and twisting everything Horton said to make it sound like a personal vendetta against him, which he had to admit it was. But the fact that Luke Felton had been heading towards the area where Venetia Trotman lived was extremely interesting. Although, Horton silently acknowledged, it was also in the direction of where Luke's sister lived. Horton was intrigued to know why Shawford had given Luke Felton a lift and impatient to know where Shawford had taken him, but as they swung into the car park at the rear of the five-storey block of modern flats there was no sign of the red BMW. Nor was there any answer to Seaton's finger pressed on the intercom.

Could Shawford be at Horton's former home near Petersfield, sitting at the table he had once sat at, lounging in the chair he'd lounged in, watching the television he'd bought, lying in the bed he'd once slept in . . . ?

He pulled himself up roughly. Tormenting himself with images like this was a waste of time and energy. It made no difference to Catherine or bloody Shawford, and hurt only him. Before he could suggest to Seaton that they head for Petersfield, the door opened and an elegant, slender woman in her early sixties stepped out.

Seaton said, 'We're looking for Mr Edward Shawford, but he doesn't seem to be in.'

'He's probably on his boat.'

Horton hadn't known that Shawford had one. Catherine hadn't mentioned it. Though why should she? They'd hardly conversed since she'd thrown him out. Had the fat slob taken Catherine and Emma out on it today? The vision of Emma on Shawford's boat hurt him badly. His daughter should be with him, on his boat. He didn't want Emma to go away to school, but for the first time he considered that it might not be a bad thing if it meant getting her away from Shawford.

He brought his attention back to the woman in front of him as she said with a smile, 'It's a motorboat. He only bought it a few weeks ago. And he's never stopped talking about it since.'

Horton said, 'I don't suppose you know where he keeps it.'

'I do. And I could probably tell you the colour, make and size of the engine, if I'd paid enough attention. It's at Horsea Marina.'

Horton thanked her and they headed for the marina. Seaton remained silent. Horton was grateful for that. It gave him time to prepare for the fact that he might find Catherine with the slimy git. He'd cope with that. But what he knew he couldn't cope with was seeing Emma there with Shawford, laughing with him, smiling at him . . . just being with him. It wasn't just Shawford, because Horton knew he'd feel the same about his daughter being with any man that wasn't her father. He didn't know what he would do if Emma was there, but the spring of rage inside him warned him it would be something drastic and highly damaging.

When they were approaching the marina, he thought he should tell Seaton something about the situation. He didn't really want to, but Shawford might bring up the fact he was having a relationship with Horton's soon-to-be ex-wife. And if Catherine were there, then Seaton would quickly cotton on.

He gave a potted version of their break-up, leaving Seaton to fill in the rest himself. Like a good cop, Seaton listened expressionless and without comment. He was too ambitious to remark on it. Horton knew Seaton was single but didn't know if he was in a relationship. In fact, he knew nothing at all about the young PC. And now was not the time to discover it, he thought as they turned into the marina.

While Seaton enquired at the marina office for the location of Shawford's boat, Horton stepped out of the car and walked down to the shore. He stared across the harbour at the ancient remains of Portchester Castle, trying to get his emotions under the iron control that he'd had to use as a child and teenager to shield himself from being hurt by others' cruelty and carelessness, whether deliberate or accidental. If Emma was with Shawford then he had to make sure that she didn't get upset or confused by any display of anger from him. He'd have to pretend that he didn't mind. It wouldn't be the first time and he knew it wouldn't be the last.

He surveyed the scene before him as a distraction from dwelling too much on what he'd lost. Just beyond the castle, but completely hidden from view, was Willow Bank and its slipway where Shorena had been moored. It would have been easy enough to slip out into the harbour from there. His eyes swivelled to the right of the castle, taking in the masts of the yachts and dinghies at the Castle Sailing Club and beyond it the large boat sheds and more yacht masts. Also visible was a red and black funnel, which looked strangely out of place among the sailing boats.

He swung his gaze southwards but Seaton hailed him. A couple of minutes later they drew up in front of one of the pontoons. Their timing was perfect because as Horton climbed out, Shawford punched the release button on the bridgehead and stepped off the pontoon. And, as Horton noted with great relief, he was alone.

Shawford looked up, did a double-take before glancing back at his boat and then, scowling, snarled, 'What do you want?'

'A word.'

'I'll give you two. Bugger off.' Shawford pressed the zapper on his key ring and the BMW clunked open.

Seaton quickly said, 'We need you to help us with our enquiries, sir.'

Shawford started with surprise and eyed them nervously. 'And they are?' he said, heaving his sailing bag into the boot.

His attempt at indifference didn't quite ring true. Horton answered, 'Luke Felton's disappearance.'

'Didn't know he had.'

He was lying, of course. Horton said, 'Strange that, seeing as he works for the same company as you.'

'Doesn't mean to say we're bosom pals.'

'But you gave him a lift on Tuesday evening at about six thirty.'

Shawford looked up and Horton saw surprise in the light grey eyes, and along with it something else, which looked to him like panic. Shawford turned away and pulled open the driver's door. 'So?'

Horton stepped closer and placed a firm hand on the open car door, forcing Shawford to press his body back against the car. Disguising his disgust behind the veneer of amiability, a skill that he'd perfected as a police officer over the years, Horton said, 'We'll get through this a lot quicker if you cooperate, sir.' He stressed the last word, making it sound like a sneer, before adding in the same light manner, 'You see, you might be the last person to have seen Luke Felton alive.'

Shawford's head jerked back in surprise. 'You mean he's dead?'

'Possibly. Now are you going to answer our questions or do I have to ask you to come to the station?'

Shawford licked his full lips nervously. 'I saw him beside the road on Tuesday evening. I pulled over and asked if he'd like a lift.'

'That was very chivalrous of you.'

'I can do without your sarcasm,' flashed Shawford.

'And I can do without your lies,' snapped Horton. 'Why did you give him a lift?'

Shawford took a breath but didn't speak. Horton could see his mind racing, obviously deciding exactly what and how much to tell them. The truth would be nice but Horton doubted he'd get it. He remained silent, keeping his eyes on Shawford, knowing it was only a matter of time and nerve before he cracked, but Seaton's clear voice broke the heavy silence.

'Where did you take Luke?'

Horton could have slapped the PC. He hadn't yet learnt that silence was a powerful weapon. But he would. Horton flashed him an angry glance. Seaton flinched. Shawford visibly relaxed.

'Portchester Castle.'

It wasn't the answer Horton had been expecting, or was it? If it was the truth, then it strengthened the theory that Felton knew about the Trotmans and had gone there to get money. It could also mean Felton had returned there on Thursday night or Friday morning and killed Venetia Trotman.

'Why there?' Horton asked sharply.

'He said it was where he wanted to go. He didn't give a reason and I didn't ask him.'

'And you just happened to be going that way,' taunted Horton.

Shawford's eyes narrowed, clearly with hatred. 'It's the route I take home from the factory,' he said through clenched teeth.

'Diverting down to the castle off the main road isn't on your route.'

'It's a few minutes diversion, no more.'

Clearly Shawford wasn't going to budge on that. There had to be a reason why he'd offered Felton a lift, and gone out of his way to drop him off at Portchester Castle. The Shawfords of this world didn't do anything unless there was something in it for them.

Seaton said, 'What did you talk about, sir?'

'Can't remember. This and that. How he was settling in, that kind of thing.'

Horton felt like saying 'bollocks'. Shawford was lying, but he was also growing more confident and Horton wondered why.

'Did Luke speak about Natalie Raymonds?' he asked.

'Who?'

That was so obviously a lie that even Shawford realized they'd know it and shifted uneasily, but he didn't make the mistake of elaborating on it, or trying to back-pedal. This time Seaton didn't break the silence. He'd learnt his lesson. And Shawford kept his nerve, finally forcing Horton to say, 'She's the woman Luke Felton murdered.'

Shawford fiddled with his keys. 'He didn't mention her.'

Horton wondered at Shawford's evasiveness. He said, 'How did you feel about the company employing a killer?'

'It's nothing to do with me. I'm sales not personnel. Now if there's—'

'Where exactly did you drop Felton?'

'In the car park opposite the castle.'

'Were there any other cars there?'

'I didn't really notice.'

Horton thought that at least was the truth. 'Anybody hanging around or walking past the castle?'

'I wasn't paying attention.'

And if Luke was meeting someone there, then he must have arrived early, because he could have had no way of knowing that he was going to be offered a lift.

'What did Luke do next?'

Shawford eyed him, bewildered. 'He got out. I turned the car round and left.'

Horton eyed him steadily, searching for the lie. It sounded and looked like the truth, but an experienced salesman like Shawford was practised in the art of lying. And Horton didn't trust or believe him one iota. He also wasn't about to let him off the hook that easily.

'Been out on your new boat?'

The question took Shawford by surprise. The fear was back in his eyes. He eyed Horton warily before snapping, 'Yes.'

'Where have you been?'

'That's none of your business.' He made to climb into the car, but Horton stalled him.

'Everything's my business when I'm looking for a missing prisoner.'

'Well, you won't find him on my boat.'

Horton raised his eyebrows and glanced at Seaton. 'Now that's an idea. We hadn't thought of that. Maybe you didn't drop him off at Portchester Castle but drove him here. You invited him on board, then killed him and pushed him overboard in the Solent.'

'You're mad!' Shawford paled.

'Am I?' Horton began to wonder whether a theory he'd posed in order to frighten Shawford might actually hold water. What motive Shawford could have for killing Felton, Horton had no idea; Seaton though was eyeing him admiringly, as though he'd solved the crime of the decade in a flash of inspiration. But Shawford was an experienced sailor and could have used his boat to get from Horsea Marina to Willow Bank quite easily, Horton thought. But why would Shawford hitch up with Felton, and why kill Venetia Trotman? However much he hated him, Horton couldn't see Shawford as a killer.

Alarmed, Shawford said, 'I dropped Luke off at Portchester Castle and went home. I got in at just after seven. You can ask my neighbour. I saw her in the lobby.'

'You might have left Felton, dead, on your boat and returned later to get rid of the body.'

'Christ! You're insane. You're trying to fit me up, just because I'm in a relationship with Catherine. I want a lawyer.'

'Why? You've not been charged,' Horton replied, feigning bewilderment. OK, so he was enjoying this.

'I know you bastards. You'll twist everything I say.'

'Had much dealing with the law then?'

'Sod off, Horton.'

Horton smiled, which seemed to send Shawford into a purple fit. His fists clenched, but with supreme effort he managed to control himself. Pity. Horton would have relished being thumped and then charging the man.

'We'll need to search your boat.'

'Then you'll need a warrant.'

'So you have got something to hide,' Horton taunted, ignoring the pleading look Seaton was throwing him. Good job Cantelli wasn't here, Horton thought. He'd be having kittens.

'You could plant something.'

'Tch, tch, you obviously don't hold the police in high regard.' Horton leaned forward and lowered his voice. 'But then I think you're a useless piece of shit.'

Shawford flushed. 'How dare you . . . Did you hear that?'

Seaton looked confused. 'Sorry, sir, must be the noise of that helicopter going over.'

'What bloody . . . Oh, I see, sticking together. Well, I don't have to put up with your crap any longer.' He climbed in the car and this time Horton didn't prevent him, but he leaned down and tapped on the window. Shawford looked in two minds whether to lower it, but finally did so with ill grace.

Pleasantly Horton said, 'We'll need you to come to the station and make a statement about giving Luke Felton a lift.'

'What, now?' Shawford snatched a glance at his watch.

Why, you got a date with Catherine? 'Yes, now. We'll follow you.'

'You can try,' said Shawford, gunning the engine.

Watching the car speed away Seaton said, 'Do you really think he killed Felton?'

Horton considered it for a moment. 'No, but I want a warrant to search his boat, and we'll take forensic samples from it.' If only to annoy Shawford, thought Horton. Aloud he said, 'You can check his story tomorrow with his neighbour, and see if anyone around Portchester Castle remembers seeing Felton there on Tuesday evening. Meanwhile, if you can give up more of your Sunday, you can take Shawford's statement.'

CHAPTER TWELVE

Shawford stuck to his story but Horton was convinced there was something he wasn't telling them. He had again denied them access to his boat and insisted on them getting a warrant, so Horton would, if only to spite the man — because he couldn't really see him kidnapping and killing Luke Felton, or being in league with him to rob and kill Venetia Trotman. But Horton had an edgy feeling about Shawford. OK, so his intense dislike of the slob was probably clouding his judgement, but his copper's instinct told him there was something not right.

From his office window he watched Shawford cross the car park to his vehicle while mentally running over their encounter at Horsea Marina. Shawford had looked shocked at seeing them but there had also been that nervous glance back at the boat, the insistence that they get a warrant before going on board, and the defensive response when Horton had asked him where he'd been. Of course, there might be nothing more in Shawford's reaction than hatred for him, but as Shawford pulled out of the car park, Horton found himself reaching for his helmet and jacket.

On the Harley he would soon catch up with Shawford, but even if he didn't, he had an inkling where he would find him, and that wouldn't be with Catherine. Horton veered off the motorway and made towards Horsea Marina. He'd been correct. Ahead was Shawford's BMW. He kept well back, even though he doubted Shawford would recognize him or his Harley. Shawford pulled into the marina and drew up close to the spot where earlier Horton and Seaton had interviewed him. As Horton watched him hurry from his car to the pontoon, he reconsidered his theory about Felton having been on Shawford's boat; was Shawford trying to hide the evidence? But Horton just couldn't see it. No, he had other ideas about what Shawford might be trying to hide.

A few minutes elapsed before Shawford emerged, looking furtive, and carrying a plastic carrier bag. Horton smiled grimly to himself. Climbing off the Harley he crossed to Shawford's car. Shawford saw him, froze, flushed and tried to look untroubled, but Horton could see he was shitting himself.

'What's in the bag?' Horton demanded.

'None of your business,' Shawford bluffed, but Horton remained resolutely in front of the driver's door, blocking him.

'This is harassment,' Shawford raged. 'I shall report you to your superiors.'

'Report all you like. Edward Shawford, I am arresting you on suspicion of the kidnapping of Luke Felton and of being in possession of items belonging to him—'

'You bastard!'

'Hand it over, Shawford.' Horton stretched out his hand and angrily Shawford pushed the bag into it.

Peering inside Horton found himself staring at what he had expected, not Luke Felton's personal effects, but a stash of DVDs and magazines. He dipped inside and withdrew a magazine. He didn't need to flick through it, or the others, to know what they contained; the woman on the front of the one he was holding gave him enough of a clue. She was dressed in a black leather tunic, thigh-high boots, a spiked leather collar, and she was wielding a whip. With his knowledge of

Shawford's relationship with Catherine — which had once included bruises that Catherine had tried to blame on him — Horton could see that Shawford liked it rough.

'It's not what you think,' Shawford blabbed. 'It's just a fantasy, that's all, a bit of fun. I like to look at it. I don't actually do it.'

Horton eyed him with disgust. His stomach churned at the thought of this man and Catherine indulging in sadomasochism. Which of them had the power? Surely not Catherine, but then he couldn't see Shawford as the dominant partner in the relationship, the one wanting to inflict pain while Catherine took pleasure in it. No, it had to be the other way around, but that made him feel angry, disappointed and sick. It threw into question everything his relationship with Catherine had been. He hoped that Shawford was telling the truth about only wanting to look at it, before another mind-numbing and paralysing thought struck him. Emma!

His body stiffened with fear and fury. He had no reason to believe that Emma had witnessed this kind of sexual behaviour between Shawford and her mother, or that Shawford's tastes ran even stronger than sadomasochism, but he didn't want him anywhere near his daughter. And certainly not in the same house while her mother indulged in whatever sick fancy turned Shawford on. He reached for his mobile.

'What are you doing?' Shawford cried.

Horton eyed him coldly. 'Getting the vice squad into your apartment, who will take it apart.' He had no intention of doing so; vice might find images of Shawford with Catherine. And he couldn't stand that. It would be all over the station. He made to punch in a number, praying that Shawford would lose his nerve. He did.

Shawford blanched. 'No, please. Not that.'

Horton made a pretence of hesitating while breathing a silent sigh of relief. He eyed Shawford steadily and with hatred. Shawford flinched. Then, thrusting his face so close to Shawford's that he could see the veins in his eyes, Horton hissed, 'If I find you within a mile of my daughter, I'll wipe your fat face in the dirt and smear your perversions all over the press. Is that clear?'

Shawford opened his mouth to say something, thought better of it and nodded curtly. After a moment Horton stepped back, but not far enough for Shawford to escape brushing against him. Shawford's nervous eyes flicked down to the bag in Horton's hand.

'I'll hang on to these,' Horton said brusquely.

He watched as the BMW sped out of the car park, then stashed the bag in the locker on the Harley and headed up the hill bordering the city. Here he drew into one of the view-point lay-bys and stared, without seeing it, at the land and seascape spread out beneath him under a low cloud. He tried not to think of Catherine and Edward Shawford together. He realized his fists were clenching as disturbing images flitted through his brain. He had to force himself to relax, to take a slow, deep breath. Distantly he could hear the throb of the traffic. After a while his heart rate settled down, though not back to normal because he knew there was something he had to do to guarantee that Shawford never saw Emma again.

Half an hour later he was pulling up outside his former home. Catherine's car was on the driveway. Good. Stiff with tension, he pushed his finger on the bell and waited impatiently for her to come to the door. It seemed like ages, but in reality, it must only have been a minute, maybe less. Her expression changed swiftly from polite curiosity to anger before she half closed the door on him as though afraid he'd storm in. He desperately wanted to, but curbed his agitation.

'What do you want, Andy?'

'Where's Emma?' Horton strained his ears for his daughter's pleasant laughter or chatter but all was silent. This was one time in his life when he prayed she wouldn't be there.

'She's on a sleepover with a school friend.'

Horton glanced at his watch to disguise his relief. He was astonished to find it was nearly four o'clock. 'Shouldn't she be back soon for school in the morning?'

'What do you want?' Catherine repeated firmly.

'To come in.'

'You can't.' She made to close the door further.

Exasperated, Horton said, 'Catherine, what are you afraid of? That I'm going to ransack the place or contaminate it in some way, or perhaps physically attack you?'

'No, but—'

'Or that once inside I'll refuse to leave until I see Emma, or refuse to go for good?' He saw that something like that had crossed her mind. Wearily, he said, 'I won't. We need to talk.'

'We finished talking a long time ago when you—'

'Oh, change the record, Catherine,' Horton cried, exasperated. 'You know I didn't sleep with Lucy Richardson, never mind rape her, so stop dragging that up as an excuse for why you ended our marriage. If you want to blame me and the job, then fine. It's better for Emma's sake than me citing your adultery. And don't deny it,' he added hastily at her black look, 'because I don't believe it and what's more I don't care anymore. I need to talk to you about Edward Shawford.'

'So, we're back to him,' Catherine hissed. 'You're jealous.'

Horton's expression hardened. Brusquely he said, 'There's something you should see. I've just taken these off Shawford.' He pulled out one of the magazines. 'But if you'd like to discuss it here on the doorstep for the neighbours to hear . . .'

He saw her startled expression before, tight-lipped, she stepped back, and for the first time since September, Horton walked through the hall and into the lounge on the left. She'd completely changed it; clearly it had been a case of sweeping him out of her life.

'Looks nice,' he said, though he didn't mean it. Everything was white except the floor, which was wood. There were white walls, white chairs, white curtains, the only splash of colour being the red cushions. She'd ditched the books, ornaments, pictures and photographs, except for one large one of her and Emma above where the fireplace had once been, but was now a plain wall. The room reminded Horton of a prison cell with splashes of blood.

She stood with her arms folded and glared at him, but behind her blue eyes he could see she was worried. 'What's this all about?' she demanded with hostility.

Clearly, he wasn't going to be offered a coffee, not even a glass of water. Even if he were he didn't know whether he'd be able to swallow it, his body felt so taut.

He tipped open the plastic bag, scattering the contents on the floor. Her eyes flicked to them and then up to him.

'Shawford had those on his boat.'

'You're lying.'

'I don't want to know what you do with Shawford, but I am concerned about my daughter being in the same house when you do it.'

'How dare you!' she raged. 'You think—'

'I dare, Catherine, because I know that you and Shawford have indulged in some extreme physical sex in the past.'

She flushed. Her mouth opened then closed tightly.

Horton continued. 'Is there anything I need to know about?'

She didn't answer.

'Is there?' he pressed.

'No,' she spat. 'I've never been into bondage and all that stuff.' She jabbed a finger at the magazines. But her eyes fell and she turned away from him.

'Ah, but he wanted to.'

She swung back, her eyes flashing with fury. 'Of course not,' she declared hotly.

It was a lie. Horton knew he was right. 'I've applied for a warrant to search Shawford's boat. Not because of that,' he added hastily, gesturing at the pornography, 'but because Shawford, so far, is the last person to have seen Luke Felton. He gave him a lift on Tuesday night. We might also need to apply to search his apartment. I'm telling you this, Catherine, because I don't want to be the source of gossip and sniggers all over the station, and I don't want Emma exposed to it. Is there anything I need to know about?'

She glared at him. 'No,' she snapped.

'Are you sure?'

'Of course I'm sure. I have never let him do anything like that,' she spat. 'And if you think I'd do anything to upset or expose Emma then you're mad.'

Horton saw the fury in her eyes and along with it was fear, because she knew what he was leaving unspoken. He didn't have to threaten her with what the courts would make of it. Catherine wasn't stupid. Again thoughts of the boarding school sprang to Horton's mind. It might save Emma from being exposed to her mother's boyfriends.

Crisply he said, 'There's a prospective parents' evening at Northover School next Saturday.' He recalled what the headmistress had told him: tea, a tour of the school, a chance to meet the teachers and the pupils, and the opportunity to ask questions. 'I suggest we both be there with Emma.'

'I . . .' She made to protest then gave a curt nod.

'And it's Emma's decision whether she goes or not. Isn't it?' he insisted, when she glared, tight-lipped, at him. 'And if she wants to go, I will pay her school fees.' Again, she nodded.

He turned and walked swiftly to the door. He could hear her following. At the door he turned to face her. 'Just be careful who you sleep with next time.'

The door slammed on him. He was perturbed to find he was shaking slightly. He rode into Petersfield and bought a coffee, hoping it would calm his jangling nerves and soothe his inner turmoil. Three cups later he found he was ready to return to work, and that meant talking to ex-Superintendent Duncan Chawley about Natalie Raymonds.

CHAPTER THIRTEEN

Removing his helmet, Horton stared up at the address Trueman had given him, thinking the former superintendent had done well for himself. The modern, two-storey brick-built house, with neat blinds at the windows and a sturdy enclosed porch tacked on to the front, was set in landscaped grounds of about two acres amid rolling fields on the borders of West Sussex and Hampshire. To the left, and attached to the property, was a single-storey brick-built extension with a large double-glazed bay window, and to Horton's right was a detached double garage block.

His observations were curtailed by the sound of a car pulling up behind him and he turned to see a silver Saab convertible draw to a halt. A man in his late thirties with cropped black hair and a sun-weathered complexion climbed out. He studied Horton with a wary frown. Horton noted the chinos, deck shoes and red sailing jacket. This was so obviously not Duncan Chawley that either Trueman had given him an old address, which was highly unlikely, or this man was related to Duncan Chawley.

'Can I help?' the man asked in a well-modulated voice, but with a hint of suspicion.

'Are you the occupant?'

'Yes, and you are?'

Horton introduced himself with a show of his warrant card. 'I'm looking for Mr Duncan Chawley.'

'He's my father. I'm Gavin Chawley.'

Horton took the outstretched hand, returning the firm grip.

'Why do you want him? Only my father's not well,' Chawley said with concern.

'I need to talk to him about one of his old cases. It is important,' Horton pressed, wondering what was wrong with Duncan Chawley.

'Then you'd better come in.'

Horton stepped into a porch, where Chawley hung his jacket before entering a large hall. He offered to take Horton's leather jacket and was hanging it up when a blonde woman hurried towards them with an anxious look on what must once have been a pretty face, thought Horton, but now looked jaded. She froze, somewhat startled at Horton's appearance.

'He's a policeman,' Chawley explained. 'He's come to talk to Dad. This is my wife, Julia.'

The woman tossed Horton a shy smile before addressing her husband. 'Is it OK if I take the children out now, Gavin? Only we're late. They're going to a friend's birthday party,' she explained to Horton, again with that hesitant smile. From the lines around her eyes and mouth, Horton thought she looked too tired for birthday parties. He wondered how many children the Chawleys had, maybe several, though he couldn't hear any.

Gavin Chawley gave his wife a smile and a nod and she slid past them and up the stairs.

'My wife and I take it in turns to go out at the weekends, because of Dad's illness,' Chawley explained, leading Horton through the tiled hall into a sunny and expansive modern kitchen and breakfast room at the back of the house. 'It puts a strain on things.'

And just as he'd seen the strain on Julia Chawley's faded features, Horton now noticed them on Gavin Chawley's more rugged ones.

'It's particularly hard on Julia,' Chawley continue
'because she's at home with Dad and the children all wee
I try to relieve her at weekends but it's not always possibl
It's not that we resent it,' he added hastily. 'It's just difficu
sometimes, particularly with the children at that age whe
they need to go to classes and friends' parties. My mother die
some years ago and when Dad got ill, we had an extensio
built so that he could live with us. He hates being depende
and I can't say I blame him; I'd hate it too, especially whe
he's always been such a fit and independent man. Did yo
know him before he retired in 2001?'

'I'd met him but I didn't work with him.'

Gavin smiled. 'He had quite a reputation. If you wa
here a moment I'll see if he's up to speaking to you.'

Horton gazed around the kitchen but there wasn't an
thing much to see, so he crossed to the glazed doors whic
gave onto a patio and immaculately tidy, almost regime
tally landscaped gardens, which seemed to stretch on for eve
The daffodils were tossing about in the light March win
and slowly setting sun. He'd go for a run tonight; a blast
sea air would help to banish those visions of Shawford an
Catherine.

Craning his neck to his right he saw the children's swin
and climbing frame and thought he'd give anything to pus
Emma on a swing. He heard the children's voices, then th
front door closing. A door led off the kitchen to his right. H
made towards it when Gavin Chawley returned.

'My father said he'd be pleased to talk to you, Inspecto
but he tires very quickly, so please don't be too long.'

Horton assured him he wouldn't. Gavin Chawley le
him through a utility room to a door, which he knocke
on before opening, and Horton stepped into a swelterin
hot but comfortably furnished lounge with wide patio doo
overlooking the expansive grounds. The room had the sme
of sickness and death about it and the thin, bald man sittin
in the reclining chair did too. He bore no resemblance to th
healthy, vibrant man Horton remembered, or to the slic

clever copper with superb eloquence. Horton couldn't help thinking, what a sad end for the detective with a reputation of being like a razor.

As Gavin Chawley announced him, Horton could see what was ailing ex-Superintendent Chawley; no one was that yellow. It had to be a liver disease.

'Will you be all right, Dad?' Gavin said anxiously.

'Of course. For heaven's sake stop fussing,' his father sniped. Horton watched Gavin silently slip out of the room. He couldn't help feeling a little sorry for him. OK, so it wasn't nice being an invalid and dependent on others, but it was also a thankless task being the carer of an embittered and ungrateful one.

Duncan waved him into a seat.

'Luke Felton's gone AWOL,' Horton said without preamble. 'He's been let out on licence.'

'Bloody typical. I take it you're here in the hope I can tell you where to find him?'

'Something like that.' Horton tried hard not to mop his perspiring brow or be shocked at such a change in the former police officer. He had no idea how old Chawley was but he deduced mid to late sixties, only he looked more like mid-eighties.

'Sorry to disappoint. I've no idea.'

'You remember the case, sir?'

'Can hardly forget what he did to that young woman.'

Horton could hear the anger in his voice. The case had obviously touched a nerve, as was still apparent after all these years. But then he knew some cases affected you like that more than others. He tugged at his shirt, which was already sticking to his back. 'Did Luke Felton know Natalie Raymonds?'

'No. We checked right back to kindergarten. No connection whatsoever between them. The poor girl just happened to be in the wrong place at the wrong time.'

Horton nodded. 'And Luke Felton happened to be on that coastal path on that day. Why?'

'No idea. He never said because his brains were scran bled by the drugs. Does it matter?' Chawley asked, eyeir Horton keenly.

'I guess not. It's just one of those points that bug me. expect you know what that's like, sir.'

He saw Chawley digest this. After a moment he sa with a frown, 'It bugged me too, and Felton couldn't tell u We could only assume he'd arranged to meet a dealer, wh either didn't show, or legged it after handing Felton his stu There were no signs of anyone else having been at the scen around Natalie's body, except for the dog walker who foun her. And we didn't trace anyone on that path at the time her death, although there was one witness who saw Felton

'Peter Bailey.'

Chawley looked surprised, then nodded knowingl 'You've been reading the file.'

'Was he reliable?'

'One hundred per cent.' Chawley eyed him with su picion. 'This sounds more than trying to find a killer who gone AWOL. Are you reinvestigating the case?'

'No,' Horton said hastily. 'I thought Luke Felton migl have known someone on Hayling Island from that tin and that's where we'd find him.' He didn't see any nee to tell Chawley about a possible connection with Venet Trotman's murder.

He could see that Chawley didn't believe him. But it w partly the truth. Horton wasn't reopening the case; he had r authority or need to do so. And Felton could have nothir to do with Venetia Trotman. He might still have been hea hunted for a job or left the area for one, as Cantelli had pose Or he could be hanging out with some old junkie mates. C lying dead somewhere having been killed by a dealer.

He said, 'How did Felton get to Hayling?'

Chawley took a few breaths before answering. 'No or on the buses recognized him and we checked the trains the nearest station, the same. There were no sightings of hi walking from the railway station to the coastal path. All w can assume is that someone gave him a lift, either this dealer who handed over the drugs just across the bridge onto the island and then kicked him out of the car, or someone he knew. Otherwise, he must have hitched a lift, just as he must have done leaving the scene of the crime, and the driver went on somewhere not knowing what Felton had done. I put out an appeal but no one came forward, except Peter Bailey.'

'Could Bailey have been mistaken and Felton caught the ferry from Portsmouth to Hayling?'

But Chawley was shaking his head. 'Checked. The ferry master didn't take Felton across. Felton's DNA was on Natalie's body, and her blood was on his clothes. He couldn't remember killing her, but he listened to his lawyer, thank God, pleaded guilty 'while under the influence of drugs' and saved us all a lot of time, not to mention the taxpayer a great deal of money. Pity they didn't lock him up and throw away the key. Scum like that are a waste of breath,' he added with bitterness.

His words reminded Horton of Neil and Olivia Danbury, who clearly shared the same opinion. Horton didn't see there was much more to be gained here. 'Did Julian Raymonds' alibi check out?'

Chawley eyed Horton guardedly. 'Yes. Witnesses knee deep came forward to say he was selling boats at the boat show all day and propping up the bar in a nearby hotel until the small hours of the morning. There was no hint of any marital problems between him and Natalie and nothing to suggest he hired someone to kill his wife. And before you ask, we found no evidence that Natalie Raymonds was playing the field either.'

And that seemed to be that. Horton thanked him for his time and stretched out a hand. Chawley's grip was still firm. Releasing his hand, Chawley said, 'Let me know when you find Felton.'

Horton promised he would and, feeling sad that Chawley had come to this, found his son Gavin waiting a little anxiously in the kitchen with a mug in his hand.

'Was my father able to help you?' he asked, puttir the mug down carefully on the sink drainer and escortir Horton back to the hall.

'He cleared up a couple of questions. Does he ever ta about his cases?'

'No. When he retired he said that's it. He wasn't one those policemen who have an urge to write their memoi or dwell on the past. Will you need to come back?' Chawl asked anxiously.

'Only when we find Luke Felton. Your father ask to be kept informed,' he added quickly as Gavin Chawl looked concerned.

'I remember him, that is, I recall the case. Dad w obsessed by it, but then he was like that with every maj investigation. He loved the job. Lived, ate and breathed it.

The comment caused Horton an uncomfortable jolt the memory of Catherine's angry words, *You think more of th job than you do of me*. Had it been true? Well, stuff it, the jc was all he had, and a daughter who he wasn't going to gi up at any cost.

He returned to the station mulling over what Dunca Chawley had told him, seeing again in his mind the gaun yellowing figure of the former detective superintende and finding it difficult to rid himself of the smell of sic ness. He reckoned they would never know why Felton ha been on the coastal path that day, because even when if they found him, he wouldn't remember. And it didn really matter anyway. That case was closed. The Venet Trotman one was wide open, unless there had been a new developments.

Uckfield said not. There was no sign of Dennings in t incident suite, so Horton assumed he must still be with t team digging up Venetia Trotman's garden, although it w now dark. 'You got any more on this Luke Felton?' Uckfie asked. 'Because Trueman's not getting very far with provir a connection between him and the victim, or Felton beir pally with any inmates or ex-cons.'

Swiftly Horton told Uckfield about Shawford giving Luke Felton a lift to the castle, but said nothing about his subsequent interview with the man and his trip to Petersfield. He finished by adding, 'I've applied for a warrant to search Shawford's boat, maybe he's lying and took Felton there, but that might just be my suspicious mind working overtime.'

'And the fact you hate his guts.'

'The feeling's mutual.'

'Shawford giving Felton a lift doesn't connect him with Venetia Trotman.'

'I know, but it is the last sighting of Felton, and in the vicinity of the victim. I'll take a look around there tomorrow with Cantelli. PC Seaton's also going to ask around in the area.'

Uckfield sniffed. 'I'll wait to see if we get anything from the search of Shawford's boat before questioning him.'

Horton addressed Trueman. 'Any news on the key found in the victim's hand?'

'It opens a portable locker, the type that's sold in any hardware store or online. I'll be able to check suppliers tomorrow. We might be able to find out where and when it was bought but that probably won't get us much further.'

No wonder Uckfield looked so bad-tempered, thought Horton, returning to his office, and even Trueman looked glum. Clearly it was one of those frustrating cases that looked set to drag on. Horton hoped the disappearance of Luke Felton wasn't going to be the same.

He glanced at the clock and saw it was too late to do more tonight. Heading for the boat there was no sign of anyone following him, but then why should his graffiti artist bother to do that when he knew where he lived? His mind returned to Shawford. He'd given them a lead and tomorrow they would see where it took them. And in a week's time, he thought with a smile, he'd get to be with his daughter.

CHAPTER FOURTEEN

Monday, 16 March

'Impressive, isn't it?' Cantelli said.

Horton stared across the moat at the flint walls of tl Roman castle and agreed. It was.

'We brought the kids here last summer,' Cantelli adde falling into step beside Horton as they headed eastwar towards the shore, keeping the castle wall on their righ 'Marie was doing the Romans at school. Did you know th the earliest Roman fortification was built here between 2ẞ and 290 AD and the first Norman castle in 1086?'

'I'm more interested in what Luke Felton was doing he last Tuesday,' Horton replied.

'Philistine,' Cantelli joked. 'Have you no feel for histor

Too much, Horton thought, but of his own rather tha any Roman soldier stationed here in a perishing north-eas erly watching for marauders in Portsmouth Harbour. To h left was a picnic area and beyond that a path that led nort wards along the shore. He could hear the drone of the ca on the motorway, about four miles to the north, even thou the wind was in the opposite direction.

Cantelli continued. 'Being so close to the harbour the castle was also a great favourite of the medieval kings. King John was a regular visitor, Henry the First stayed here before travelling to France and Henry the Second made several visits in 1163 and 1164.'

'I didn't know you were a historian,' Horton re-joined with a hint of sarcasm.

'I have hidden depths. For example, I also know that Henry the Fifth sailed from Portchester Castle in 1415 for the Battle of Agincourt, and Queen Elizabeth the First was a guest at the castle in 1601.'

Horton threw him a pitying glance. Cantelli grinned. 'I know, not the kind of useful background you had in mind. Still, you never know when it might come in handy.'

'I doubt Luke Felton came here to soak up the castle's history.' But what did he come for? Was it more than a coincidence that Luke had wanted to be taken to the same location as where the murdered woman lived?

Cantelli slipped a fresh piece of chewing gum into his mouth before turning up his jacket collar against a stiff breeze that was blowing up Portsmouth Harbour. 'Must have been a bit draughty for those Roman soldiers in their skirts and sandals.'

Horton smiled fleetingly and gazed across a choppy sea at the boats bobbing about on their moorings. Opposite he could see the boats in Horsea Marina. 'According to Shawford's evidence he dropped Luke here at about six thirty. Let's see if Felton could have reached Venetia Trotman's house on foot.' They turned right, heading in the direction of Willow Bank. Soon they had left the castle behind them and were walking along the footpath before it petered out and they stepped down onto the shore. Horton told Cantelli about his visit to Catherine, and Shawford's sexual tastes. Cantelli looked concerned. 'Surely Catherine wouldn't put Emma at risk,' he said.

'Maybe not, but that boarding school suddenly looks a very attractive option.' For a start, neither Catherine nor her father would be there to poison his daughter against him, an he might even get to see Emma over some weekends and i the holidays. All he had to do was persuade her it was for tl best, and that might not be easy. He wasn't going to force h into it though. If she really hated the place, and the thougl of being away from her mother, then he'd have to think (something else. He couldn't expect Catherine to stay celiba until Emma reached eighteen.

They drew up at the bottom of the concrete slipwa where Shorena had been moored.

'It's not much of a walk,' Cantelli said.

Horton glanced at his watch. It had taken them ju under half an hour. 'If Felton did come this way on Tuesda it would have been dark, and he must have known the hou was here because there's no sign of it from where we' standing.'

Horton raised his eyes to the tangle of bushes and tre hiding the house. He climbed up the slipway, with Cante following. Locating the gate and beyond it the blue and whi scene-of-crime tape flapping in the breeze, he nodded at P Allen who was standing guard inside the garden. 'Foun anything?'

'Not even a dog bone. Just calling it off now, sir.'

Horton stared at the house. 'If Luke came here with tl intention of meeting and killing Venetia Trotman, then wh wait until the early hours of Friday morning to do so whe he could have killed her on Tuesday night? And why allo Shawford to give him a lift when it would have been safer t have no witnesses?'

'Perhaps he'd arranged to meet someone at the sailir club, or the pub back down the road.'

'Ask them, Barney.' They headed back to the cast where Cantelli departed for the nearby pub. Horton contii ued on the shore path northwards. Ahead he could see the re and black funnel he'd noticed yesterday from Horsea Marin

His thoughts this time turned towards his graffiti artis There had been no more messages pinned to his yacht (

scratched on his Harley and no sign of anyone watching him. Perhaps whoever it was had grown tired of his little game and had decided to torment someone else. Horton hoped that might be the case, but he wasn't counting on it.

He drew up at a junction in the footpath; to his left it led into a car park and a small industrial estate beyond, ahead to a boatyard, boatshed and basins. He doubted Luke would have come this way, because why not ask Shawford to drop him at the industrial estate instead of the castle? Unless, of course, he deliberately wanted to hide the location of a rendezvous.

He rang Walters. 'Check Kempton's list of visitors to see if any of them come from the Bromley Industrial Estate.'

While Walters checked, Horton took the path ahead. He was soon picking his way through a number of small sailing dinghies and canoes on the quayside towards a large boatshed on his left and the red and black funnel on his right — which, it emerged, belonged to a derelict paddle steamer, clearly in the process of renovation. A small blue van was parked in front of it on the quayside.

'There's no one from the industrial estate on the list,' Walters said.

Horton eyed the sign on the boatshed. 'How about the Youth Enterprise Sailing Trust?' Young people could mean drugs. Had Luke come here to meet with a dealer who supplied the kids?

'No one from there either. I've checked with the council parks department, who claim the last Rookley to be buried in the cemetery was in 1957.'

And Horton doubted Rookley had been visiting whoever it was. But it reminded him about the funeral party he'd seen while tailing Rookley through the tombstones. He asked Walters to find out who the funeral directors had been.

Horton tried the door to the Youth Enterprise Sailing Trust office but found it locked. He turned his attention to the paddle steamer. It was a sorry sight with its rusty portholes and paddles, its leaning and collapsed funnels. There was a chain across a sturdy temporary gangplank with a "No

Entry" sign on it but Horton, eyeing the blue van, surmise someone was on board.

Lifting the chain and replacing it behind him, he climbe on board and stepped onto a small area of the deck laid wit temporary planks of wood. Surrounding it was the origin wood, rotted and riddled with holes, and beyond, rustin anchor chains and piping. Ducking his head, he entered narrow corridor before stepping right into a wide main cab punctuated by solid iron struts and lined either side wit small square windows. The floor had been re-decked but no polished, the windows repaired, the ceiling restored; and man in white overalls was doing something in the far corn with some cables. In the centre was a long work bench wit some new planks of wood on it and a plane, while in th corner were paint pots, more wood and a variety of carpen try tools, which Horton hoped were locked away at nigh Horton showed his warrant card and produced a photograp of Luke from his jacket pocket. In answer to his question th man, in his early sixties, shook his head.

'I haven't seen him.'

Horton wasn't surprised. 'Looks a big job this,' he com mented conversationally, and in genuine interest.

'You're not kidding. It's one of the old Portsmouth Isle of Wight paddle steamers. Built in 1936, mothballed the late 1960s, became a restaurant, then a night club, the left to rot until we rescued it. Had to have it lifted onto barge and brought across the Solent. How we managed without it collapsing I'm still not sure, but then underneat the rot is a good solid iron hull.'

'You're hoping to sail it when it's restored?'

'God, no! It's going to be a floating activity centr accommodation and lecture room for the youngsters w have here. Specially adapted, of course. They're all disable in some way,' he added in response to Horton's baffled loo 'It means we'll be able to take more kids, and all year roun not just for a limited season like we do now.'

'You're a charity then?'

'Yes, run purely on voluntary donations and legacies. Damn hard work getting the money but people can be generous. The lease on this place is paid by a local businessman. And thanks to a recent legacy from an old lady, we hope to get this young lady finished a lot sooner than expected. I used to work here when it was Hester's Shipbuilding, electrical fitter. Now I just help out when I can, like a lot of us volunteers. Butchers, bakers, accountants, lawyers. Policemen,' he said pointedly.

But Horton had stopped listening after he'd mentioned Hester's. His mind darted back to the Natalie Raymonds case file and to one of the statements: that of the witness who'd seen Luke on the Hayling Coastal Path, Peter Bailey. If Horton remembered correctly, Bailey had worked for Hester's. So did a lot of people, he told himself before asking, 'When did Hester's close?'

'Autumn of 2001.'

Horton made his farewell but had only gone a few steps when he turned back. 'When's the season?'

'April to October.'

'So there are no young people here this time of year?' He certainly hadn't seen or heard any.

'No.'

The theory of Luke dealing drugs here then went up the chute. Having promised to look in again when he wasn't on duty, he found Cantelli with PC Seaton in the sailing club. Breaking off his conversation with a woman, Cantelli crossed to Horton and Seaton followed.

'I met Sergeant Cantelli in the pub where I was asking if any of the staff remembered Luke Felton,' Seaton explained. 'They didn't. I've also asked in the castle bookshop and café, and I showed his picture to some of the dog walkers earlier this morning in case they also walk their dogs here of an evening, but no one remembered seeing Luke. And there wasn't a service at the church that evening.'

'No sightings of Luke here either,' Cantelli added. 'And no member went sailing into the sunset on Tuesday night

because it wasn't high tide until just after eleven p.m., so r
boat could get out until about nine o'clock.'

So, dead end, or was it? His conversation with the ma
on the paddle steamer and the mention of Hester's w
scratching away at Horton's mind like a dog with a flea. 'Le
talk to the witness who saw Luke Felton on the coastal pat
Peter Bailey.'

'Why?' asked Cantelli, baffled.

'I'll tell you on the way,' Horton replied.

Cantelli couldn't see what the significance of Pet
Bailey having worked at Hester's Shipbuilding had to c
with Luke Felton's disappearance and said so. Neither d
Horton, but he said, 'Indulge me.'

'That usually leads to trouble,' grumbled Cantelli goc
naturedly. 'How do we know that Bailey's still living at tl
same address? He might have emigrated or died.'

'Well, we'll soon find out.'

CHAPTER FIFTEEN

'It was a long time ago,' Peter Bailey said, reluctantly letting them in and leading them through a faded hall into an equally faded sitting room. It was icily cold, which reminded Horton of Venetia Trotman's house, but there the resemblance ended. The acrid smell of male sweat mingled with that of fish, dust and decay and the room looked as though it had last been decorated sometime in the 1970s. Its orange walls, yellowing net curtains, threadbare maroon carpet, sparse and dated furniture and a television that could qualify as an antique, all confirmed to Horton that Peter Bailey was as oblivious of his surroundings as he was of his appearance. He peered nervously at them over the top of smeared gold-rimmed spectacles, with a chip in the right lens. His silver eyebrows knitted across a forehead in a thin face etched so deep with lines that the expression corrugated iron sprang to Horton's mind. His white monk's hair sprang up around a freckled pate, making it difficult to put an age on him. Late fifties or late sixties? It was hard to tell.

Cantelli lifted the small pencil from behind his ear and opened his notebook. 'You saw Luke Felton on the coastal path on Hayling Island on the nineteenth of September 1997.'

'On the afternoon that girl was killed, yes.'

'Can you remember the time?'

Bailey removed his spectacles. 'It's in my statement.'

'Of course.' Cantelli smiled, as though he was dim f forgetting that. 'But if you would confirm . . .'

'It was just after four o'clock or thereabouts.'

'What were you doing on the path, sir?'

Bailey looked puzzled. 'Why all the questions, Sergean Luke Felton was convicted and sentenced. I thought this w finished with a long time ago.'

'Luke Felton's been released on licence.'

Bailey's skin blanched and he stared wide-eyed at ea of them in turn. 'I don't understand,' he stuttered.

Cantelli quickly explained, finishing with the news th Felton was missing. 'We're looking for anything that mig help us find him.'

'You can't think he's coming after me?' Bailey uttere clearly horrified. Horton noticed that his left leg had start to jigger and the hands holding his spectacles were shakin

'I doubt he'd even remember you, sir, he was so spac out on drugs,' Cantelli said reassuringly. 'Perhaps you cou just tell us what you can remember of that day.'

Bailey looked far from pacified. In fact, his face look like a chewed-up sock.

Horton added, 'It might help us to find him and se him back to prison for breaching the terms of his licence.'

Bailey turned his anxious gaze on Horton. 'I can't s how what I have to say can possibly help you do that.'

'If you wouldn't mind, sir,' Cantelli firmly insisted.

Bailey rose and crossed to the large bay window. Hort caught Cantelli's eye and urged silence. Not that he real needed to. Cantelli knew the score.

Clearly Bailey was gathering his thoughts. In the silen Horton listened for sounds of a Mrs Bailey, or anyone el living in the house, but there was only the whirring of wh must be a refrigerator. It certainly wasn't the central heatin Was he a bachelor, or perhaps a widower? Or had Mrs Bail grown tired of being cold and walked out on him? Horton wouldn't blame her if she had.

Bailey took a deep breath and turned back to face them. With his nerves under better control, he began.

'I'm a twitcher, bird watching's my hobby. I was on the Hayling Coastal Path that day because the contractors had been working on restoring the old Langstone Oyster Beds and after completing the project in May it was discovered that rare seabirds had started nesting there.' He swivelled his eyes between them, adding, 'The oyster beds were restored not for fishing but for nature conservation. It's a Site of Special Scientific Interest and home for tens of thousands of seabirds.'

Horton already knew this, and so too did Cantelli, but they said nothing, letting Bailey talk on.

'As a result of the work an island had been formed in one of the lagoons and had become home to little terns. Did you know they're an internationally rare seabird and subject to the European Union's Birds Directive?' Bailey had regained his colour and was looking animated.

Cantelli contrived to look amazed while Horton nodded encouragement, thinking that perhaps Mrs Bailey had grown tired of playing second fiddle to the little terns.

Bailey resumed his seat. Sitting forward he continued eagerly. 'One pair of little terns had settled on the small island and had raised two young. It was amazing. I watched them for ages. It was a remarkable day for me, which was why I remembered seeing that man, Felton.' His face clouded over.

'I was returning to my car, which I'd parked where the old railway halt used to be, when Luke Felton passed me. He was walking down the path towards the seafront, or I should say slouching. His head was down. He had his hands in his pockets and a woolly hat rammed on his head.'

'How did you know it was Luke?' asked Horton sharply. 'You couldn't have seen his face if his head was down and almost covered by a hat.'

Bailey flushed, this time with agitation rather than enthusiasm, and his leg started to jigger again. 'I described the clothes to the police officer who interviewed me, and th fitted the description of those Luke Felton had been wearin scruffy jeans, muddy trainers, a navy jacket and navy woolle hat. He was about five feet ten, and thin. You see, when heard the appeal on the local news by that police superi tendent for anyone seen on the coastal path that day I can forward and gave my statement.'

So that explained that, but Horton felt uneasy. 'Did yo see a woman? Five feet four, long brown hair, slim, wearin running clothes.'

Clearly by Bailey's troubled expression he knew exact who Horton meant. 'Natalie Raymonds. No. I know whe her body was found though, but I didn't walk that far. I' often wondered if I had done whether I might have been ab to prevent her death.'

Looking at Bailey, Horton doubted it, though he su posed his sudden appearance might have frightened Lul Felton off. There was a short pause before Horton dropp in casually, 'Had you ever seen Luke Felton or Natal Raymonds before?'

Bailey looked blinked hard. 'No. I usually stayed at tl northern end of the coastal path and around the marshes. I those days I was still working and my mother was alive, so couldn't always get away. She was an invalid for many year She died four years ago.'

And that, thought Horton, explained the neglecte unloved air about the house.

'Where did you work?' asked Cantelli with polite inte est, though both he and Horton already knew.

There was a moment's hesitation before he answer uncertainly. 'Hester's Shipbuilding. I was a design draught man, but I was made redundant in 2001 when it closed dow After that I took whatever I could, mainly contract work. I st do a bit from time to time, although I don't really need to wo now Mother's dead, but it gets me out of the house.'

And Horton would like to get out of this miserab house too, but there were more questions to ask. 'Can yo describe exactly what you did and what you saw while you were bird watching the day you saw Luke Felton?' Seeing that Bailey was mystified by his question, Horton added, 'I take it you had binoculars.'

'Oh, yes, I see.' Bailey relaxed a little and considered the question. Horton wasn't sure how it would help but there had to be more. Or he hoped there was. 'I took some time watching Binness Island in Langstone Harbour—'

'Was the tide up or out?' Horton interrupted.

'Up. I remember because the dredger was going out of Oldham's Wharf and I was concerned it would frighten the birds away.' He frowned in thought. 'There were three fishing boats trawling the channel and a couple of sailing dinghies from the club by Oldham's. That's all I can remember.' The leg jigger was back.

Horton said, 'Did you see anyone else on the path?'

'No. I was surprised because it was a nice day, warm and sunny.'

'You'd have thought more people like you, keen bird watchers, would have been looking at the little terns.'

There was the hesitation again, and another frown. 'Yes, you would,' Bailey answered, eyeing Horton anxiously.

Cantelli said, 'Were there any other vehicles in the car park when you returned to your car?'

Bailey put a hand on his knee as though trying to stop it jigging. 'I don't see how this will help you find Felton.'

Cantelli simply looked at Bailey enquiringly while Horton remained silent.

'There weren't any cars,' Bailey said moodily.

'What time would this have been, sir?' Cantelli pursued.

'I don't know, about four thirty, I guess,' replied Bailey tetchily.

Cantelli took his time jotting this down. 'No dog walkers there then, sir? It's a popular spot for that, especially on a nice day.'

'Well, I didn't see any,' Bailey snapped, his voice rising in irritation. 'I just saw Luke Felton.'

'And the little terns.' Cantelli smiled. He got no respon from Bailey. At a sign from Horton that only Cantelli wou have seen and interpreted he made a great show of closi his notebook and putting it in his jacket pocket while sayin 'Thank you for your help, Mr Bailey.' He rose, and add apologetically, 'Would you mind if I use your toilet? T much coffee before I came out.'

Somewhat reluctantly Bailey said, 'Upstairs, first do on your right.'

Cantelli smiled his thanks and slipped out.

Chattily, Horton said, 'Where's the best place for bi watching around here then?'

Bailey looked taken aback at the question. 'Are you keen bird watcher?'

'When I'm out sailing, yes. Otherwise, I don't have t time for it.'

'Of course . . . with your job . . . There are lots of plac around the coast and each season brings its visitors. There we Slovenian grebes off the oyster beds in February, and a—'

'What about around Portchester Castle?' Horton c him short.

Bailey started and his face lost some of its colour. 'W there?' he stuttered.

Horton shrugged. 'You mentioning Heste Shipbuilding made me think of it. You must have walk along the shore there many times and seen rare bird Horton heard the toilet flush. Cantelli would have a go nose around upstairs, and not just in the bathroom.

With something akin to relief, Bailey said, 'Oh, yes, course. I used to during my lunch hour but I haven't be over that way for years.'

Truth? Bailey could have been there last Tuesd evening, but why would he want to meet Luke Felton wh he was clearly terrified of him?

Horton heard Cantelli's tread upon the stairs. H entered the room with a slight shake of his head and a smi at Bailey.

Horton rose. 'If you recall anything more about the day you saw Luke Felton, please let us know.'

Bailey quickly promised he would, clearly eager to get rid of them. Outside Cantelli heaved a sigh of relief. 'He depressed me.'

Horton was inclined to agree. 'That description of Luke might have fitted hundreds of youths.'

'The investigating team must have matched the clothes Bailey described with those belonging to Felton.'

Yes, and found Natalie's blood on them. 'Did they contact the fishing boat and dredger crews? They might have witnessed something.'

'I think that's probably stretching it,' Cantelli said, as Horton jotted down the vehicle registration number of a twelve-year-old maroon Ford parked in the narrow driveway of the 1950s semi-detached house. Cantelli was doubtlessly right and Horton didn't like to return to ask Duncan Chawley, though if he dug deeper in the case file, he might find records of it.

Pointing the car in the direction of the station, Cantelli said, 'It doesn't help us find Felton, unless it was Bailey who Felton went to meet at Portchester Castle on Tuesday night.'

'He looked uncomfortable when I mentioned the castle, and I think he lied about not going there, but I can't see why he should agree to meet Felton. He seemed terrified that Felton was out and might approach him. But run a check on his car, Barney, you never know, he might have been picked up for speeding in Castle Lane on Tuesday night.'

'I doubt we'd be that lucky, but I'll also check with the sailing club in case he owns a boat.'

'I think the only boat he'd own would be the kind he'd put in his bath.'

'You never can tell,' said Cantelli optimistically.

Maybe, but Horton was sure Cantelli was wrong on that score. As the sergeant swung into the station car park Horton noted Bliss's car in its allocated space. That meant he'd have to brief her, but he had no sooner stepped inside his office than Bliss hove onto his horizon looking like Captain Shark[…] about to execute one of his crew, and Horton guessed that [h…] was the intended victim.

'Do you know where I've been for the last fifteen mi[n]utes, Inspector?' she blazed, slamming his door behind he[r]. 'With Chief Superintendent Reine, listening to how incom[…]petent my team is and how you've compromised a high-lev[…] drug operation.'

Horton had been expecting it. He remained silent [as] Bliss continued.

'Your paperwork is shoddy and overdue, you do n[ot] adhere to proper procedure, you spend too much time inte[r]fering in other cases when you can't solve the ones that yo[u] have, and clearly you have an issue with authority. I hav[e] therefore requested that you be removed from CID an[d] posted to a more suitable position. Results are what we ne[ed] in CID, not meddling and messing up critical operations.'

Again, Horton said nothing. There seemed no point [in] defending himself because clearly she wasn't going to liste[n].

Bliss continued. 'DC Walters will also not be a mem[…]ber of my team. He's too slow and idle. I was in two min[ds] whether to keep Cantelli but I need some continuity, an[d] Sergeant Cantelli will do as he's told if he values his chanc[e] of promotion.'

Promotion! Cantelli! The sergeant wanted that about [as] much as a dose of swine flu.

'I'm putting in a request for some new officers. You['ll] hear about your transfer shortly and tell DC Walters [to] expect his. From the beginning of April this team will [be] a vastly different one. Meanwhile you will attend to yo[ur] paperwork. You will not get involved with Superintende[nt] Uckfield's murder investigation, and you will not make an[y] attempt to locate Ronnie Rookley. You will find Luke Felto[n]. Is that clear?'

Horton nodded curtly and let out a long sigh as sh[e] swept from his office. If she had just calmed down, sh[e] would have learnt of the possible connection betwe[en]

Venetia Trotman's murder and Luke Felton. But she hadn't even asked him to update her on any developments. Well, that was her lookout.

He rose and walked briskly into the CID office. Without preamble he announced, 'DCI Bliss has requested that I be removed from CID, along with you, Walters. But Cantelli gets to stay under the ice maiden while a whole new bunch of razor-sharp detectives are brought in to solve every crime in Portsmouth within two minutes flat, without moving from their desk and with immaculate paperwork to show for it. So, as this is my last case in CID, I want Luke Felton found and I don't much care who we upset locating him. Which means, Barney, you might risk all future chances of being promoted, and the joy of working for DCI Bliss.'

Cantelli shrugged. 'Guess I could do with the exercise on patrol with you, Walters.'

Walters almost swallowed the ginger nut biscuit he was eating. With his mouth full he said, 'I've got Luke Felton's prison medical file, guv.'

'And?'

'Felton started his sentence at Winchester but he was transferred to the Isle of Wight after three weeks on medical advice, where he had hypnotherapy as part of his drug treatment. The woman who was treating him lived there and still does.'

This sounded promising. 'Nice of the authorities to accommodate him,' Horton muttered, wondering why Luke had got such special treatment to be granted alternative medicine and a transfer. Could he possibly be on the Isle of Wight with his hypnotherapist? The island wasn't accessible from Portchester Castle; or rather it was by private boat, but if heading to the Island then surely Luke would have wanted a lift to Portsmouth Harbour or Southsea where he could have caught the ferry or hovercraft.

'The hypnotherapist is called Lena Lockhart,' Walters continued. 'I've got her home and office address, but she's not at her office. I haven't tried her home yet.'

Horton knew he should ask the local police to intervie her; that was what Bliss would say. But Bliss wouldn't be h boss for much longer. And he might as well go out in styl He glanced at his watch.

'I'll pay her a visit,' he said, knowing he was gambling c finding her in. She might be on holiday or with a client; sl might know very little they didn't already know about Lul Felton. But if Luke had contacted her then he didn't wa her prepared with some phoney story. And if Luke was the then he didn't want him running off. Collecting his helm and jacket he headed for the door, with Cantelli shaking h head after him.

CHAPTER SIXTEEN

A tall woman with long legs, clad in tight jeans and a loose-fitting white shirt clasped to her small waist by a wide black shiny belt, opened the door to him. She was in her late thirties, with long curly dark hair, chocolate-brown eyes and an attractive elfin face. Horton didn't blame Luke Felton for wanting to see her regularly. He reckoned most of the prison population must have jerked off the moment she walked through the gates.

'I don't see why I should betray a patient's confidence,' she said, waving him into a seat in the small flat which backed onto the railway line in Ryde. Out of the corner of his eye Horton could see the red and black former underground train drawing to a halt at the small station below them.

'I didn't know you were a doctor?' he said.

She flushed. 'I'm a hypnotherapist,' she declared defiantly, as though waiting for him to scoff. He didn't. He told her he wanted to talk about Luke Felton, but he didn't mention that Felton was out on licence or that he had gone AWOL, and she gave no indication that she knew this.

'And you were helping Luke Felton with what?' he asked.

'It'll be on his prison records.'

'I thought you might help us save time.'

'Why don't you ask Luke?' Then her eyes widened ar her face paled. 'Has something happened to him? He's n killed himself?'

Her slim hand flew to her perfectly shaped, red-li sticked mouth. Beautifully manicured nails with red poli reminded him of Olivia Danbury, but her words remind him of Ashley Felton, who also believed his brother capab of committing suicide. And that made him consider the boc found in the harbour, before recollecting that Dr Clayto had ruled out suicide and that it was Luke. It was still poss ble that Luke, rejected by his brother and fed up with bei treated like a prisoner at work, had got a lift from Shawfo to Portchester Castle where he'd simply walked into the se But there were better places to do that — along Southsea se front for starters, where he wouldn't have had to wait thr hours for the tide to come in.

'Has he threatened to?' Horton asked, curious. Walte had made no mention that Luke's prison record had show him to be depressed or suicidal.

Lena Lockhart sank heavily on to the chair opposi Horton and said wearily, 'I thought I'd helped Luke to g over his depression.'

'What was the cause of it?'

'Prison, I would have thought, wouldn't you?' sh replied tartly, her brown eyes flashing.

So she had a thing for Felton. And had Felton con here on his release? If he had, he'd already moved on, becau even though Horton couldn't see into the bedroom his fine tuned ears and copper's antennae didn't detect anyone el being here except them.

Sternly he said, 'He was convicted of murder.'

'Yes, but he didn't do it. He didn't kill Natalie Raymond

Horton smirked. 'That's what they all say.' He want to provoke a reaction and he got one.

She jumped up, glaring at him. 'And sometimes it ha pens to be true.'

‘How can he remember?’ Horton interrupted incredulously. ‘He was out of his mind on heroin.’

‘Yes. But under hypnosis he didn’t recall it at all.’

‘Surely the drugs would have obscured his memory?’

‘No,’ she declared emphatically.

Horton eyed her steadily for some seconds. She was adamant in her belief that Felton had been innocent. Was it just emotion talking? He had several unanswered questions about Natalie’s death himself; perhaps Lena Lockhart could help him get some answers.

‘Tell me,’ he said more gently, and genuinely interested.

She eyed him sceptically. He’d have to try a little harder to convince her. Leaning forward he said, ‘I know nothing about hypnotherapy, so treat me as a complete idiot. Explain to me how it helped Luke and why you believe he didn’t kill Natalie Raymonds.’

She hesitated for a moment, eyeing him warily, unsure whether to trust him. Then his sincere expression obviously made her decide she could. She resumed her seat, though she didn’t completely relax.

‘Hypnosis can help improve the psychological and physical well-being of an individual,’ she began a little warily. ‘In the case of drug addiction, it can be used to help change a subject’s attitude and mental thought processes towards using drugs, reducing the urge to take them. Oh, I know it’s not been scientifically proven, but I’ve seen it work. And it worked with Luke.’

Suddenly he saw that their relationship went further back than the Isle of Wight prison and even Winchester. ‘Did you help Luke on his drug treatment programme before prison?’

She nodded. ‘After he was sentenced for the attack on an elderly lady, part of the condition of him being given a community sentence was that he underwent a drug treatment programme. I was living and working in Portsmouth then and I helped Luke handle his withdrawal symptoms. They were pretty severe. But Luke was determined to come off

drugs and stay off. So I was staggered when I read that he
been sentenced for killing that girl while on drugs. I co
tacted Winchester prison and offered to help him. He ha
just tried to kill himself so they were keen to invite me ove
I knew the prison doctor, and he recommended that Luke l
moved to the Isle of Wight where I could treat him.'

'Go on,' he encouraged when she stalled, wonderin
angrily why they'd only been given the edited highlights
Felton's records and not the full story.

Leaning slightly forwards she said, 'What I try to do
change an addict's thought processes so that he or she doesn
feel the urge to use substances any longer. Through hypnosi
I attempt to modify behaviour by increasing and heightenin
mental awareness so that the addict is more inclined to recei
suggestions and ideas. But before that I need to get to the co
of the subject's inner feelings, especially about themselves, ar
try and understand why they resorted to taking drugs.'

'And what did you discover about Luke?' His genuin
interest must have encouraged her because she seemed to fo
get about client confidentiality. Or was it because she believe
Felton was dead? Horton wasn't about to enlighten her.

'Luke was a middle child, and we all know what th
means. Middle child syndrome. The middle child in a fami
of three often feels that he or she doesn't quite belong. He h
to fight to receive attention from his parents. The first chi
always has a special place in its parent's affections and ge
heaps of attention, love and protection. The second child ge
some love and attention, but not as intense as the first chi
and only until the new baby comes along, then the midd
child is suddenly side-lined for a younger sibling. The midd
child feels it's being ignored and becomes insecure. It fee
out of place and can become troublesome, or a loner, as
the case of Luke. His elder brother, Ashley, was charismati
confident, an achiever, and his younger sister, Olivia, tl
much yearned for girl, spoilt, cosseted.'

And from what he'd seen of both Ashley and Olivia l
thought that Lena Lockhart was correct in her assessmen

Recalling Ashley Felton's luxury apartment facing the harbour, Horton said, 'Luke's brother seems to have done well for himself. He runs a recruitment company.'

'I know, and according to Luke, Ashley was the apple of his parents' eye. Good at sports, likeable, popular, and clever without even trying.'

Horton wondered if Cantelli had managed to ask Charlotte about the Feltons. He'd not mentioned it, so Horton supposed not.

Lena Lockhart was saying, 'Luke was always urged by his parents to be more like his brother. He slogged for his A levels and got brilliant results, but at a cost — his health and nerves. And when he won a place at Oxford, he thought his parents would be over the moon. Ashley had gone to university too but not Oxford, and he'd come out with a first-class honours in business studies. So Luke felt he had to match that. But Luke was reading history. His father, an accountant, couldn't really see the point of it and told him so, and his mother kept saying how well Ashley was doing working for a blue-chip company as a management consultant at that time. Whether this was as bad as Luke portrayed, I don't know, but it's what he felt. Olivia, four years younger, was attractive, cooperative, enchanting and a budding actress.'

Horton's ears pricked up. He recalled his first meeting with Olivia Danbury and her vehement declarations that she had not seen Luke and never wanted to see him. At the time he'd thought her emotions were genuine unless she was a good actress; perhaps the latter was the case.

'Did she go to drama school?' he asked.

'Yes. She graduated in June 1997 and married Neil Danbury in September the same year, a week after Luke was arrested for the murder of Natalie Raymonds. Olivia blamed Luke for ruining her wedding and wrecking her career.'

'I can understand her feelings about the wedding, but how could it have wrecked her acting career?' Horton asked curiously.

'Luke says she lost confidence. I guess she didn't wa
the fact that her brother was a murderer dragged up eve
time she got a review.'

And the media would drag it up, thought Horton.
was the kind of juicy titbit the public loved. Some acto
or actresses wouldn't have minded, perhaps even used it
a lever to propel themselves further into the limelight: th
'look at tragic me' and 'how I've overcome the shame of m
family'. It would make good Sunday newspaper reading. Bu
Olivia Danbury was obviously different.

Lena said, 'Perhaps she found being Mrs Danbury w
a more lucrative and satisfying role. Neil Danbury took ov
Luke's father's firm when he died while Luke was in priso
Luke didn't go to either of his parents' funerals, though h
would have been given permission to attend with a guard. H
said he wouldn't have been welcomed, and he didn't want
bring more shame on his brother and sister.'

All this was useful background, but it didn't help hi
find Luke Felton. 'So Luke cracked up.'

'Yes. Once at Oxford the pressure really hit him. H
never saw himself as clever and he found it difficult to fit
and to have relationships. He was the lump, the odd one ou
the awkward one. And the more he was told that the more h
became it, withdrawn, quiet, introverted.'

Her words stabbed a painful memory in Horton of
particularly nasty piece of work he'd met when he'd been i
the children's home. A thin crow of a woman had delighte
in telling him that his mother had walked out on him becau
he was useless, rebellious, no good, and a lot worse. It ha
taken months of patient confidence-building by his last fost
parents to help him deal with the mental cruelty, but nothin
could ever erase it. He gladly brought his mind back to Len
Lockhart as she continued.

'Luke felt that nothing he did could ever please his pa
ents, and with his inability to stay focused he drifted fro
one thing to another until he started taking drugs. I belie
it was to get attention. Drugs were a cry for help. But

didn't get him the help, or the understanding and sympathy he craved. Instead, he got told how much more worthless he was than his brother and sister, so he slipped into deeper addiction and got into more trouble until the attack on that pensioner.'

She leant forward; her expression keen. Horton could see her enthusiasm for what she did shining through. Or was that enthusiasm for one particular client, he wondered cynically.

She said, 'Luke was truly horrified at what he'd done and had a genuine desire to kick the habit and start afresh. And that's why I knew hypnosis would work. A hypnotist can help the client to get a control over his life in many ways.'

'But it didn't work,' said Horton bluntly. 'Luke reoffended two years later, only this time a young woman lost her life at his hand.'

She sat back with a sigh and pushed a hand through her long hair. 'I know, but I'm convinced Luke didn't kill her. And now he's . . .' She rose and crossed to the window.

He should tell her. But how did he know that Luke Felton wasn't dead?

After a moment she turned back. Horton could see the sorrow etched on her face. He felt a bit of a heel, but if it helped him get closer to finding Luke then he'd cope with it.

She continued. 'When I met Luke for the second time here on the Isle of Wight, he was distraught at what he'd done, even though he couldn't remember a single thing about it. So, we started again.'

Horton heard the train clattering past. He wondered how close she had got to Luke Felton emotionally and physically since he'd been released from prison. As he witnessed the sadness in her eyes, he thought it was time to tell her. But first one more question.

'What was Luke's temperament like? When he didn't get his way, did he sulk or fly off the handle? Was he moody?'

'He was moody but not violent. His moods were caused by his remorse and his hatred and dread of being locked up.

He wasn't aggressive but he was angry with himself. I feel s bad about failing him.'

'I'm not sure that Luke is dead.'

Her head came up. 'But you said—'

'He's missing and could possibly be dead. I'm trying t find him.'

'So that you can put him back in prison,' she flashed.

'He's breached the terms of his licence.'

'Yes, for a crime he didn't commit.'

But Horton needed convincing of that. 'Tell me wh you believe he's innocent.'

She looked as though she was about to clam up befo she registered the manner and tone of his question. Taking breath, and getting a grasp on her emotions, she said, 'Aft a traumatic incident a subject under hypnosis may be able t recall with complete accuracy details that their subconscio mind has remembered but their conscious mind has ove looked or blotted out. I hoped that when fully aware agai Luke might be able to recall everything that he said while h was in the trance. But Luke's trances were so deep that h had difficulty remembering what he'd said during them. S I recorded them—'

'Have you still got the recordings?' Horton interrupte eagerly.

'Yes, but they're confidential.'

'Not if it will help me to understand him.'

She eyed him sceptically. 'But why do you need t understand him? Especially now he's broken the terms o his licence.'

She was testing him. Horton understood that. H said, 'Because I'd like to know if he really did kill Natal Raymonds.'

'You're doubtful. You think he might have been inn cent,' she cried, almost jubilant.

'I didn't say that.'

She sprang up and began to pace the small lounge. 'If could prove that Luke didn't kill Natalie . . .'

‘Why should you want to?’ Horton asked quietly.

Her eyes flashed at him, then she sighed and added in a more subdued manner, ‘Because he deserves it. He was tormented by the fact that he had killed her. I don’t believe he did. And I’ll tell you why, Inspector Horton, because when Luke was under a trance he never once mentioned seeing her, being with her, her name, where her body was found, nothing. He talked about darkness and water.’

Horton eyed her sceptically. ‘Maybe because he killed her in the dark. And he was certainly by the water.’ But sunset wasn’t until 7 p.m. in September and Luke had been seen by Bailey at 4 p.m. Could he have killed Natalie in daylight and then sat there drugged until dark? Possibly.

Lena said, ‘He also talked about a gate.’

‘There are plenty of gates in the countryside.’ And one Horton had seen near that copse where Natalie’s body had been found. It meant nothing. He needed more convincing than this.

She drew herself up and said, ‘Luke wasn’t alone. When he came out of the trance, he couldn’t recall anyone, but under hypnosis he kept saying, he, water, gate, dark. I can see that you don’t believe me but you will. The tapes are in my office in Ryde,’ she declared belligerently.

‘OK. Let’s get them.’ He rose.

Eyeing his motorbike clothes, she added, ‘I’ll meet you there.’ She gave him the address.

He reached her office before she did. It was a room over a luggage shop with a doorway to the right and situated halfway up the steep incline of Union Street. Standing outside he gazed at the view northwards. The Solent was a dark grey green, flecked with white where the waves were being whipped up by the strong winds. Across the water he could see the tower blocks and high-rise office buildings of Portsmouth. The hovercraft was speeding towards Ryde, leaving a trail of foaming white in its backwash, and a car ferry was ploughing the waters heading for Portsmouth. A large container ship was following a cross channel ferry out of the harbour. While waiting for her to arrive, Horton po dered what Lena Lockhart had told him. Had there bee someone with Luke Felton? Bailey hadn't mentioned anyo but it could explain how Luke had got on to Hayling Islan and off again, though not why Bailey hadn't seen this oth person. It could also explain the tie that Natalie had bee strangled with. But if there had been another person at th scene why hadn't SOCO found evidence of it? He suppose the delay in discovering Natalie's body had hindered tha but it hadn't stopped Felton's DNA and fingerprints fro being found. And even if someone had been with Felto that didn't mean he hadn't killed Natalie; this other perso could have given him the tie. Even if he hadn't killed Natal himself, Luke was still an accessory to the murder.

A car pulled in to the side of the road and Lena climbe out. The door to the street was open. 'I take Sundays an Mondays off,' she explained, leading him through a narro hall and up the staircase where he saw three closed doo before they climbed a second flight of dusty stairs. 'I sha this building but there's hardly anyone around. I think mo of the rooms are vacant.' Reaching the last door off a corr dor, she made to insert her key then stepped back, puzzle 'That's strange, it's open.'

Horton stiffened. 'Don't touch anything,' he cautione quickly, stepping in front of her. He saw immediately th the door had been forced open. His heart skipped a beat.

'Who—'

'Quiet,' he hissed.

She snapped her mouth shut, looking alarmed. His hea was racing along with his mind as he considered the implic tions of this discovery, but there would be time to dwell o that later. There was no sound from within. Taking a brea he pushed towards the door, glimpsing Lena's look of co cern. Then, raising his foot, he violently kicked it open an charged in. Once inside he froze. His eyes quickly took in th devastation around him and the fact there was no one her

Turning, he called out, 'It's OK.'

Lena came up behind him. Her eyes widened as she surveyed the scene.

'Where do you keep the tapes?' Horton asked. He watched her gaze travel the room before alighting on a cabinet to her right. It was open, its contents scattered around the floor.

She said, 'They're in that box file.' As she made towards it, Horton stalled her.

'Stay where you are. Don't touch anything.' Gingerly he stepped forward, stretching his fingers into latex gloves. Bending down he picked up the bright blue file, knowing full well what he would find. And he did. Absolutely nothing.

CHAPTER SEVENTEEN

He sent Lena across the road to a café, saying that he wou join her as soon as he could. She made no protest, still shake by the incident. Then he called the local police, hoping th his old adversary DCI Birch was on a day off and wouldn get to hear of the break-in. He reported it as such, with r mention of it being linked to a missing offender. He didn see any need to involve the island's detectives, and the Is of Wight relied on Hampshire's SOCO team so Phil Tayl would be here soon. While Horton waited for the patrol un to arrive, he called Taylor.

'I'm on a boat in Horsea Marina.'

Of course, Shawford's. Horton cursed. 'How long w you be?'

'Just finishing.'

'Good. I want you over on the Isle of Wight.' Hortc quickly relayed what had happened. He arranged for Sergea Elkins to bring Taylor and his team to the island on tl police launch. He wasn't sure what Bliss was going to s about the additional expenditure, but he'd be off the tea soon, so what did he care?

He surveyed the devastation before him. Lena h informed him before leaving for the café that it didn't look though anything but the tapes had been stolen, and she told him that the last time she'd been in her office was Saturday, leaving it at 2 p.m. It transpired that only a couple of other rooms in the building were let, and in addition to the luggage shop on the right of the entrance there was a clothes shop on the left. Someone might have seen the intruder, thought Horton. He'd get the local police to ask.

Lena had confirmed that the reports she'd written about Luke Felton and his treatment would be on Luke's prison medical file. Walters hadn't mentioned it, but then Horton hadn't given him much chance to elaborate before dashing off to catch the ferry. If he hadn't seen the break-in, he might have said Lena was lying about the tapes to try and vindicate Luke Felton. But the break-in was no phoney and from his experience he thought her story had a ring of truth about it. He was heartily glad that he had come.

He instructed an officer to remain outside the office and to call him on his mobile the moment Taylor and his SOCO team arrived. On no account were they to admit anyone else without calling him first. Then Horton nipped across the road and found Lena looking forlorn in a dark corner of the café, which also doubled as a pub, and which was getting increasingly busy as the evening drew closer.

Fetching them both a coffee, he placed the cup in front of her and sat down.

'Why would someone steal those tapes?' she asked.

'Why do you think?' He knew she must already have worked it out. She wasn't stupid, just shocked.

After a minute her face lit up and she said excitedly, 'Luke was telling the truth. He didn't kill Natalie Raymonds.'

'He still might have done,' Horton said, not wanting to be drawn and recollecting Bailey's testimony and the evidence. 'But it seems you may be right. Luke might not have been alone.' And he wondered what Duncan Chawley would make of that.

'And you think this other person has stolen the tapes. But why wait until now? I've had them for five years.'

That was a question Horton had been mulling ove along with several others. He said, 'Have you seen or hea from Luke since he was released? It's important you tell n the truth, Lena.'

'I swear to you I haven't. I knew Luke was applying f parole, but that's the last time I heard from him. I haven been working at the prison for a year.'

Her flushed face hinted to Horton that maybe she ha become too involved with her clients, one in particula Perhaps someone had found them doing something th wasn't professional or acceptable behind prison walls.

He let it go — that was not his concern — and said, think the person who was with Luke Felton when Natal was killed has only just learned about the tapes.' Whic meant that Luke must have told him. So who could Lul have trusted and confided in? His mind ran through tl list of possibilities. His brother, Ashley? Or his little siste Olivia Danbury? But why would either of them have bee involved in the murder of Natalie Raymonds? Could Lul have told Neil Danbury? Horton thought it unlikely judgir by Danbury's previous remarks.

Then there was Kelly Masters, but Horton couldn't s why the personnel officer at Kempton's would want to ste the tapes, and she could hardly have been involved in Natalie murder. But she could have told someone about them, if Lul had confided in her after a session of mad passionate love, rather frenzied sexual intercourse. Who though? One nan sprang to mind. Edward Shawford. Hence his Good Samarita act of giving Luke a lift. Taylor's search of Shawford's bo now seemed to have been an exceptionally good idea.

What about Matt Boynton, Luke's probation office Again, Horton couldn't see any link between him and Natal Raymonds. And even if Luke had told Boynton about tl tapes, how would Boynton have known who to pass tl information on to? The same went for Ronnie Rookley.

And clearly if there had been someone with Luke th day, as was now highly probable, why had he set Luke up take the blame for Natalie's death? It had to be drug related, surely.

Horton considered the options. What if Natalie had been a dealer, and had been about to cause trouble for her supplier? The supplier, whoever he was, had used Luke as a scapegoat for Natalie's murder, luring him to the coastal path with the promise of drugs. Maybe Rookley knew this supplier. He'd gone to meet him in the cemetery after they'd questioned him about Luke's disappearance in the greasy café. And Rookley had either been told to clear out, or the supplier — Natalie's killer — had silenced him, as he might already have silenced Luke.

Suddenly Horton felt afraid for Lena Lockhart. 'Is there anyone you can stay with for a while?' he asked.

She looked up, bewildered. 'Why should I?' Then, catching his drift, her eyes widened. 'You think I'm in danger?'

'No. It's just a precaution,' he tried to reassure her, but she eyed him cynically.

'You think that whoever stole the tapes is Natalie's killer and that he might come after me because I can testify to what Luke told me.'

Something like that, thought Horton, but he didn't say so. 'It's best to be on the safe side.'

She frowned, considering this. After a moment she said, 'I've got an aunt in Brighton. I could go there for a few days, but I'd have to cancel my appointments.'

'I think it might be best. And you should leave right away. I can get someone to accompany you home and we'll get you on the ferry.'

'You'll let me know what happens, though, and when it's safe to come back.'

'Of course.' He felt relieved. He'd be a lot happier with her out of the way. 'I don't want to know the address,' he said, reaching for his mobile phone. 'Just give me your mobile number.'

She did. His phone rang as he finished entering it in his address book. Taylor had arrived a lot quicker than he had expected, but he wasn't complaining.

'I've not had a chance to get anything over to the la yet from Shawford's boat,' Taylor mumbled nasally. 'Bu everything's clearly labelled so there's no risk of cross-con tamination or getting things mixed up.'

Horton believed him. Taylor was efficiency itself.

At the entrance to Lena's office building Horton aske her to wait just inside the door and if she'd mind having h fingerprints taken, along with a swab for DNA purpose 'Just to eliminate you,' he explained. She agreed. When th process was complete, he gave instructions for one of th PCs to follow Lena home and to go inside with her while sh packed. 'Follow her to the ferry and see her safely on boar Make sure no one follows you and get a list of all the pa sengers, both car and foot.' Just as a precaution, he though He couldn't see anyone watching them as they drove away

He asked the other PC to check with the occupants the building, and the adjoining retail units, to see if an one had seen or heard anything between Saturday afternoo and that morning. Then he joined Taylor in Lena's offic Holding up the empty box file, now encased in an eviden bag, Taylor said, 'There aren't any prints.'

Horton had anticipated that, but there might be som thing: a hair, a drop of spittle, anything. And Taylor wou find it if it was there. Horton waited until the officer return with the news that no one had seen or heard anythin Disappointed, he left instructions for the PC to remain un Taylor had completely finished and then to call a locksmi and make sure that Lena's office was fitted with new loc and firmly sealed.

Standing just inside the hall, he called Cantelli, wh said, 'Peter Bailey's got a clean driving licence and he doesn keep a boat at the Castle Sailing Club. I've also checked wi Horsea Marina, Portsmouth, Langstone and Chichester ha bourmasters and there's no boat registered to Bailey. Th computer unit can't find anything on Luke's computer show he corresponded with anyone, and Walters says th none of Kempton's visitors admits to talking to Luke, let alone offering him a job.'

'I think we can forget that theory.' Horton quickly relayed what had happened and explained his ideas.

Cantelli listened in silence before saying, 'So someone connected with Rookley looks our best bet.'

'Yes, although I'm not ruling out the others yet, especially Shawford. But we need to find out who was supplying in 1997, who Luke knew, and find a connection between that and Rookley or Crown House.' Which meant Horton needed the surveillance tapes and a list of Rookley's contacts from the drug squad. It was unlikely Superintendent Oliver would give him that without Bliss's or Uckfield's permission, and Uckfield wouldn't be interested because this new development meant that Luke Felton had no connection with the murder of Venetia Trotman. 'See if you can persuade Olewbo to give us the information, Barney. I've asked him once and he said he'd see what he could do, so jog his memory for me.'

Horton rang off and headed for the ferry. While he was waiting to board it, his phone rang. He expected Cantelli, but it was Dr Clayton.

'I've got a match on your body in the harbour,' she said, somewhat excitedly.

Horton hadn't exactly forgotten about the body, but it had slipped down his list of priorities. 'Who is he?' he asked keenly.

'I'll tell you when you get here.'

Horton hesitated, wanting to know more yet eager to get back to see if Olewbo had sent him anything yet. 'Can't you tell me over the phone or call Sergeant Cantelli?'

'No,' she said firmly. 'You need to see this, Andy.'

He could tell by her voice this was big news. He felt a tremor of excitement as he speculated mentally as to who it could be. As the marshalling steward waved him on board, he said, 'I'll be with you in fifty minutes.'

CHAPTER EIGHTEEN

Gaye Clayton sat back twiddling her pen, looking an mated and a little smug. 'Your body in the harbour is Ja Turner, age forty-nine, reported missing by his employe the International Development Fund, based in London, o the fourth of March. He'd gone on leave on the twentie of February and was due back on the second of March. Th concierge at his London apartment confirmed he last saw M Turner at six thirty when he left his exclusive and expensi riverside apartment. That's my description, not the report' I recognized the address.' She smiled. 'Want to see what h looked like before he became breakfast, lunch and dinner fo the Solent sea life?'

Horton walked around to Gaye's side of the desk an peered at the image on her laptop computer. He found hin self staring at a slender-faced man with light grey eyes, shor straight brown hair, a narrow mouth and an honest expre sion, if there was such a thing. Jay Turner looked like th man you'd meet behind the counter in the post office o council office.

Quickly he skimmed through the rest of the repor There wasn't much. Turner was single. The concierge said h hadn't been carrying any luggage when he'd left and hadn said where he was going. Neither had he indicated he'd been going on holiday. Jay Turner didn't own a car. He had no health problems, or any other problems that anyone knew about. He was a quiet man who was always polite but not overly friendly. Shy, was the concierge's description. Horton wanted to know more about him, and why he'd washed up on their shore.

'Does he have any relatives?' he enquired, thinking with relief that some other policeman would need to break the tragic news to them.

'No idea, and I doubt you'll even get the chance to ask.'

Horton stared at her, puzzled. She leant across and scrolled down the page until he saw with surprise exactly what she meant and the reason for her excited manner. The record was flagged, which meant that Jay Turner had been someone incredibly important, not so ordinary and maybe not so honest after all.

Gaye added, 'The moment he was identified an automatic alert was triggered, but I've no idea who it was sent to. No doubt someone will be here soon, or at the station, to ask about your body. They're probably already on their way.'

Horton wondered who they were. The Metropolitan Police? Serious Organized Crime Agency? National Intelligence? MI5? MI6? Interpol? Europol? Well, they'd find out soon enough. And this would be one case — if indeed it was murder — neither he nor Uckfield would need to worry about, because they wouldn't get a look in. Perhaps, though, there was nothing suspicious about Jay Turner's death either, Horton thought, recalling Dr Clayton's findings. Turner had probably had a heart attack while out walking and fallen into the sea, or been swept into it by the tide.

Gaye said, 'There's nothing from the lab yet on the analysis of his clothes, skin or organs, but if he's that important I doubt I'll get the results anyway. They'll be whisked away to whoever is on the end of that alert. There's not much either of us can do about Mr Jay Turner, but there is more we can do on our mystery lady.'

Gaye punched something into her computer and th
time Horton found himself examining a computer-enhanc
image of Venetia Trotman before her face had been battere
Short dark hair framed a lean, angular face with high chee
bones, dark brown deep-set eyes, a strong, slightly promine
nose and a wide mouth.

'You've done a good job,' he said admiringly, recalli
the woman he'd met last Thursday afternoon.

'Your detailed description helped, plus what I had
work on from the body. I've emailed the photograph to I
Dennings but while I was reconstructing her face on n
computer, I wondered if one of my colleagues might l
able to tell you more about her. John Lauder's a forens
anthropologist. I've sent the photograph over to him aski
if he could come up with a biological profile for her throu
analysing her skeletal attributes, and the reason I say th
is because her appearance struck me as being more Easte
European than British or American. Of course, that mig
have no bearing on your case whatsoever, or I should s
Superintendent Uckfield's case, but in view of the fact sl
doesn't seem to exist in this country I thought it might hel

'I'm sure it will. At the moment we've got nothi
except that key.' And the foreign caller, he thought.

'No joy with that?'

'Not yet.' Although he hadn't checked with Truema
today, and by now it was possible he might have mo
information.

Gaye said, 'Well, let me know if and when you g
more on her. I'm curious, and a little sorry for her. Mayb
shouldn't be. For all I know she could be a mass murdere
But until someone comes to claim her, she stays in cold sto
age. And . . .' Gaye shrugged. 'I don't know, call it woman
intuition, but I think she deserves better than that.'

Her words inadvertently conjured up thoughts of h
mother. Horton had wondered many times if she were de
and waiting in cold storage for him to claim. There w
no national database of unclaimed bodies in the UK so l

couldn't trace his mother that way. The only time they'd be alerted about an unidentified body was if the DNA or fingerprints matched someone on the missing persons database, which was what had happened with Jay Turner. In his mother's case, though, there were no DNA or fingerprints recorded and none of her belongings left to take them from. There was only Horton himself. He'd not had his DNA run through the missing persons database; maybe he should.

He stared at the photograph of Venetia Trotman and wondered if Gaye Clayton could age the photograph of his mother, which he'd stared at yesterday morning on his computer. He didn't want it done officially because he'd have to reveal his interest. Maybe Gaye Clayton could also take his DNA and search for a match. He knew he could rely on her discretion not to repeat anything about his mother. He hesitated though. Was he ready for that yet? The answer was no. But there was something she might help with.

Removing from his jacket pocket the piece of paper which had been left on the hatch of his boat and contained the drawing of the symbol, he said, 'Any idea what this means?'

She took it and studied it from several angles before glancing up at him. 'Is it connected with Venetia Trotman or Jay Turner?'

'Neither, and I'd prefer to keep this between ourselves for now.' That earned him a quizzical raised eyebrow.

She examined the drawing for some seconds more before saying, 'I've never seen it before, but I have a friend, her name's Perdita, she's an expert on symbology. Do you want me to ask her what she makes of it?'

He did. It would save him making it official. And although he could have asked the lab to analyse the original for prints and other traces, he reckoned anyone clever enough to deface his Harley and get onto the pontoon without being spotted wasn't going to be stupid enough to leave his traces all over it.

He headed back to the station, where Walters informed him he had the name of the undertakers who had arranged the funeral last Friday. Horton told him to talk to the tomorrow and visit the cemetery. 'See if you can find tho gravediggers and get a lead on what Rookley was doing that cemetery, and whether they saw him with anyone.' T Cantelli he said, 'Tomorrow we'll have another chat wi Ashley Felton and Matt Boynton. Luke might have sa something to them about Natalie's death, other than wh he told Lena Lockhart about it being dark and mentio ing water and a gate. He might also have confided in Kel Masters,' he added, recalling her sexual appetite and Luke enforced celibacy.

'I managed to corner Olewbo in the canteen. He sa he'd sent you an email.'

'Good.'

Horton had just finished briefing them about Ja Turner when Bliss marched in, trailing two well-built me in dark suits. Swiftly Horton registered their grim expressio and recollected his conversation with Dr Clayton. He w surprised the big boys had arrived so quickly, much quick than he'd expected, which meant they'd probably come b helicopter. If that was the case, Jay Turner must have bee someone extremely important . . . or extremely dangerous.

'Inspector,' Bliss commanded, sweeping past him in his office. The men in suits hung back until, with a quic glance at Cantelli, Horton followed her.

The younger of the men closed the door behind Horto while the older one took up position at Horton's desk an waved him into the chair the other side of it. Bliss stoo beside Horton looking annoyed, probably because he hadn told her about Jay Turner immediately after he'd returne from the mortuary. Another black mark against him in th rapidly mounting heap of them, and that was even before sh knew about his trip to the Isle of Wight.

Tersely she made the introductions. 'This is Command Waverley and Superintendent Harlam from the Seriou Organized Crime Agency. They want everything you hav on the body found in Portsmouth Harbour last Friday.'

'Jay Turner,' Horton said, getting no reaction from Waverley or Harlam now beside him. He hadn't expected one. They were trained not to show emotion. He was intrigued, though, and swiftly considered what Jay Turner might have been involved in: drugs or people trafficking, corruption or kidnapping, or perhaps all four. A natural death was now looking highly unlikely. Could Turner have been rendezvousing with someone on board a yacht in the Solent or English Channel and been disposed of? Horton had no idea what the International Development Fund did, but the mere word 'International' coupled with the Serious Organized Crime Agency smacked of an overseas connection.

'There isn't much to tell,' he said, and relayed what they knew, which was practically nothing.

Waverley looked bored before he'd even finished speaking.

Rising he said, 'The body's being moved to London.'

That would please Dr Clayton.

'Superintendent Harlam and I will be stationed here for the next couple of days. DCI Bliss will be our liaison officer.'

She didn't smile, but Horton could tell she was wetting her knickers with delight, and probably calculating how this might help her climb the greasy pole even quicker than she had anticipated.

Waverley continued, 'You can continue with your other cases. DCI Bliss assures me you have many.'

She threw Horton a final glare before sweeping out behind the two men. He moved around his desk and sat down. Whatever Jay Turner had been involved in he doubted he'd find out unless Bliss decided to tell him, though maybe she would if it demonstrated her importance.

A tap came on his door and Cantelli entered. 'Big brass?' he asked, sitting down. Horton swiftly relayed what had happened. Cantelli listened, then consulting his notebook, said 'Jay Turner was born in Portsmouth, and educated at the University of London where he got a degree in Modern Languages, specializing in Russian. He then joined one of the big firms of accountants, qualified as a chartered accoun ant and worked there until he became a management co sultant in 1992. He joined the Civil Service in 1993, whe he worked for the Diplomatic Service until he joined tl International Development Fund in 1996. I also access his missing persons file but there's no next of kin mentione and I got the three monkey syndrome when I tried to follo it up with the station which recorded him missing, so I call the concierge at his apartment. His job must be a bit lone because he liked a chat.' Cantelli smiled. 'He says Mr Turn was a nice quiet man, never had any visitors that he'd see or let into his apartment, but then he was hardly ever ther Not much point in having such an expensive flat, he said, ar not using it, but then there were a lot of people like that London. Mr Turner worked abroad, Europe somewhere, b the concierge wasn't sure where exactly. Turner was usual away for three to six months at a time then back for four five weeks, but even then, he was hardly ever around.'

'The elusive Mr Turner,' Horton said thoughtfully.

'Want me to dig a bit deeper?'

'I doubt you'd get very far. We'll leave Mr Turner Waverley and Harlam and concentrate on Luke Felton.' H told Cantelli to go home.

'I think you should do the same, Andy. You look bea

Horton did feel weary. The sleepless nights were catc ing up with him and his head was aching. He needed tin and space to sift through all the information he'd glean throughout the day and he couldn't do that here. A run alo the seafront would help.

'I won't be long. I just want to check what Olewbo sent over.'

Cantelli looked at him in exasperation before leaving. few minutes later, with full access to the files — for whic he silently thanked Olewbo — Horton was scrolling throug endless images of the occupants of Crown House comir and going, including the shuffling, shifty figure of Ronn Rookley. But there were none of Rookley meeting wi anyone. And none of Luke Felton and Rookley together. And there was only one of Luke Felton entering Crown House on Monday evening. Judging by the time, he was obviously returning from work, and he didn't go out again.

Horton's head was thumping and his eyes felt as though they'd dried up and rolled back into their sockets. He rubbed at them with a fist, which only seemed to make them worse. This was pointless. He needed more than pictures, he needed Olewbo's inside information, and he needed to know who had been big on the drug scene in the area in 1997.

He might as well call it a day. Then his finger froze, and he blinked hard at the image on the computer. Sitting forward, he scrutinized it closely and then the date and time in the top right-hand corner. He sat back and ran a hand over his head. What was Ashley Felton doing at Crown House last Thursday evening? The obvious answer was that he'd gone to visit his brother. He hadn't said though. Why not? He'd told them that Luke had visited him on 6 March and asked for money, but he'd made no mention of seeing him again just under a week later — or to be more precise trying to see him, because by then Luke Felton had already disappeared.

Horton printed off the picture then switched off his computer. There didn't seem any point in briefing Bliss about the developments on the Luke Felton case when she had bigger fish to fry, and talking of fish he fancied some, along with chips.

He bought some after an invigorating run along a blustery, chilly, dark seafront and ate them hungrily on board the yacht, mulling over the Luke Felton case. Every new piece of information they uncovered only seemed to serve up more questions than answers, and still brought them no closer to where Felton was.

Making a coffee, he took it up on deck in the hope that the fresh night air might provide inspiration, or illumination. The wind had dropped a little and the moon, moving into its last quarter, was visible through a cloud-scudding sky, throwing glimpses of silver light on the boats in the

yard above the marina. His eyes flicked up to his Harley
he wondered what Dr Clayton's contact would make of tl
symbol. All was quiet. Then his eyes narrowed as a dark shaj
detached itself from the cover of one of the boats. Hortc
froze. If the bastard was back and scrawling something el
on his Harley, he'd have him by the throat. He slamme
his coffee mug down, and raced up the pontoon and in
the boatyard in time to see a hooded figure moving swift
through the hulls of the boats towards the road. As thoug
sensing his presence, the figure turned. Horton caught tl
glimpse of a man's face, and registered strength and hardne
without noting details, before the figure turned back and ra
towards the road.

Horton tore after him. The man glanced back befo
swerving to the left. Horton followed. He was gaining c
him, then suddenly the figure vanished. He must ha
jumped down on to the shore, but when Horton drew u
there was no sign of anyone, not even a ruddy seagull.

Scouring the dark horizon and remaining perfectly sti
Horton strained his ears for the sound of footsteps on tl
shore and the crunching of shingle, but only the hum
traffic and the wind reached him.

Leaping down on to the shingle, Horton turned eas
wards towards the entrance to Langstone Harbour and
row of upended tenders and rotting houseboats. With h
heart pumping fast, he steeled himself for an attack, h
senses heightened. With bated breath he advanced ginger
until he reached the first overturned tender. Stretching o
he upended it, springing back, prepared to be met with h
knife-yielding graffiti artist. But there was nothing and n
one. He repeated the act with the next tender and the follo
ing one, his senses so strained that he felt like a rod of stee

The man had moved incredibly swiftly and silently,
though he'd had practice at being unobtrusive. He couldr
simply vanish. Horton stood stock still and listened agai
but there was no sound save the gentle wash of the sea c
the shore and the hammering of his heart. He walked c

towards the semi-derelict hulk of an old houseboat, losing what little light he'd had from the street lights as the shore curved further away from the road. He cursed himself for not having a torch and prayed for the moon to make even the most fleeting of appearances, but the cloud had thickened and the air suddenly felt heavy with the promise of rain. He told himself it would be far more sensible to return tomorrow in daylight, but he knew the man would be gone by then.

This was foolish. But still he pressed on until he was standing beside the blackened hulk of the houseboat and could push open what was left of the rotting door. Steeling himself for a possible attack, and holding his breath, he crashed the door open with his foot and waited. Nothing. Or at least no one rushed out with a knife to kill him. But that didn't mean no one was waiting inside.

The door fell off its tentative hinges and crashed to the floor. The silence after it was deafening. Still no movement from inside. Knowing he was a fool to continue, Horton stepped over it and into a small black interior that smelt of mud, seaweed, rotting wood and decaying filth. The houseboat was empty. Or was it? As his eyes adjusted to the dark interior, he caught sight of something in the far right-hand corner. Two steps, avoiding the gaping holes in the rotting wood, took him towards it. The moon made an appearance, sending slivers of light through the gaps in the rotted wood. Horton took a tissue from his pocket and turned over food packets and tins. How long had they been here? They looked recent. Is this where the figure he'd seen was living? Was it a tramp he'd frightened off?

Horton bent to look closer and stiffened as he noted paper and something else — a black felt pen. The sound of a motorbike pulling away caught his attention; he knew this wasn't the shelter of any tramp. It was, or had been, the temporary home of his graffiti artist.

CHAPTER NINETEEN

Tuesday, 17 March

Horton eased a hand around the back of his neck, trying to r himself of a headache caused by lack of sleep, and attempt not to look as tired as he felt.

'Rough night?' Cantelli asked, concerned.

They were on their way to Ashley Felton's apartment.

'You could say that.' Horton told him about the symb pinned to his yacht, the hooded figure and the fact that ea lier that morning he had returned to the rotting housebo and collected up the debris, which he'd taken to the forens lab along with the felt pen. In daylight it was clear to Horto the man had been living rough, which made him wond how he could afford a motorbike. He'd asked Sergeant Stri to check the reports for any stolen bikes.

Cantelli listened in silence with a frown, and with repeat glances in his rear-view mirror. 'I can't see anyone followi us on a motorbike,' he said, worried. 'Maybe you should st with us for a few days until we can find out who this stalker i

'Thanks, but I'll be all right.'

'I seem to remember you saying something like th before, and you were almost fried alive.'

'I'll move the yacht later. It's high tide this afternoon.'

'Well, see that you do. Anyway, I'm glad Dr Clayton's friend is investigating that symbol. And perhaps Joliffe and the lab will come up with a match on fingerprints.'

Horton sincerely hoped so. He changed the subject. 'I called DCI Stuart Pritchard this morning. He was a DS on the drug squad in 1997. I did my training with him at police college. I wondered if he might remember the major players on the drug scene at the time of Natalie's death.'

'Does he?'

'He was in a meeting so I left a message for him to call me. I don't hold out much hope of it leading to anything though, because if Natalie was killed by a supplier, then it's probably one still unknown to us. Someone clever enough to use Luke Felton and frame him for her murder and get away with it.' He wondered if it might be the same person that Superintendent Oliver had been after. If so, then Horton wasn't hopeful of catching him.

'I asked Charlotte about the Feltons last night,' Cantelli said, negotiating the heavy traffic through the city. 'She didn't know the Felton children, but Sonia Felton was very proud of her eldest son, Ashley, who was then something grand in management in London. And Olivia was the apple of her father's eye.'

Which was what Lena Lockhart had told him.

Cantelli was saying, 'She told Charlotte that Luke was difficult to reach. A quiet boy, a bit of a loner. He'd dropped out of university and didn't seem to want to do anything. Charlotte says that Sonia and Neville Felton rowed over the best way to deal with Luke. Neville wanted to throw him out, but Sonia wouldn't hear of it. When Luke was charged with attacking that pensioner and stealing her money while high on drugs, Sonia was mortified. She was off sick for a long time. Charlotte says Sonia blamed herself for not getting close to him, for not loving him enough. The Feltons helped him through the drug rehabilitation programme and Luke promised he'd never go back to drugs. His father got him a job somewhere, Charlotte doesn't know where. It w after his community service anyway. I expect it was with o of his clients. When Luke was charged with killing Natal Raymonds, they were devastated. It killed Sonia. It wasn her fault but Charlotte says she thought it was.'

Horton considered what Cantelli had said. It pretty mu married up with what Lena Lockhart had told him abo Luke, but it wasn't the picture Ashley Felton had painted his brother. What was it he had said? He asked Cantelli.

'I wondered about that. Ashley Felton said that Lu had a terrible temper, that he used to fly off the handle the smallest thing, especially if he didn't get his own way.'

'So who do we believe?'

'No contest,' Cantelli declared. 'Charlotte wouldn't s that if she hadn't heard it.'

'No, but perhaps Sonia Felton saw her middle son in different light.'

'That doesn't account for what Lena Lockhart told yo Though I guess she might have seen a different Luke Felt because of prison, and Ashley Felton could have said that abo Luke because he feels guilty over not helping his brother.'

And he looked more than guilt-ridden when he open the door to them a few minutes later. Dressed in casu clothes, Ashley Felton once again led them through t small lobby into the open-plan room. The table was litter with crockery and cutlery from several meals, and among t debris were strewn papers and a laptop computer. The roo stank of stale cigarette smoke and whisky, and a fug hu over it. Horton wished they could throw open a windo but Ashley Felton seemed to be allergic to fresh air — a suffering from a cold, judging by his constant sniffing.

'I didn't feel I could go into work not knowing whe Luke was. Besides, I can work from home,' he explaine reaching for his cigarettes. 'Have you got some news abo Luke?' He sat down and lit up. He seemed a far cry from t confident, charming man Lena Lockhart had described.

Horton asked if Luke had talked about his drug treatment programme in prison.

'No. As I said we only talked briefly, and he didn't mention it. He just asked for money to help him move out of Crown House.'

'Did he ever confide in you that he didn't kill Natalie Raymonds?'

Ashley Felton's hand froze. Horton noted it was shaking slightly. 'I don't understand,' he stammered. 'What are you saying?'

'There's a possibility that Luke wasn't alone that day and that the person with him could have been Natalie's killer.'

'But Luke confessed.'

'We have evidence that throws new light on the case,' Horton said, eyeing him carefully.

'Jesus!' Ashley Felton leapt up and stalked across the room. Horton said nothing and neither did Cantelli. After a moment he turned back to face them. He looked tortured and his voice shook as he said, 'What evidence?' The ash from his cigarette fell on to the wooden floor.

Horton answered. 'Luke underwent hypnotherapy treatment while in prison and he recalled certain things about the murder. His sessions were recorded.'

'You've got tapes?'

Horton thought Ashley Felton looked on the verge of collapse.

'Where were you between Saturday midday and Monday midday, Mr Felton?'

'Here. Why?'

Truth or a lie? Horton wasn't sure but Ashley Felton didn't want to look at him. Could Luke have confided in him? Could Ashley have sailed across to the Isle of Wight and stolen Lena's tapes? Could he have killed Natalie Raymonds and framed his own brother for her death?

'Alone?' asked Horton.

'Yes.'

Looking worried, Felton leaned over and stubbed h half-smoked cigarette out in the ashtray. Reaching into h pocket Horton unfurled the computer photograph and la it in front of him. Evenly he said, 'Why did you go to Crow House on Thursday evening at eight thirty-three p.m.?'

Felton slowly straightened up and fixed his bloodsh eyes on Horton. 'I went to see Luke, but he wasn't there. felt bad about refusing to help him with the money. Aft he'd gone, I couldn't stop thinking about it.' He sniffed an ran a hand through his fair hair. 'You see, I said some dread ful things about how he'd killed Mum and Dad. I really to into him. He didn't retaliate. He said he would never troub me or ask me for anything ever again. I thought . . . well, grew worried that I might have driven him to do somethin drastic. We were told that he had tried to kill himself prison and I'd said something like "good riddance". It w tormenting me. I had to see him. When I got there, I fe even worse because I could understand why Luke wanted get out of the place. But he wasn't there. I thought that l must have managed to get a sub from Kempton's and ha found himself somewhere else to live. I wasn't happy abo not being able to see him to make it up to him, but I thoug that I'd get the chance at some stage. Then you showed u to tell me he was missing, and as time's gone on and he's n been found I thought . . . No, I know,' he corrected, 'th Luke must be dead. He's killed himself.'

Horton studied him closely. Felton looked haunte by what he'd done, but was that about refusing to help h brother? It was possible, but Horton could see there w more to Felton's agitated manner than guilt. And he kne the cause of it, he'd recognized the signs: the shaking hand bloodshot eyes, dilated pupils, agitation, talkativeness, co stant sniffing.

Evenly he said, 'How long have you been addicted cocaine?'

'I'm not!' Ashley Felton started. His eyes fell and l turned away.

'Is that why you went to Crown House? Did you think Luke would know someone who could help you?'

He spun round. 'No. I went there to apologize.'

'Did Luke say he could get you some coke?' Horton held Ashley's tormented eyes.

After a moment his body slumped. He sat down heavily and reached for another cigarette. 'No. I went to ask him if he could get me some. My supply in London's dried up.'

And Horton knew that could only be because Ashley could no longer afford it. When they looked into his financial affairs, his guess was that Ashley Felton would be up to his eyes in debt.

Coolly, Horton said, 'Luke didn't come here asking you for a sub, did he? In fact, he didn't come here at all because he didn't know where you were living. This address isn't held on any directory of company directors. We've checked.' Cantelli had done so before they'd left and he'd discovered that Ashley Felton had only bought this apartment in November.

Felton fidgeted nervously but said nothing.

Horton continued. 'You contacted Luke and asked him to meet you at Portchester Castle on Tuesday evening.' That got a reaction. Ashley's head came up. 'No!'

'What did you do, Ashley, when he refused to help you? Did he threaten to tell your sister and brother-in-law about your drug addiction? Or perhaps he remembered that you were that other person with him on the coastal path when Natalie was murdered. And that you killed Natalie.'

'No!' Ashley sprang up. 'I didn't even know Natalie and I was in London when she was killed.'

At a sign from Horton, Cantelli put the photograph of Ronnie Rookley in front of Ashley. 'Did you see or talk to this man?' he asked.

Ashley rubbed a shaking hand across his eyes. He was perspiring heavily. It seemed to take him a while to focus on the picture in front of him, but when he did, he shook his head. 'No. I went inside and asked someone where Luke's room was. I knocked and hung about but there was no answer.'

Horton eyed him closely. Was he lying? Perhap Rookley said he'd get Ashley drugs. Stabbing at the pictu of Rookley, Horton said, 'Did you arrange to meet this ma in the cemetery on Friday morning where he said he'd giv you something?'

'No. I tell you I've never seen him.' Horton studied hin forcing Ashley to add, 'If I'd got something do you think I be in this wretched state?'

He had a point. 'When did you start taking drugs asked Horton.

Grudgingly Ashley replied, 'About eighteen months ag at a party in London. Business was tough. It seemed to hel me through, but now . . .' He shrugged.

'Did you take drugs in 1997?'

'No.'

'Did you know Natalie Raymonds?' Horton asked agai

'I told you. No. I wasn't even in the country then. I wa working on a project in Germany. You can check with m former employers.'

Horton wasn't going to take it at face value. Ashle Felton clearly wasn't a supplier, but maybe Natalie had bee and had refused him more drugs. Would that have bee enough for him to kill her and frame his brother? It wa possible.

He said, 'Who's your London supplier?' He didn expect an answer so he wasn't disappointed when he didn get one. 'We'll need you to make a statement. And we'll nee to check your movements.' Not only over the last week bu also in 1997, Horton added to himself. They'd also get a wa rant to search this flat and Felton's boat. Ashley Felton cou have taken his brother out on his yacht on Tuesday nigh killed him and dumped his body in the sea. And he could b lying about not knowing or meeting Ronnie Rookley.

Cantelli slipped out to call a patrol car.

Horton said, 'How did you know Luke was living Crown House if you didn't see or contact him?'

'Matt Boynton told me.'

Of course. Horton recalled the first meeting with Boynton and Ms Attworth; she'd said that they'd contacted Luke's brother and sister.

'I didn't kill Luke, Inspector,' Ashley said wearily. 'But I think he must be dead.'

'Do your sister and brother-in-law think that?'

'Olivia does, and I don't think she much cares either. And Neil believes that Luke's back to taking drugs and is on the streets somewhere, probably London.'

They watched him climb into the police car before returning to their own vehicle parked on the quay. Horton scanned the area but there was no sign of anyone on a motorbike. He didn't dare to hope that he might have frightened his stalker away.

He said, 'Ashley might not have been involved in Natalie's murder, but he could have met Luke at Portchester Castle and asked him if he knew where he could get some drugs. And when Luke refused and threatened to tell his sister or the authorities about his brother's addiction, Ashley gave him a lift back to his yacht in the Town Camber where he killed him and then disposed of the body. He then went to Crown House on Thursday, to meet Rookley, who told him to be in the cemetery on Friday morning where he'd sell him some drugs. Only Rookley thought he'd earn some extra money and said he'd inform on Ashley if he didn't cough up. So, Ashley killed him too.'

'You think Ashley Felton could have attacked you at the locks?'

'He's about the correct build. You'd better contact the London drug squad when we get back, Barney. We'll see if his DNA matches anything Taylor found at Lena Lockhart's office. We'll let him stew in a cell while we talk to Matt Boynton and Kelly Masters. He might feel more like talking after a couple of hours.'

'If he's not crawling up the wall by then. Good job Sonia Felton isn't alive to see what's become of her golden boy,' Cantelli said sadly.

Horton agreed.

CHAPTER TWENTY

They drew a blank with Boynton, who said he and Lul didn't talk about the past, but were more concerned wi focusing on the present and the future. He claimed to kno nothing about the tapes, though he did know that Lul had undergone hypnotherapy sessions as part of his dr treatment programme. 'It's on his prison file,' Boynton ha explained when asked how he knew. Of course, thoug Horton, as they headed for Kempton's and Kelly Master He wondered if Shawford would be there.

On his way he called the lab to see if they had anythi from the search of Shawford's boat and got a lecture on ho they too needed sleep, were desperately short of manpowe were grossly overworked, and weren't superhuman being Pity. A few of those would come in handy.

As they turned into Kempton's, Horton noted that ne ther Shawford's nor Catherine's cars were in the car par He wondered if Catherine had spoken to Shawford abo the pornography. He couldn't see her not doing so. Wou she dump Shawford? He'd thought it highly likely after the encounter on Sunday. But would he get to keep his jo Horton didn't know. He was relieved to see that his fathe in-law's car was also absent.

At reception, Cantelli asked for Kelly Masters. He got a wary look from the receptionist, but she rang through to the personnel officer and two minutes later Kelly teetered out on her high heels, huddled in a black coat with a thunderous expression on her fleshy face.

'We'll talk outside,' she said crisply, brushing past them.

They followed her into the car park and beyond it to the main road, where she took a packet of cigarettes from her coat pocket and lit up.

Abruptly, Horton asked, 'What did you and Luke discuss between the sheets? Oh come on, Kelly, we know you and he were at it.'

Her eyes narrowed. 'So I slept with him. That's not a crime, though I can't say it was a memorable experience.'

'I expect he was out of practice,' Cantelli muttered.

She flashed him a hostile look. Horton said, 'And what did Luke tell you?'

'I stopped listening after a while. It was boring stuff about prison.'

Cantelli said, 'Did he mention anyone in particular? Any inmates, friends or anyone he was close to?'

'No. Just how bad it was being locked up. Is that it? Because I've got to get back to work.'

'We'll walk back with you,' Cantelli said politely. She didn't look too happy about that and didn't move.

Scowling she added, 'He talked about prison then went to sleep.'

Horton said, 'How often did you see him?'

'Every day.'

'You know what I mean, but I'll rephrase it for you. How often did you sleep with him?'

'That's none of your business.'

'It is when Luke Felton might be dead.'

She flashed him a startled glance.

'How often, Kelly?' Horton asked more harshly.

'Twice,' she spat. 'I gave him the benefit of the doubt. I thought he might be better second time around. He wasn't.'

'And?'

'And what?' she cried, exasperated.

'He told you the same thing all over again?' Horton sa incredulously.

'More or less. He said he wanted to put Natalie Raymond killing behind him and move on. And that's it, apart from wh he muttered in his sleep, something about water and darkne and bailing.'

'Bailing?' Horton picked up eagerly. That was new. 'A in bailing out?'

'I don't know. It might have been bailey. Now I've g work to do.' She threw her cigarette down and ground it o viciously with the sole of her shoe.

This time they let her go. Turning to Cantelli, Horto said, 'Are you thinking what I am?'

'She could be mistaken. Or perhaps Luke Felton remen bered Peter Bailey from the trial.'

Horton called Lena Lockhart on her mobile. After co firming she was safe and well, he asked her if Luke had me tioned anything about bailing or bailey. He could hear h thinking about this for a moment.

'No, sorry. Is it important?'

Horton wasn't sure. He let her go and rang Walters.

'I showed one of the gravediggers Rookley's ugly mu shot but he didn't recognize him,' Walters said. 'I'm ju waiting to speak to the other gravedigger, who's due ba from the dentist soon, but I've got the name of the funer directors who handled the burial you saw on Friday. I check that out after I've had something to eat,' Walters adde pointedly. 'I haven't had anything all morning.'

Horton wasn't sure that Walters' 'anything' meant t same as most people's. He glanced at the clock on the das board and saw that it was almost one thirty. It was also tin to move his yacht to another marina and safety, yet he hes tated. 'If I move it, Barney,' he explained as they headed ba to the station, 'it might delay me finding him.'

'Or him finding you,' Cantelli said. 'I thought that was the point.'

'If he returns, I'll be prepared.'

'Or asleep. Even you can't keep awake for ever.'

'I don't think he will return. Not now I've blown his hideaway.'

Cantelli snorted his views on that. 'I'll ask for a patrol along Ferry Road. I've not noticed anyone tailing us.'

'Maybe he's got to sleep some time too.'

After grabbing something to eat, Cantelli went to interview Ashley Felton while Horton rang through to Trueman. He briefed Trueman about the stolen tapes and his interviews with Felton, Boynton and Kelly Masters, ending with, 'I think it confirms that Luke Felton has nothing to do with the Venetia Trotman murder.'

'I'll tell the super.'

'And then stand well back,' added Horton, because Uckfield would need to start looking for another suspect. It also meant he had no reason to be involved in the Venetia Trotman murder, except that he wanted to be. Ridiculous though it was, he felt he owed her something.

There were no signs of Waverley or Harlam and Bliss didn't make her presence felt either. Horton called Sergeant Stride, who said that no motorbikes had been stolen in the Portsmouth area over the last month — which was good for motorbike owners, not so good for Horton's mission to unmask his mysterious persecutor. DCI Pritchard hadn't returned his call, so Horton tried him again, only to be told he was in a meeting. If it was the same meeting it was a very long one.

He then called the lab and managed to get hold of Joliffe this time. Joliffe said there was no match on any of the fingerprints taken from the houseboat debris, but he would see if they could get a match on DNA, which would take longer. Horton felt frustrated at the delay but consoled himself with the fact that it ruled out a convicted villain, recently released and after his blood. Did that make the case stronger for h graffiti artist being someone connected with Zeus, the allege jewellery thief that Superintendent Sawyer was after, and wh might have known Horton's mother? Horton wasn't sure.

His phone rang. It was Walters. 'The other gravedigg remembers you, guv, and he remembers Rookley.'

Thank heaven for an observant man. 'And?'

'He didn't see where Rookley went because he w watching the committal, but after it he saw Rookley agai talking to someone at one of the graves. He couldn't see wh because he had his back to the gravedigger, but he describe him as a well-built man but not fat, dressed in a dark ove coat. He couldn't see the hair colour because he wore a h and they were standing under a black umbrella.'

'Not much help there,' Horton grumbled, though o person flitted into his mind. Neil Danbury. But then tho sands of men were well built and wore dark overcoats; t description also fitted Ashley Felton, who had a reason to dealing with Rookley, while Neil Danbury didn't.

Walters continued. 'The gravedigger says it didn't lo as though they were arguing, and neither did they look though they were discussing the dearly departed. They we en't standing over a grave or nothing.'

'Ask him if Rookley left with this man.'

'Already have. He doesn't know. He had to go in t opposite direction to dig another grave.'

Horton cursed. 'Get around to the funeral directors.'

'But guv—'

'You can grab some lunch as you go.'

Restlessly, Horton applied himself to his paperwo while his mind busied itself elsewhere. He thought abo Venetia Trotman and the man with the foreign accent wh had reported her death. Trueman hadn't said they'd got an thing from analysing his voice pattern, so they must still waiting on the report. Then there was Jay Turner washe up in the harbour. Where had he come from? Why had ended up on their shores? Had he been killed? And where w

Rookley? He'd vanished completely, like Luke Felton. Could both be connected to drugs? Did Ashley Felton know more than he'd told them?

Horton fetched a coffee, hoping the caffeine would clear his mind, and took it back to his office. Drinking it, he stared across the car park, deep in thought. If Luke had been trying to remember who had been with him on that fateful day, why hadn't he called Lena Lockhart and asked to listen to the tapes in the hope that it might stimulate greater recall? Perhaps he didn't want to remember but wanted to put the past behind him and move on, just as Boynton had told them. Horton knew that was easier said than done. Kelly had told them that Luke remembered bailing, which meant he'd either been on a boat at some stage or, as Cantelli had suggested, was getting the word confused with Peter Bailey who gave evidence at his trial.

He turned back to his desk. The fact that the tapes had been stolen proved that someone had been with Luke when Natalie was killed. So why hadn't Bailey seen this man?

He sipped his coffee as he assembled his thoughts. One reason could be because Luke had agreed to meet the man and Natalie in the copse. The accomplice could have driven there and parked up nearby, or he could have come by boat from Portsmouth, and taken Luke Felton back to the Portsmouth shore by boat in the dark, hence bailing. Yes, he liked that idea. Another option was that Bailey was lying about seeing Luke Felton. And why would he do that? Because Bailey was the accomplice and Natalie's killer.

Mentally, Horton ran through their previous interview in that depressing house. Bailey had seemed agitated and had looked decidedly uncomfortable when Horton had mentioned Portchester Castle. Why? Could Bailey have met Luke Felton there on Tuesday, afraid that Luke had started to remember certain things about that day?

Horton sat up. With a frisson of excitement, he quickly grasped the theory and began to push it further. Why would Bailey want Natalie Raymonds dead? And why should he wish to frame Luke Felton? Bailey was hardly their drugs sup plier. And how would he have known either of them? Horto supposed he could have seen Natalie Raymonds when she been running along the coastal path. But how would Baile have known Luke Felton, and more importantly his back ground, well enough to get him to agree to a meeting i that copse? There were two possibilities. Bailey had eithe worked or socialized with Luke Felton, which seemed doub ful unless the job his father had got Luke had been at Hester Shipbuilding, or Bailey already knew him. Peter Bailey didn have a criminal record, so he couldn't have been involve with Luke during his community service for the attack o the pensioner in 1995, unless . . .

With his heart racing, Horton quickly turned to h computer and called up the case files for 1995. When h found the one he wanted, his eyes devoured the text on th screen. Several minutes later he sat back, with a grim smile o satisfaction. There was a great deal more to Peter Bailey tha met the eye and considerably more than he had told them Bailey also had a very strong motive for wanting Luke Felto convicted and put away for a very long time.

CHAPTER TWENTY-ONE

Peter Bailey sat hunched over a cold cup of tea with a slimy skin on it in the interview room, looking forlorn and pathetic. Horton eyed him closely. His grey monk's hair was damp with sweat and unkempt, his trousers were smeared with earth, and the fingers, which fiddled with his spectacles, showed traces of dirt under the nails.

Horton had discovered that Bailey's mother was the pensioner Luke Felton had assaulted and robbed in 1995. Ethel Elmore had remarried after her first husband had died in 1963, when Bailey was twelve. He'd kept his father's name. And if it was that simple, thought Horton, watching Bailey's grubby fingers, then why hadn't Superintendent Duncan Chawley made the connection in 1997?

'Maybe he did,' Cantelli had said, 'but because Chawley had Luke Felton in custody and he'd already confessed he kept quiet about it. It was one case swiftly cleared up and a brownie point to him.'

Horton didn't like it. It was sloppy work and threw into question Felton's guilt.

Cantelli began the interview in a casual, friendly manner, almost as though he wasn't particularly interested. 'How did you lure Luke Felton into meeting you on the coast path in 1997?'

Bailey eyed them both guardedly 'I didn't.'

'No? Perhaps you took him there in your car then.'

Bailey shifted nervously but said nothing.

Cantelli smiled. 'It's OK, Peter, we understand. If l had done that to my mother, I'd have wanted to get my ow back and finger him for Natalie's murder.'

Bailey's head came up. 'I didn't. I saw him slouchi along that path.'

'And you did what?' Horton interjected sharply, maki Bailey start.

'Nothing.'

Horton laughed derisively. 'You expect us to belie that, the man who had attacked your mother?'

Bailey's grey skin flushed. He replaced his glasses a studiously avoided eye contact.

Horton sat back and in a lighter tone said, 'How oft did you see Natalie Raymonds running along the coast path?'

'I didn't.'

'Never? On all the occasions you went there to spy c the little terns?' Horton said, feigning surprise.

'No.' Bailey fidgeted.

'I think you did, Peter, and maybe that's when tl idea first struck you. You thought her a perfect victim, good-looking girl, alone, regular in her running habits.'

'I don't understand.' Bailey stared at each of them turn with a bewildered air.

Relentlessly Horton continued, 'Perhaps you even spol to Natalie. Maybe you fancied her and she laughed at you told you to push off. Hurt and humiliated, an idea began form in your mind on how to get back at her and at the san time get revenge on the man who had hurt your mother.'

'I don't know what you're talking about,' Bailey sa sullenly. 'I saw Luke Felton the day that girl was killed. I never met her before.'

'Maybe you didn't mean to kill Natalie. You just meant to put that tie around her throat, squeeze it a little to make her unconscious and then leave Felton to take the blame for assaulting her, but when you felt the power you had over her, a better idea sprang to mind. She wouldn't be able to laugh at you again if she was dead and Felton would be convicted for her murder. And just to make sure, you came forward to say you'd seen him on the path. It was justice for what he did to your mother. But then Luke was released on licence and started remembering. He called on you and begged you to tell the truth. But you couldn't have that, so you killed him. What have you done with his body, Peter? Buried him in the garden?'

Bailey's eyes widened with horror. 'I don't know where he is. I swear it. I thought that . . .'

'Yes?'

Bailey's body slumped. He stared down at his trembling hands and muttered, 'He ruined our lives, Mother's and mine. I couldn't leave her after that.'

'You wanted to?' Cantelli asked gently.

Bailey's tormented eyes swung up to Cantelli. 'I'd been offered a job abroad but after the attack she became an agoraphobic. She never stepped outside the front door from that day until they carried her out in her coffin ten years later. That's what Luke Felton did to us, and what did he get for his crime, for wrecking our lives? Community service.' There were tears in his eyes now as he added, 'It was pitiful. A disgrace. He was made to clear up litter along the shore at Portchester Castle. I saw him there one lunchtime when I was working at Hester's. I wanted to confront him but I couldn't. It's just not in my nature.' Bailey dashed a hand across his eyes.

'So you arranged to meet him at Portchester Castle last Tuesday night with a view to killing him. Where did you take him, Peter?'

He stared at Horton, confused. 'Nowhere. I didn't meet him. I haven't seen him.' Suddenly the tears began to roll down his creased face. 'My mother was the gentlest, most trustir woman you could find. She didn't deserve what he did to he He killed her as good as if he'd stuck a knife in her heart.'

'And is that why you killed him, Peter?' Cantelli aske softly.

Bailey stared at him with anguished eyes. He sniffe noisily and ran a hand under his nose. 'No, but it's why lied. You're right, I didn't see Luke that day. I made it u I wasn't anywhere near the coastal path. I was at home wi my mother.'

And if Bailey was now telling the truth, where did th leave them? thought Horton. And where did it leave the ori inal investigation? With a ruddy great hole in it.

Bailey began to gabble. 'I didn't think my eviden would help to convict him. I thought the police would fir out before it got that far, but then Felton admitted the crim I thought he must have been there. Everyone said he did i I didn't feel guilty. I remembered what he had done to n mother and thought that at last I'd got some kind of justic I put him out of my mind until you showed up asking que tions and I thought he might have remembered somethir about her murder and discovered I'd lied. I thought he migl come after me.'

'Maybe Felton did come after you, and you killed hin pressed Horton, quietly this time.

Bailey forced his head up with an effort. 'No.'

'He knew you'd lied and he wanted revenge for the yea he'd spent inside. You had to kill him. Maybe it was self-d fence. A jury would have sympathy with that.'

Bailey was shaking his head. 'I haven't seen him.'

Horton gave Cantelli a sign to continue. 'Where we you last Tuesday from six o'clock onwards?'

'At home.'

'Can anyone vouch for you?'

Bailey looked thoroughly dejected. 'No.'

After a moment Cantelli said brightly, 'Been gardenin Peter?' He jerked his head at the dirty fingernails.

Bailey blinked at the change of subject and stammered a reply. 'I stumbled into a bramble.'

'In your own garden!'

'I didn't have my spectacles on.'

Bailey looked at them both with pleading in his fearful eyes. Horton said, 'We'll search your house and garden.'

'You'll find nothing.'

The truth or a lie? Horton told Bailey he'd be held on suspicion of the murder of Luke Felton while they conducted a search of his premises. Bailey made no protest, he didn't even ask for a solicitor or a warrant, but granted them permission to go ahead with a dumb inevitability that Horton found depressing.

Outside Cantelli said, 'Could he have killed Natalie Raymonds?'

It was a question that Horton had been asking himself during the interview. Was Bailey capable of such a crime, and one that had required careful planning? The answer was yes. Bailey had been a design draughtsman, which meant he had an eye for detail, and he had a powerful motive.

'If he did, then unless he admits it we'll not be able to prove it. We might get lucky with the search, though, and find evidence to connect him with Felton's disappearance. And we might even find Felton's body. I'd like you on the search, Barney.'

Their conversation had taken them back to the CID office where Walters had returned footsore, wet and in bad humour. 'The old lady they were burying on Friday was a Margery Blanchester, she was ninety-one,' he said, throwing himself down in his chair with a heavy sigh. 'None of the funeral directors match the description the gravedigger gave me, and I can rule out five of the eight mourners because three are women and the other two are men in their seventies. I'll do the rest tomorrow.'

Horton consulted his watch and was surprised to see it was just after six, but there was someone he wanted to see before calling it a day and he wanted Cantelli with him.

'Why do you want to interview Julian Raymonds Cantelli asked, as they headed out of the city towards Haylir Island.

'If Chawley didn't check that Bailey was related to tl pensioner Felton attacked, then what else didn't he check?

'Raymonds' alibi?'

'He says he did, but if Chawley knew Bailey was lyir and kept silent to get a conviction it's shoddy work, and means we can't trust a single thing in that case file, except tl pathologist's report. Chawley told me he'd checked Natalie background and looked for links between her and Luke, b how can we be sure? There's nothing in the file to indica any of Natalie's friends were interviewed, and there's n record of where she went to school, where she worked, notl ing. And if we put that with Lena Lockhart's testimony, ar the missing tapes, then we've got a vastly different case c our hands. One that needs reopening.'

'I don't think Olivia Danbury will be too pleased abo that.'

Or her arrogant and overprotective husband, thougl Horton, and neither, he suspected, would Julian Raymonds b

The door of Raymonds' house was opened by a wel groomed blonde woman in her early forties. Cantelli swift made the introductions in the pouring rain.

'This is about letting that killer out of gaol, isn't it?' M Raymonds snapped. 'I don't want Julian upset. He's bee under a lot of pressure and his health's not good.'

Horton tried a sympathetic look. He said nothing ar neither did Cantelli. With an irritable sigh she was forced admit them and they followed her neat little figure down tl hall into a gleaming white living room that made Horto wish he'd brought sunglasses. It reminded him of wh Catherine had done to what had once been his home.

Sitting hunched over a laptop computer was a thin, bal ing man in his fifties with several papers spread out arour him. Beyond him, Horton could see the lights of Portsmou across the dark expanse of Langstone Harbour.

'It's the police,' Mrs Raymonds announced briskly.

Raymonds looked up, more alarmed than upset. Mrs Raymonds had been right though; her husband didn't seem in the best of health. Horton wondered what was wrong with him. His troubled eyes flitted warily to Horton and quickly away again. For a moment there was a brief flash of colour on his hollow cheeks before it faded once more into greyness.

Politely, Horton said, 'I'm sorry to trouble you, Mr Raymonds, but I need to ask you a few questions about Natalie.'

Raymonds lowered the lid of his laptop. 'It's all in your files. I've nothing to add.'

'We have new evidence showing that Luke Felton might not have been alone when your wife was killed.' And the person with him, thought Horton, could still have been Peter Bailey.

Raymonds' eyes flicked up to his wife, who was standing ramrod straight, arms folded, lips pursed, glaring at Horton. She caught her husband's glance and gave a slight shake of her head.

Catching it too, Cantelli said, 'Any chance of a cup of tea, Mrs Raymonds?'

She looked as though she was about to tell Cantelli what he could do with his tea, but whether Cantelli's charming smile or the slight nod from her husband changed her mind, Horton didn't know. She huffed out of the room with Cantelli following. If anyone could charm her then Cantelli could. And at the same time pump her for information.

Horton took the seat opposite Raymonds. 'Did you ever hear Natalie talk about a man on the coastal path? A birdwatcher, about late forties, looked older, medium height, slender build, wearing spectacles?'

Raymonds shook his head but Horton saw anxiety in his tired eyes. Horton prompted, 'She might have made fun of him, joked about him trying to chat her up.'

'She never said.'

Horton hadn't really expected any other answer, but he sensed a hint of unease, and something more underlying

Julian Raymonds' manner. What was it: concern, ange resentment, fear? He said, 'How often did she run along tl path?'

'When she felt like it.'

'There wasn't a regular time then?'

'Not really. It depended on the weather and what sl was doing that day.'

That didn't necessarily mean Bailey hadn't selected h as his victim. He could have seen her on several occasio on the path. But if he hadn't, as he claimed, then who el had wanted Natalie dead, and why? And who wanted Lul Felton to pay for it? Julian Raymonds?

Eyeing Raymonds closely, Horton said, 'Is there anyo who would have wanted Natalie dead?'

Raymonds bristled. 'I know what you're driving at b I can tell you I didn't kill her. I had only just married he for God's sake.'

'Maybe you made a mistake. It was a whirlwin romance.'

'I loved Natalie,' Raymonds insisted, but his stateme rang false. Horton kept his gaze on the thin, stooping ma not allowing his excitement to show. He knew he was on tl edge of learning some new and vital piece of informatio that could turn this case around. After a moment Raymon sighed. Horton wondered if he was about to hear a confessio

'Oh, what does it matter now? You might as well kno the truth. I thought Natalie loved me, but she only loved m money, which will soon be gone along with this house. I' bankrupt, cleaned out. Not that that's Natalie's fault. Tl recession finished me off. I didn't realize until I married h what really turned her on: money and power. I had bo then, and connections with some influential people. Natal loved that.' He ran a hand over his face. Horton could he the soft rumble of voices coming from the kitchen.

After a moment Raymonds continued in a flat wea tone, 'Natalie had affairs. She was having one when she w killed, but I've no idea who with.'

Horton's pulse quickened. At last, the truth. So much for Chawley's investigation. 'How do you know that?' he asked keenly.

'Because she was different. She always was when it was going on. Brighter, happier and more passionate. I thought it would pass like the other affairs. I turned a blind eye because I couldn't bear the thought of losing her. When she was killed, I was devastated. I thought that maybe a jealous wife or partner had killed her, but when Luke Felton was arrested, I was shocked. He wasn't her type. For a start he didn't have money or power. And Natalie would never have had an affair with someone so scruffy, or a drug addict.'

And that ruled Bailey out too, certainly of being Natalie's lover. But he did have that motive for wanting to destroy Luke Felton, and Raymonds had one too. As though reading Horton's mind, Raymonds added, 'And if you think that gives me a reason for killing Natalie, then I can tell you there were several witnesses who can swear I was at the boat show when Natalie was murdered.'

Mrs Raymonds burst into the room, with Cantelli, sipping at a mug, in tow.

'If you're going to accuse my husband of such a vile act then you can charge him, and we want a solicitor present,' she cried.

'Leave it, Sharon,' Raymonds said, waving away his wife's protests. To Horton he said, 'I've kept silent about Natalie's affairs because no one asked me about them. Superintendent Chawley had Luke Felton for her murder, the evidence seemed overwhelming and he confessed to it.'

'Can you tell me anything about her lover, anything at all?' Horton hoped he didn't sound as desperate as he felt.

But Raymonds shook his head.

'What about previous lovers?' asked Cantelli, quickly picking up on Horton's conversation with Raymonds.

'I've no idea who they were. I didn't want to know.'

Angrily, Sharon Raymonds interjected. 'It all happened a long time ago. My husband is ill, we don't want it raked up

for the newspapers to splash all over their front pages agai
Natalie is dead and good riddance, I say. Whoever killed h
did us all a favour.'

'Sharon!'

'It's true,' she declared. 'All right, so I shouldn't ha
said that about wishing her dead, but she used you, Julia
and made your life hell.'

Horton said, 'Did Natalie take drugs?'

'No,' Raymonds answered without hesitation. 'She va
ued control too much, which was why she enjoyed usi
men, she had emotional and sexual control over them. A
she wouldn't do anything to destroy her body or looks.'

'Did she ever deal in drugs?'

'Not that I know of.' He looked genuinely shocked.

There didn't seem anything more Raymonds could t
them, and he was, Horton had to admit, looking serious
ill. He told Raymonds they'd need a statement at some sta
and that there was a strong possibility the case would be re
pened in light of new evidence. That made Raymonds lo
even worse. In the car he asked Cantelli what he'd got fro
Sharon Raymonds.

'Julian Raymonds has cancer, is broke and she lov
him.'

'If this lover story is true, Barney, then Bailey certain
doesn't fit the bill, and it's as he claims, he saw an opport
nity to put Luke in the frame for her murder after Chawl
had given his press conference asking for any sightings of
man in his twenties on the coastal path that day. He on
half expected to be believed, not knowing that Chawl
already had DNA and fingerprints. Luke was there, and wi
Natalie's killer. Whoever killed her hadn't counted on a fal
witness coming forward but wasn't going to look a gift hor
in the mouth when it did. It wasn't a spur of the mome
murder, it was meticulously planned and premeditated,
had to be to implicate Luke. So Natalie must already ha
told this lover the affair was over but agreed to see him o
last time. He brought a drugged Luke Felton with him mo

probably in a boat on the high tide, which is why Luke kept mentioning water and bailing. It must have been a small boat to get up on to the shore and perhaps the water got in. Bailey said the tide was up when he was bird watching, and he's correct, high water was at two twenty-nine p.m. on the nineteenth of September 1997. Which means the killer could have access to the shore between twelve thirty and four thirty. Let's say he came in the boat at three thirty or even four o'clock, killed Natalie and left a drugged Luke there to take the blame.'

Cantelli took it up. 'He becomes aware of his surroundings after it grows dark, stumbles over the body and gets his DNA all over Natalie and blood on his clothes, and staggers onto the coastal path—'

'Sees the gate, which is directly opposite—'

'And then somehow makes his way back to Portsmouth.'

'He wasn't picked up until the Monday in Southsea and it was clear he'd been sleeping rough. He didn't catch the ferry so perhaps he hitched a lift. Or . . .' Horton paused before voicing the thought that had occurred to him earlier. 'Perhaps Natalie's killer took Felton back to the Portsmouth shore in his boat and dumped him there. But who was her lover, Barney? It has to be someone with money or power, or both according to Raymonds, and someone who knew Luke Felton.'

'Ashley Felton had money and power.'

'But he was working in Germany.'

'I haven't had time to check that yet. He could be lying. Though I can't see him wanting to frame his brother and destroy his parents. What about Neil Danbury? I haven't met him, but I've seen his house and there's a lot of money there.'

'Not in 1997 there wouldn't have been.'

'But he inherited Neville Felton's practice. He could have had a fling with Natalie, who threatened to tell all before the big day. Perhaps she was going to waltz into the church at that moment when the priest says "Does any man know any just cause or impediment why these two should not be joined in holy matrimony?" That would have put the kibo: on his future career. He kills Natalie, frames Luke becau: he's already got a criminal sentence, and then inherits tl business from his father-in-law.'

'I'd warm to that version,' Horton said, recalling h interview with Danbury at the police station. 'And I haven forgotten Edward Shawford. He could have been Natalie lover, though I don't see him having the brains to plan h death and frame Luke Felton for it, or having money an power.'

'That's because you're prejudiced.'

Horton grunted acquiescence. He wondered thoug how Shawford would have known Luke in 1997. But the what the devil did he know about Shawford's past anywa He only knew of his present sexual tastes: sadomasochism.

Horton sighed. 'It's late, Barney. Let's sleep on it Tomorrow they might get some fresh evidence from tl search of Bailey's premises and car. And tomorrow he'd re-in terview Edward Shawford.

CHAPTER TWENTY-TWO

Wednesday, 18 March

Cantelli left to oversee the search of Peter Bailey's premises after making sure that Horton hadn't received a nocturnal visit from his stalker.

'All quiet on the marina front,' Horton reported, trying not to show any traces of fatigue. He doubted he was fooling Cantelli. The sergeant looked as though he'd been awake half the night worrying about it, which made Horton feel guilty. Perhaps he was being selfish. Strangely enough, though, he'd managed a few hours of untroubled sleep without any dreams or sounds of motorbikes disturbing him.

Walters went off to track down the remaining mourners at the funeral, which left Horton free to interview Edward Shawford. He promised Cantelli he'd take someone with him and was just wondering if PC Seaton was on duty when his phone rang. It was Dr Clayton.

'John Lauder's come through with some information on your mystery lady,' she announced excitedly.

'That was quick,' Horton said, surprised.

'Being a forensic anthropologist, he's usually only got a few old bones or a skull to work on, or if he's really lucky a complete skeleton. So when I sent him photographic image measurements and the full autopsy report it was a doddl or so he claims. Plus, I said it was urgent. I'll tell you wh he's discovered when you get here. And before you ask, ye I have told Superintendent Uckfield, or rather DI Denning But the reason I want you here isn't for the pleasure of seeir you again, nice as that usually is, but Perdita's also got son interesting information on your symbol, which I haven't to Dennings.'

That changed everything. Shawford could wait.

On his way to the mortuary Horton speculated as t what both Lauder and Perdita had discovered. Would th former help Uckfield find his killer? Horton sincerely hope so. Perhaps he already had a lead on it. And what about th symbol? Was its interpretation going to point him in th direction of Zeus and his mother? Horton felt a quickenir pulse as he pulled up in the hospital grounds.

He found Dr Clayton in her office staring at a lapto computer screen. She looked up with a smile.

'I was right,' she cried triumphantly. 'According to Joh Lauder, your mystery lady is not of British or American or gin, she's from Eastern Europe. Lauder thought Russian first, but when he investigated further, taking skull and faci measurements into consideration, and based on the inform tion I gave him, he says she is Georgian.'

Horton's mind quickly tried to grapple with this ne information and what he knew about Georgia, which w about as much as he knew about astrophysics. He recalled th anonymous caller and his foreign accent. There had to be link there surely? And no doubt Trueman had already mad it, along with contacting the Georgian authorities to see if h could get a match on Venetia Trotman's fingerprints and DN He'd probably also sent her photograph and description ov to Georgia and Europol, asking them to circulate her details.

He said, 'She might originate from Georgia but we don know when she lived there, if she ever did. She could ha been born in the UK to Georgian parents.'

'You want sugar on it?' Gaye rolled her eyes. Then she smiled. 'If you recall, I noted that she had very little dental work—'

'I haven't seen the report.'

'Of course, it's Superintendent Uckfield's case. Well, Lauder has confirmed my opinion that the dental work was not carried out in the UK.'

And Horton wondered what Uckfield would make of that. He was keen to find out, but not keen enough to forget the other pressing matter that had brought him here.

Not bothering to disguise his excitement he asked, 'And the symbol?'

Gaye beckoned him around to her side of the desk. 'Extremely interesting and highly significant, given what I've just told you.' She pointed to the screen and he swivelled his gaze to it. She continued. 'On the face of it, it looks like the pagan "deadly" symbol: a cross and a circle above it. But the cross intersects at the bottom not in the middle.'

Horton found himself staring at an enlarged picture of the symbol which had been left on the hatch of his yacht.

'Perhaps whoever did it can't draw,' he said, recalling Cantelli's hasty and perfunctory research.

'There is always that, but Perdita says if you look closer you can see that there is some kind of small bar across the right axis near the bottom, not far from where the cross intersects.'

Horton peered at the screen as Gaye flicked on an enlarged image. He saw clearly what she meant. It was the same on his Harley, only he hadn't been studying that for artistic merit, minute detail or even interpretation, he'd been too angry.

Gaye went on. 'On the pagan deadly symbol there is a circle resting on the axis of the cross, but in this drawing, it is high and above the cross. It also has a jagged edge and isn't a true circle. And before you say it, I suggested it could be because someone's hand was shaking when they drew it and they were incapable of drawing a perfect circle.'

'And her reply?'

'She thought the circle was more star like, and much t high to be associated with the deadly symbol.'

'Well, that's a relief. Unless it means something wors

'There are also two shapes either side of the cross.'

Which Horton had seen on his Harley as two sm etched lines. But he hadn't bothered to examine their sha or include them in the drawing he'd shown Cantelli becau he thought the vandal was having fun scratching squigg lines. In the drawing pinned to his yacht, the shapes were f more distinctive, something he hadn't paid much attentic to when he'd ripped it off.

'On the left,' Gaye said, pointing, 'is a small letter "l with something like a hangman's scaffold on the top, ar on the right is a small line with almost a circle adjoining it

'Aren't they just random marks?' he asked, knowing th they obviously weren't.

'Perdita says not. The one on the left, the extended "b she believes represents, in its simplistic term, the Georgi letter "L".'

Horton eyed her with surprise, his mind leaping wi thoughts and ideas.

'I thought that might get you excited. Now you kno why I wanted you here. It ties in with what Lauder has to us about our mystery lady. And there's more.'

'Go on,' he said.

'The other symbol she thinks is the Georgian letter f "U". Putting that together with the cross and the star li circle at the top, Perdita believes the "L" symbolizes t word "Lion", and the "U" stands for "Unicorn". The Lic generally represents courage, strength and nobility and t Unicorn, purity and virtue. Perdita claims that we're lookir at a coat of arms of Kartli.'

'Where?'

'That's more or less what I said, but I looked it up c the Internet, and asked Perdita. Kartli is a historical region central eastern Georgia better known to classicists as Iberia.

used to be a separate country with its capital at Tbilisi, which is Georgia's capital, but it's now divided up. The Georgians living in the historical lands of Kartli are known as Kartleli. Why should someone leave you this note?'

'And etch it on my Harley.'

'My God! I wouldn't like to be the person responsible for that when you catch him.'

Horton wondered if he ever would. But he also felt a great sense of relief that his stalker wasn't connected with Zeus. Given that Lauder said Venetia Trotman was from Georgia, then if the author of this note was her killer why draw attention to himself? And why become his stalker? The answer came as quickly as he'd posed the question. His stalker and the anonymous caller were the same person. He hadn't killed Venetia Trotman but wanted Horton to discover who had. And there was more. Horton's mind was teeming with ideas. He needed to talk to Uckfield urgently, but first he asked Gaye to look up the word Shorena.

Hastily thanking her, and asking her to pass on his gratitude to Lauder and Perdita, he hurried back to the station after promising her he'd tell her all later.

'Over a drink,' she called out after him.

Horton found Uckfield in the incident room along with Trueman, Dennings and Marsden. He'd anticipated an atmosphere of excitement — the news that Venetia Trotman was Georgian was a breakthrough — but what he saw, much to his surprise, was dejection and in Uckfield's case sullen anger.

'Why so gloomy?' he asked in puzzlement, removing his leather jacket.

Uckfield answered him grumpily. 'Why do you think? You've ruled Felton out of the investigation and we've got sod all else.'

'But Lauder's analysis of Venetia Trotman changes everything.'

'What analysis?'

Horton focused his gaze on Dennings. The idiot hadn't told Uckfield or Trueman.

Flippantly, Dennings said, 'Dr Clayton's friend clain she's from Georgia.'

'John Lauder is a forensic anthropologist,' Horton co rected, stiffly. Uckfield glowered at Dennings.

'So, she's a foreigner.' Dennings shrugged but glared Horton, clearly not pleased with him butting in and showir up his incompetence.

Trueman caught on instantly. 'Your anonymous tip-o could also be someone from Georgia.'

'Yes. And there's more.' Horton's thoughts were tun bling through his head like tickets in a tombola. Quickly l told them about the symbol etched on his Harley, whic drew raised eyebrows from Trueman and a 'bloody hell' fro Uckfield. Horton then said, 'And there's Jay Turner.'

'Who?' Uckfield asked.

Excitedly, Horton said, 'My body in the harbour tur out to be Jay Turner, who is of great interest to Command Waverley and Superintendent Harlam of the Serio Organized Crime Agency. Turner was born in Portsmout and educated at the University of London where he got degree in Modern Languages, specializing in Russian. H was last seen alive in London on the twentieth of Februar He left on foot, didn't own a car and wasn't carrying ar luggage. Cantelli discovered that Turner began working f the International Development Fund in 1996 and regular spent three to six months working overseas, and the rest the time he was hardly ever in London.'

Uckfield opened his mouth to speak, but Hortc quickly continued. 'We learn that Venetia Trotman ori inates from Georgia, and judging from the lack of any I I wouldn't mind betting she's here illegally. Her husban Joseph Trotman, bought Willow Bank in 1997 and paid his bills in cash. Venetia told me her husband had died thr months ago, but how do we know that for certain? His dea hasn't been registered because his identity is false. I wouldn mind betting that Joseph Trotman equals Jay Turner ar that he met Venetia when he was working in Georgia.'

'You've got evidence?' Uckfield interjected sharply.

'No. I'm assuming it because Turner worked for the International Development Fund, and spoke Russian.'

Uckfield addressed Marsden. 'Get everything you can on this International Development Fund. Find out if they operate in Georgia and if so since when.'

'There's something else,' Horton added. 'The missing yacht is called Shorena. It's a Georgian girl's name meaning remote.'

With renewed vigour, Uckfield turned to Trueman. 'What do you know about Georgia? Recent events not ancient bloody history.'

'It's complex,' Trueman said.

Uckfield rolled his eyes. 'Edited highlights please,' he pleaded.

As Trueman delved into his encyclopaedic memory he also tapped into his computer. 'Georgia is in south-western Asia, bordering the Black Sea, and sharing borders with Armenia, Azerbaijan, Russia and Turkey. It's largely a mountainous country with the Great Caucasus Mountains in the north and the Lesser Caucasus Mountains in the south. Georgia is of great strategic interest to Russia and the West, because it sits in the path of potentially lucrative oil routes. But relations with Russia are extremely tense. Georgia also featured in the Greek legend of Jason and the Argonauts—'

'As in he of the Golden Fleece?' interrupted Uckfield.

'Yes.'

'Well, I hope we don't end up with skeletons dancing all over the ruddy place.'

'It's also got Black Sea port facilities at Poti and Batumi,' Trueman added, 'which are becoming increasingly important as main cargo terminals for the Caucasus and Central Asia.'

'And for smuggling people out of the country,' added Horton meditatively, 'which could be the reason for Waverley's interest.'

Uckfield said, 'Could Jay Turner aka Joseph Trotman have been using his yacht and Willow Bank for that?'

It was possible, but Horton said, 'I'd have thought he have been picked up by now if he had.' Immigration and cu toms regularly patrolled the Solent. 'But he could have h another route, or varied them. Or he might have been involve in something else illegal, large-scale corruption for exampl Hence the Serious Organized Crime Agency's interest.'

Uckfield sprang up and began to stalk the incident suit Horton could see the way his mind was working; how he love to get one over on the men in suits from London. S would Horton, but the moment Commander Waverley g a sniff of this it would be out of even Uckfield's hands. An Horton was keen to find out why the gentle, dark-haire Georgian woman had been killed, and by whom. He was al eager to get his graffiti artist off his back.

He said, 'If Turner did work in Georgia, then he migh have been involved in taking bribes from suppliers an siphoning off money for himself from government contrac The money could have been converted into jewellery or gol and some of that might be what's stashed away in that locke And why Venetia Trotman was so desperate to keep hold the key.'

'So, who killed her?' asked Dennings grumpily.

'Not my anonymous caller,' Horton replied. 'But h could have been inside Venetia's house when I was there. H saw me at the house when I was there looking over the boa and followed me to the marina where he etched that symbol o my Harley.' And Horton knew he must be the man who ha been hiding out in the derelict houseboat, and following hi without being seen. A man highly experienced at covert wo and survival tactics. 'After keeping an eye on me, and seeing wasn't about to spirit Venetia away, he returns to Venetia find her dead. He realizes I couldn't have killed her, becau he'd been watching me most of the night, so he calls me.'

'How?' asked Dennings.

'I left a card with Venetia with my direct line numb on it. It didn't give my position or job, but he knew I was police officer, and the only way he could have known th was because he'd followed me here. And he's been tailing me to see who I'm going to lead him to.'

'And how the blazes do we find him?' exclaimed Uckfield, leaving unspoken the remainder of the sentence — without telling Waverley and his boy.

Horton said, 'He's still in Portsmouth, and he'll stay here until we find her killer — or he does.' Uckfield eyed him shrewdly.

Horton added, 'I've asked Joliffe to check the fingerprints on the debris I found in the derelict boathouse with the Georgian authorities.' Horton had called him as soon as he'd left Dr Clayton. 'They might be able to give us a name and a photograph. I think you should also check if any motorbikes have been stolen from sea ports around Britain, excluding here — I've already checked, there aren't any. He probably came into the country via a port.'

Uckfield said crisply, 'Dennings, get on to it and chase Joliffe for those fingerprints. Go over every single bit of evidence looking for connections with Georgia and see if we can get anything from SOCO to match DNA to Jay Turner. Trueman, contact Europol and Interpol and the Georgian authorities. Marsden, when you've got all you can on this International Development Fund, see if you can find anyone who can confirm Jay Turner's overseas postings without Waverley knowing. None of you are to say anything to Commander Waverley, Harlam or DCI Bliss. If we're wrong, I don't want shit all over my face.'

Horton watched Uckfield cross to his office before turning to leave. He didn't expect thanks, but a grunt of gratitude might have been nice. His eyes swivelled to Dennings. All he was likely to get from him, judging by his expression, was boiling fury.

Dennings followed Horton into the corridor. 'If you think you can get me kicked off this team by showing me up then you can think again.'

'Can I help it if you're not up the job?' Horton made to leave but Dennings grabbed his arm. Horton stiffened and

felt his fists clench, but Dennings would love that. He he
Dennings' hot, angry eyes.

'We'll see who's up to their job,' he hissed.

Horton stared at the hand on his arm and back in Dennings' face. Evenly he said, 'Then you'd better do it. you can.'

As Horton turned, he could feel Dennings' hate-fille eyes boring into his back. He headed for Kempton's whe he hoped he'd find Edward Shawford, otherwise he'd ha to track him down at his boat or his apartment. And he st had Luke Felton to find.

CHAPTER TWENTY-THREE

Shawford's red BMW was in Kempton's car park. Good. And so were Catherine's and her father's cars. Not so good. Horton hoped he wasn't going to have to interview Shawford in front of his father-in-law and estranged wife, but as he drew to a halt, the stout figure he was seeking burst through the doors. There was a thunderous expression on his flabby face and a large briefcase and cardboard box in his hands. Horton climbed off the Harley and waited for Shawford by his car.

'What do you want now?' Shawford rounded on him. 'Isn't it enough you've got me fired and broken up my relationship with Catherine?'

Horton could have crowed with delight. And he didn't care if he showed it. Mission accomplished. He'd got this warped bastard out of Emma's life. Clearly the cardboard box contained Shawford's personal desk paraphernalia. He wondered how Catherine had managed to get rid of Shawford without revealing the reason why she wanted him out and risking an unfair dismissal claim. Perhaps Shawford had volunteered to go; he wouldn't have wanted his sex life paraded in the newspapers.

He said, 'You got yourself sacked.'

'I was made redundant because of the recession Shawford sneered. 'Catherine's taking over my role but w both know that's a load of bollocks. You told her about tho magazines.'

Horton stifled his concern at the thought of Catheri being away from Emma on business trips abroad. Wh would look after his daughter? He wished it could have bee him, but he knew how impractical that was, unless he ga up his job. But then she'd be at Northover boarding schoo Catherine seemed to have it all worked out. Time to think that on Saturday, when he'd be with Emma and Catheri at the school.

He said, 'And I'll tell others, including the vice squad, you don't stop pissing me about and tell me the real reas why you gave Luke a lift to Portchester Castle.'

Shawford could see that he wasn't bluffing. Horto knew that Catherine wasn't featured in any homemade porn videos, so the threat of the vice squad was real this time.

Shawford shifted the box in his arms and ran his tong over his lips. Nervously he said, 'I gave Luke a lift becau he started to remember things about the murder of Natal Raymonds.'

Horton swiftly hid his surprise. Although he had co sidered Shawford might be involved in Natalie's murder he not really believed it. 'You knew her?' he asked, watchi Shawford closely.

'We had an affair.'

God! Horton wished he'd cautioned him and had him that interview room. Shawford could retract this, and prob bly would. He thought over what Julian Raymonds had sa about his wife enjoying power and control. Maybe Natal Raymonds was the dominant partner, indulging Shawford sadomasochistic perversions.

'When?' Horton asked sharply.

Shawford shifted, and not because of the load he w carrying. His roving eyes avoided contact with Horton 'June 1997,' he mumbled. Then his head came up and added earnestly, 'It only lasted a couple of weeks. It was over long before she was killed.'

'Why didn't you come forward with this information?' demanded Horton angrily.

'Why should I?' Shawford answered in surprise, seeming to recover some of his composure. 'It was just a fling, a bit of fun. We met on a corporate hospitality sailing event.'

'And where was her husband while you were having this bit of fun?' Horton snarled, pushing away with anger the thought that Shawford might also have been having 'fun' with Catherine behind his back before the Lucy Richardson debacle had caused their marital break-up.

Shawford sniffed and peered at the ground. Horton wondered if Shawford had been married in June 1997. He could ask and check records. Perhaps Natalie had threatened to tell Mrs Shawford about it, which would have given Edward Shawford a motive for killing Natalie. But that didn't explain why he would want to frame Luke Felton.

Harshly Horton said, 'Why did Natalie chuck you over?'

Shawford didn't even bite at the assumption that it was she who had given the stud of the century the push.

'She found someone else. I don't know who though,' he added quickly.

'Luke Felton?' suggested Horton.

Shawford eyed him incredulously. 'Not Natalie's type. Not enough money. She liked a good time, and she liked power. Some women do.'

'Can't see why she bothered with you then,' quipped Horton, but again Shawford had corroborated what Raymonds had told him. If Natalie had blatantly thrown herself at other men in front of her husband, then jealousy was a powerful motive for killing.

Shawford bristled. 'I don't have to put up with—'

A glare from Horton silenced him. 'So you saw Luke waiting beside the road on Tuesday evening, and grabbed your chance to ask him what he remembered of the day Natalie was killed without anyone at work listening in.'

Shawford nodded. 'He told me he hadn't killed her ar said that it was only a matter of days before he cleared h name. I told him he'd never get the case reopened. I didn want him to, because I thought it might come out that knew Natalie, but I didn't kidnap or kill him to shut hi up,' he added hastily. 'Luke said there was someone wh believed him who was influential and was keen to help hi see justice done.'

That certainly wasn't Peter Bailey, unless he had lied Luke, which was possible. And if it had been Ashley Felto then why hadn't Luke said something like 'my brother determined to help me clear my name'? The same for Ne Danbury.

'Who was he meeting at Portchester Castle?'

'I don't know. It's the truth,' Shawford insisted quickl as Horton looked doubtful. 'That's all he said, apart from th fact that it was where it all began, and he remembered wat and the bailey.'

Horton seized the last two words eagerly. 'The bailey?

'I assumed he meant the moat and the outer bailey Portchester Castle. Though what that has to do with Natalie death I've no idea, and he didn't elaborate. He knew nothir about my affair with Natalie, or at least he didn't mention i He told me he didn't even know her.'

'Did he say how he ended up on the coastal path Hayling?'

Shawford shook his head. 'We didn't discuss it in deta and I wasn't interested. I'd got all I needed. I dropped hi off in the car park and went home.'

Horton eyed Shawford closely. It sounded like the trut He turned on his heel and climbed on his Harley, not bot ering to look back at Shawford. He hoped it was the last he see of him.

He headed for Portchester Castle. Luke had to Shawford that was where it had all begun, and he had con here on Tuesday evening to meet the person he thought w going to help him clear his name, the one who had in fa killed Natalie Raymonds and framed him for her murder. By coincidence, it just happened to be near the site where a woman had been brutally murdered in her garden two days later. The castle then, Horton thought, pulling into the car park, had to hold the key to Luke's disappearance and to the murder of Natalie Raymonds. And if Shawford was telling the truth about Felton mentioning the bailey, and if Luke hadn't met Peter Bailey here on 19 September 1997, then why come here, pondered Horton, entering the castle grounds through a large ancient stone archway. It was miles away both by road and sea from the coastal path where Natalie had been killed.

Horton stood inside the fortifications and stared at the ruins. Nothing new sprang to mind, so he went in search of the castle souvenir shop and bought a guide book. Returning to the Green, he quickly skimmed through the book, learning that the gate he had entered by was called the Landgate. This made sense because it faced landwards, while the entrance on the other side of the Green, with its iron grille set in the stone archway, facing onto the sea, was called the Watergate. Somewhat obvious. And that's what Luke had recalled in his trance: water and gate, but not two separate words, one — Watergate.

Horton also read that he was standing in the outer bailey. So, could Luke have arranged to meet Natalie's killer at the Watergate in the outer bailey in 1997? And had he repeated that arrangement last Tuesday? It seemed likely. Surely he'd have remembered if the person who had killed Natalie had been his brother or brother-in-law, but then he supposed the drugs had obliterated that memory.

Horton located the steep, twisting stone steps to the keep and ran up them, emerging at the top where a biting wind caught him full in the chest, and stung his face with an icy chill that was more reminiscent of January than March. He didn't mind. He found it refreshing after the stench of Shawford.

He was glad to see that he was alone, except for a single gull which was crying overhead as if it had witnessed something terrible. And maybe it had, he thought, as it div to skim the surface of the water — Venetia Trotman's murd and the abduction and killing of Luke Felton, because Hort was even more convinced now, after Shawford's story, th he was dead. He watched the gull fly towards the entrance Portsmouth Harbour, where Jay Turner's body had wash up, and his mind once again returned to Venetia Trotman. H was equally convinced that Joseph Trotman was Jay Turn Had he died accidentally? Perhaps he'd gone out on his yach Shorena, and fallen overboard? But that would mean someo had been with him, because the yacht hadn't sailed itself ba to Willow Bank. Perhaps Venetia had sailed it back and h kept silent over her husband's death. Maybe she'd pushed hi overboard. Or had Jay Turner's killer met him somewhe along the coast, killed him and dumped his body in the se That thought brought Horton back to Luke Felton.

He cast his eyes over the scene spread before him hopi inspiration would come, just as it had when Dr Clayton ha told him about Venetia Trotman being Georgian. Beyon the priory church, to his right, hidden by bushes and tree was Venetia Trotman's house. Again Horton considered t coincidence of her death, both in time and location, wi Luke Felton's disappearance. Was there a connection? B no, he had already discounted that.

Swinging his gaze in the opposite direction he saw t cranes and ships in the commercial ferry port. Was Luke body in the sea? Had the person he'd arranged to meet he enticed him onto his yacht, then killed him and thrown h body overboard, it just hadn't yet surfaced along the coas Ashley Felton had a boat, so too did Shawford, but he di counted the latter. Was Neil Danbury a boat owner? W Danbury too vehement in his hatred for Luke Felton? W his protective stance towards his wife simply an act?

And where the devil was Ronnie Rookley? Had scarpered because the drug squad were onto him, just as Ja Belton the café proprietor had done, or had Rookley know too much about Luke's vanishing act?

Horton frowned as his mind ran through the facts and speculations. One thing struck him, the year: 1997. That was when Joseph Trotman had purchased Willow Bank and when Natalie had died. Did it mean anything or was he just making connections where none existed? Probably, he thought with a sigh, turning his gaze on the opposite stretch of water and the shores of Gosport. Had Venetia Trotman's killer come from one of the marinas or moorings at Gosport? Or had Luke's abductor, and probably his killer, come from there?

Or perhaps he'd come from the east, where Horton now turned his gaze. He could see the masts of the yachts in Horsea Marina. But if Venetia's killer, or the person Luke was rendezvousing with, had come from that marina, that would have meant going through the lock and being seen. So better to launch a tender from the shore right here, perhaps from the back of a car in the castle car park. Or perhaps the killer kept a tender at the sailing club, which Horton could see to the north, and beyond it the old paddle steamer moored in the basin of the Youth Enterprise Sailing Trust.

He rubbed his temple; his head ached with all the thoughts running through it. The sky was darkening. This was geographically a long way from where Natalie had been killed on the Hayling Coastal Path. Why bother to transport Luke all the way to Hayling Island from here on 19 September 1997, either by car or by boat? And if Luke and the killer had travelled to the coastal path by boat, as he'd discussed with Cantelli, then that would have meant sailing through Portsmouth Harbour, along Southsea Bay, down into Langstone Harbour and across to that copse, a long and convoluted journey. One Horton now thought highly unlikely.

So if Luke hadn't been taken to the coastal path by car or boat, then how had he got there? Simple, he thought, staring out at the sea, the dawn of realization sending a thrill through him. He had never been there. Natalie's killer had met him here, enticed him to a car or more likely a boat, drugged him and held him until after Natalie's death.

Oblivious to the rain that was now driving off the se Horton's mind raced as he pulled together everything he learnt. Could it be Bailey? Was the lover theory a diversio Had Bailey used Natalie Raymonds as a means to get eve with Luke Felton for destroying his mother's health? Ha he singled her out and planned her death with the meti ulous precision his job as a draughtsman demanded? He kept tracks on Luke Felton since his conviction for assaultir his mother, waiting for the right moment and opportuni to execute his plan. He had met Luke here, perhaps on tl evening of 18 September after finishing work at Hester' He'd got Luke on board a boat, which he had kept her Bailey could be lying about not owning a boat. He gave Lul drugs — though how Bailey would have got hold of the puzzled Horton, but he pushed that aside for now. Just he did the fact that Luke had told Shawford he had the he of someone influential. Bailey could easily have lied abo his status.

Making his way hurriedly down the steps, Horton call Cantelli. 'Any joy at Bailey's house?'

'Nothing so far except dirt, dust and his mother clothes.'

'He must have disposed of Luke's body elsewher Horton quickly told Cantelli about his interview wi Shawford and his thoughts about Bailey. 'Re-intervie Bailey. If he used a boat in 1997 then he could have repeat his actions, only this time he took Luke out into the Sole and dumped his body overboard. He could easily have trail a boat because his car has a tow bar fitted.'

'The tow bar hasn't been used in years. I've checke And there's no record of him owning a boat. Plus, I've bee thinking. I don't think he's got the bottle for it.'

'He has the motive.'

'But how would he have got hold of heroin?'

That bugged Horton.

'And there's Ronnie Rookley,' Cantelli added.

'He could have nothing to do with Luke's disappearanc

'Maybe not, but if he has, would Bailey have disposed of him too? I think Bailey would run a mile if he came face-to-face with Rookley.'

Cantelli was right. It didn't add up. Horton couldn't see Bailey dealing with and getting the better of Ronnie Rookley. So they were back to the lover theory. And that left Ashley Felton and Neil Danbury. 'Return to the station, Barney, and see if you can confirm Ashley Felton's German alibi for September 1997, and for Friday the thirteenth of March. He could have met Rookley in the cemetery. Also organize a team to go over his yacht. Check if Neil Danbury owns a boat, and his whereabouts on Friday the thirteenth.'

He called Walters. There was no answer, so Horton left a message for Walters to call back urgently, hoping he might have a lead on who Rookley had met in the cemetery.

Heading back to the Harley, Horton reconsidered the case. Who would Luke have willingly accompanied to a boat for a drink before being drugged, if not his brother-in-law, Neil Danbury, or his brother, Ashley? It had to be someone he knew well, who he was friendly with, even regularly drank with . . . His eyes fell on the Castle Sailing Club. His mind was a chaos of thoughts. Snatches of a conversation grabbed at him. Ashley Felton had told them that Luke was a very good sailor. Cantelli had asked in the club if anyone had seen Luke there on the Tuesday evening he disappeared, and no one had. But they hadn't asked if he had been a member of the club in 1997.

Horton drew up sharply as the realization smacked him in the face. They'd been asking the wrong questions. It wasn't a case of who had framed Luke, or even why; neither was it a question of who would have had the opportunity to frame him, but who could have done it so convincingly and so competently without Luke Felton ever having been on the Hayling Coastal Path in 1997? Horton knew there was only one answer.

CHAPTER TWENTY-FOUR

Julia Chawley opened the door to him. 'I'll check my fathe in-law is up to speaking to you,' she said, anxiously, and scu ried away leaving Horton to follow her through the hall ar into the kitchen. There was no sight of the children, althoug he could hear faint sounds of them coming from upstairs.

He crossed to the breakfast area and pushed open the do to the right, which he'd noticed the last time he'd been here. H stood among the toys, gazing at the children's paintings on tl walls, remembering how he'd been called upon by his daught many times to admire her artistic endeavours. He hoped he share that experience again. The paintings were of houses, wi children, larger than the houses, playing beside them; but the were many of boats. One had a large red and black funnel.

'He's ready to see you now, Inspector.'

He spun round. She had crept up so silently behind hir Her shy smile reminded him of Venetia Trotman.

She led him to the sick room, where after tapping light on the door and admitting him she faded away. Dunca Chawley was in the same position and in the same chair on Horton's previous visit. The room was also just as ho although Chawley — dressed in a woollen sweater and with thick checked rug over his legs — was impervious to the hea

'Mind if I take my jacket off?' Horton said. The sweat was pricking his brow and his shirt was sticking to his back within seconds.

'Be my guest.' Chawley waved a bony hand at him.

Horton clambered out of his heavy leather jacket. 'I'm sorry to disturb you, sir,' he began, 'but we've not been able to find Luke Felton and there are a couple of things that have come to light about the investigation into the Natalie Raymonds murder.' He perched on the seat opposite Chawley, trying not to think about that smell of death, recalling what the sailing club secretary had told him: Luke's father had been a member of the club and Luke had been a regular visitor there even after his fall from grace and the attack on Bailey's mother, mainly because his father had been held in such high respect. But the Feltons hadn't been the only members.

'Like what?' Chawley's yellow eyes narrowed.

'Like the fact that Peter Bailey has admitted to lying about seeing Luke Felton on the coastal path the day Natalie was killed in order to pay Felton back for attacking his mother.' He held Chawley's gaze, which despite his illness showed no emotion. He added, 'Which means that Luke Felton was never there, and if he was never there then someone—'

'You don't have to spell it out, Inspector,' Chawley quipped. 'I may be ill but I'm not an imbecile.'

Coolly Horton said, 'You knew Bailey was lying from the start.'

'Yes.'

There was no hesitation. No denial. And there wouldn't be. Chawley had lied about Peter Bailey, so what else had he lied about? A great deal, if Horton's deductions were correct. He eyed the former superintendent steadily.

Chawley said, 'I knew you were the type of copper who wouldn't stop digging until he had all the answers, like I used to be.'

'Until the Natalie Raymonds case,' Horton said evenly.

Chawley didn't answer.

'You knew Luke Felton didn't kill her.'

Again Chawley remained silent. That was tantamou to admitting it. Horton didn't feel sorry for Chawley no but angry. 'You let an innocent man go to prison while t real killer got off scot free.'

'Felton was scum,' Chawley said calmly.

'His parents weren't,' Horton replied stiffly, recalli what Cantelli had told him. 'They were destroyed by wh they believed their son had done.'

Chawley's eyes held Horton's without showing a flick of remorse or regret. Containing his anger, Horton sai 'Luke Felton was drugged and held captive. Evidence w planted on Natalie's body to frame him for her death and y you never spoke out. Who were you protecting?'

And that was the critical factor, thought Horton, the o thing he'd missed until now. All of Chawley's actions on th case, all the gaps in the investigation, pointed to one thin protection. He was cross with himself for not spotting it soon but sometimes a thing has to be shoved under your nose seve times before you see it. No one could have planted the eviden so carefully, swept away all discrepancies at the crime scene competently and completely, except a police officer.

Tautly, Chawley said, 'A good officer's career and fan ily would have been destroyed if I hadn't done what I did. wasn't going to allow that to happen. I've no regrets.'

'Who was it?' Horton asked tersely, knowing that h wouldn't be thanked for exposing this. The media wou love it, the public's confidence would be shattered and t Chief Constable would have to take the flak on the eve of h retirement. Horton wished he could simply walk away but wasn't in his nature. He hated corruption.

'DCI Sean Lovell was having an affair with Natal Raymonds.'

Horton hastily hid his surprise. His mind conjured u the man he'd worked with on the drug squad years ago: ea going, friendly Sean Lovell, a devoted husband and fath

No. It wasn't possible. Sean wouldn't have had the money Natalie craved, but he would have had the power, especially if Natalie had been dealing in drugs and Sean had given her protection from being exposed.

He eyed Chawley closely as the sick man continued. 'Luke was a junkie, and violent. He was no use to society. Whereas Sean was a good officer, one of the best, and he fell hopelessly in love with Natalie. She was a real looker, one of those women who could have any man eating out of the palm of her hand within minutes.'

And Sean Lovell had died of a heart attack not long after the case. Could that have been provoked by stress?

'How did he meet her?' Horton asked brusquely.

'I blame myself for that. Sean was with me at the Castle Sailing Club when Natalie came in with Julian. I could see that they were immediately attracted even though they played it cool. I said nothing. Sean was married. But he was infatuated with Natalie. He asked her to leave Julian and said he would leave Tina. Natalie laughed at him. She said they were having fun, so why ruin things. Sean was devastated. He simply lost it and before he knew it, she was dead. He didn't know what to do so he came to me and confessed. I wasn't going to let his career go down the pan because of a tart like Natalie, so I told him to say nothing, that I'd handle it.'

'So you planted the evidence against Luke at the scene of the murder.'

'Yes. And then Bailey came forward to say he'd seen Luke on the path. And Luke Felton was so pilled up, he couldn't remember what he'd been doing. He believed it when we told him he'd killed Natalie.' Quickly Chawley added, 'I know it's hard to believe of Sean. I couldn't believe it myself at first. But Natalie Raymonds was one of those predatory women. She knew exactly how to use sex to get what she wanted, whether that was money, power, fun or revenge. She'd pick her victims carefully, seduce them, suck them dry and then kick them over. She took pleasure in other people's pain and saw every man as a challenge, a conquest.'

Horton knew the type. Icily, he said, 'And what did sh want from Sean?'

'She wanted him to worship her and she wanted t destroy his marriage.'

'Why?'

Chawley gave a dry laugh. 'To show she could. It wa part of her power. And she had photographs and videos o them together. She would use them to blackmail him whe ever she wanted.'

Chawley's body slumped, as though exhauste both mentally and physically, and his breathing becam more laboured. Concerned, Horton said, 'I'll fetch you daughter-in-law.'

But Chawley managed to raise a hand to still him an croaked, 'No, give me a minute.'

Horton did. It gave him time to think over what he' just learnt. Most of the pieces fitted with what he kne and had discovered but for three things. The first was a gu reaction, a feeling that Sean couldn't have committed suc a heinous crime; the other two were more tangible. But h could see that Duncan Chawley hadn't finished yet. Horto wanted to hear it all before he spoke.

After a moment Chawley continued more slowly, a though the effort was costing him dear. 'Sean called me aft he'd killed Natalie. I told him to stay there until I came. anyone turned up, he was to show his warrant card and sa he'd responded to an anonymous call and the team were o their way. But no one came. He was a wreck. He wanted t give himself up. I heard all he had to say and told him to kee quiet. I knew that I would be in charge of the case and I' see it went unsolved, but that was before Bailey gave me th gift of Luke Felton.'

Horton listened without showing a reaction, while h mind assimilated what Chawley was telling him.

Chawley roused himself and with a new urgency said, ' this comes out, it will all have been for nothing and the mem ory of a good cop will be tarnished. Not mine but Sean's.

can hardly matter to me when I've not got long to live. But think of what it will do to Tina and the force,' he said, echoing Horton's earlier thoughts. 'And for what? Luke Felton was a drug addict and would probably have killed or assaulted some other poor pensioner or innocent person. Locking him up meant keeping him off the streets for fourteen years.'

'But that's not how it happened, is it?' Horton now said sharply, despising Chawley and not caring if he showed it. 'You couldn't simply plant Luke's fingerprints on Natalie's body and the bottle immediately after Sean called you, because you wouldn't have known where Luke was. You needed him not to be able to remember where he was on the nineteenth of September for him to become your scapegoat, and that meant Natalie's murder was planned and no impulse killing.'

Chawley eyed him steadily. After a moment he nodded slowly and gave a weary sigh. 'You're right, of course. I thought it would look better for Sean if I told you it was a spur-of-the-moment killing, done in anger, unpremeditated, but it wasn't. After being rejected, Sean planned how he would kill Natalie and how he would frame Luke for it. Heroin had been seized in a raid in Havant and put in the drug safe, but it hadn't been entered in the log. Sean simply falsified the entry and took enough to lay Luke out. He arranged to meet Luke, drugged him and then drove to Hayling, parked his car in a side street near the southern access to the coastal path and met and killed Natalie and planted the evidence.'

Horton didn't care for what he was hearing. His body was tense, his mind a jumble of thoughts, as Chawley continued. 'I didn't know what Sean had done until just before Bailey called to say he saw Felton on that path. Sean was breaking under the strain. He told me.'

'And instead of doing what you should have done, you covered it up.'

Chawley nodded. He leaned back in his chair. His face was even more drawn than when Horton had entered and the flesh seemed to have fallen from his frail body. Horto didn't feel pity, only fury.

'It's a convincing story,' he said, with an edge of steel i his voice that made Chawley look up. 'And it's almost tru except for one fact. Sean Lovell didn't have an affair wi Natalie Raymonds. You did. You killed her and you fram Luke Felton for her murder.'

Chawley eyed him with an expression devoid of em tion. There were no denials, no outraged protestations. Ju silence.

Harshly, not bothering to disguise his disgust, Hort said, 'You arranged to meet Luke at Portchester Castle, whe you kept a boat. You took him there, plied him with drir and drugs that you stole from the drugs safe or more like took off some addict without declaring it or charging hir Then, taking hairs from Luke's body and his clothes, yc pressed his fingerprints on a bottle of water and you dro to meet Natalie Raymonds in that copse as arranged, par ing your car some distance away in a side street. Then yc strangled her using your tie, and planted the evidence ar Natalie's fingerprints on the bottle of water to make it loc as though it was hers. You were quickly on the scene, headir the investigation. When Luke was found and the eviden matched, it was a result. Bailey's false testimony clinched and Luke's memory was a blank. And I'll tell you why I kno it was you,' Horton continued ruthlessly. 'Apart from the fa that I would never believe Sean to be capable of an affa let alone a murder, there's the matter of the mobile pho records. Natalie's mobile calls were never checked, becau if they had been your telephone number would have be listed. But there's something even more convincing to sho that you killed Natalie Raymonds. There's Luke Felton disappearance.'

A frown puckered Chawley's lined brow. 'I can't s how—'

'He's dead.'

Chawley's face paled. 'Then why—?'

Horton shook his head in wonderment. 'You know why,' he said scathingly. 'Because Luke started to remember things about Natalie's murder and that meant it was too dangerous for him to live. He had to die.'

Scornfully Chawley said, 'You can't think I killed him! I haven't even got the strength to move from this chair.'

'No, not you,' Horton said, rising. 'Which means someone else has gone to great lengths to protect Natalie's killer, and Sean Lovell's wife couldn't have done that.'

'Who then?' Chawley demanded angrily, but it was bluff. Horton saw the fear in his yellow eyes.

At the door he paused. Bitingly he said, 'You're a copper, work it out.'

He found Chawley's daughter-in-law hovering anxiously in the kitchen. 'Is he all right? Should I go in?'

Horton removed the picture of Luke Felton from his jacket pocket. 'Have you seen this man?' She started nervously and eyed him apprehensively. 'It's OK,' he added quickly. 'You won't get into trouble for telling me.'

'He came here a week ago last Saturday.'

It was as he'd thought. That would have been 7 March, and Luke had disappeared on Tuesday the tenth. It was also before the covert drug operation had started on Crown House. Luke must have got Chawley's address from interrogating the internet, the hi-tech unit would probably be able to confirm that when they finished trawling through Luke's internet browsing history. Horton didn't know how many Chawleys lived in the area but Luke would have ruled out the obvious and focused on the possible and come here. What he had hoped to achieve, Horton could only speculate. Blackmail? Had Luke's memory recovered so sufficiently that he knew Duncan Chawley had framed him? Or perhaps he had come here in the hope of persuading Chawley to get the police to re-open the case on the basis of his remarks under hypnosis.

She added, 'I was just coming back from shopping and almost ran him over as he was walking down the driveway

away from the house. Gavin rushed out in his car after hir
I saw him stop and the man got in. I don't know where th
went and Gavin said I wasn't to mention it to anyone whe
he got back. Is it important?'

It was, but Horton wasn't going to tell her that. He sai
'Do you own a boat?'

Her genuine surprise gave him the answer before sł
said, 'No.'

'I thought you must, given all the pictures your childre
paint of boats.'

'Duncan used to have a motorboat, but he sold it whe
he got ill. We often take the children to the harbour. Th
like to paint while Gavin is working.'

'But your husband does sail?' Horton recalled that Gav
had been wearing chinos, deck shoes and a red sailing jack
on the Sunday he had first called here.

'Oh yes, often with friends—'

'Like last Sunday?'

'Yes. And he teaches dinghy sailing during the seaso
Unfortunately, I don't like the sea. It terrifies me and mak
me sick.'

'Where's your husband now, Mrs Chawley?'

She glanced at the clock. It was five thirty-five. 'At wor
Why?' she asked anxiously.

'And that's where?' Horton asked, although he alreac
knew the answer. One of the paintings had given him that

'The Youth Enterprise Sailing Trust. He's chief executive

CHAPTER TWENTY-FIVE

Horton told her a police officer would be with her soon and that he would prefer it if she didn't call her husband. He couldn't stop Duncan Chawley calling him though. Julia Chawley looked frightened but agreed to do as he asked.

Outside he called Walters. 'Margery Blanchester,' he said, before Walters could moan about something. 'Find out who the beneficiary of her will is.' Horton remembered what the volunteer on the paddle steamer had said: Thanks to a recent legacy from an old lady, we hope to get this young lady finished a lot sooner than expected.

Then he rang Cantelli. 'You were right. Bailey didn't kill Natalie Raymonds, and neither did Ashley Felton or Neil Danbury. Duncan Chawley did. He tried to make me believe it was Sean Lovell.'

'Then he must be sick in the head. Sean would be totally incapable of that,' Cantelli cried vehemently.

'That's more or less what I said. Get over here, Barney. Charge Duncan Chawley with the murder of Natalie Raymonds and arrange for him to be taken into hospital. Make sure someone stays with him at all times and a woman police officer stays with his daughter-in-law, Julia. As soon as you've done that, meet me at the Youth Enterprise Sailing Trust.'

'Why there?'

'It's where I'll find Gavin Chawley.'

'I don't envy you telling him what his father did.'

'He already knows.'

'Ah.'

Horton headed for Portchester, checking his mirrors f any signs of the Georgian following him. He'd seen no one c his way to the Chawleys'. There were a couple of motorbike but both overtook him on the small stretch of dual carriag way. He turned off at the industrial estate and headed dow the road towards the shore until he was outside the You Enterprise Sailing Trust. No lights showed from the buildi but Gavin Chawley's car was parked in the yard and the was a light shining from the cabin of the paddle steamer. H made his way quietly and carefully up the gangplank, ar stepped on board. The cold wind was raging up the harbou howling around the boat and squeezing itself through all t rotten wood and broken, rusted pipes. Horton was surpris Gavin hadn't bolted; Duncan must by now have spoken his son to tell him he was on his way. But then where wou Gavin go? Perhaps he thought he could bluff it out. Ar perhaps Horton should wait for back-up. But it was too la now, and besides, Cantelli would be here soon.

Gavin Chawley, wearing a white overall over a light gr suit, was carefully planing a piece of wood in the middle the unfinished main cabin. 'Dad said you'd be coming,' said briefly, glancing up before turning his eyes back to h task.

'Then you know why I'm here,' Horton answered the same easy manner, taking a step further inside the cabi

Gavin continued shaving the wood, his strong han pushing the plane away from him, methodically, slowly ar easily. His weather-worn face screwed up with concentr tion. 'He said it was something to do with Luke Felton disappearance.'

But Horton could see that Gavin knew more than tha 'Did your father tell you that he killed Natalie Raymonds?

There was a perceptible tightening of the hands on the plane but Gavin Chawley's rhythmic movement never faltered. 'Sean Lovell killed Natalie. Dad was only trying to protect him.'

Something about Gavin's remark nudged at Horton. He rapidly replayed the conversation he'd just had with Duncan Chawley. 'How do you know Sean Lovell killed her?' he asked, making sure to maintain the same even tone set by Gavin.

'Dad told me.'

'Why?'

A flicker of annoyance crossed Gavin Chawley's face. 'Because of Luke Felton's visit.'

Eyeing Gavin closely, Horton said, 'How did you know it was Luke Felton visiting your father?'

With a glance of exasperation Gavin said again, 'Dad told me.'

'I see,' Horton said slowly. 'So after Luke's visit you went in to your father and said who's that and what did he want, and he told you that Sean had killed Natalie?'

'Yes.'

Wrong, but Horton contrived to look baffled. 'But how could you have had time, when your wife told me that you raced after Luke Felton and didn't return for hours?'

A flash of irritation crossed Gavin's broad features. After a moment he said, 'I opened the door to Luke. He told me his name and I asked my father if he wanted to see him. I remembered the name from Dad's cases. He said to let Luke Felton in and that he'd come to see him about Natalie Raymonds' murder, and that's when he told me about Sean Lovell killing her and how he had to protect a fellow police officer.'

Horton gave an exaggerated frown, deciding to play dumb. 'But if Sean Lovell killed Natalie, why did you go after Luke?'

'To protect my father,' snapped Chawley, pausing from planing the wood, and glaring at Horton as though he was an idiot. 'He had covered up the fact that Sean killed her ar I didn't want it coming out and destroying his reputation. wanted to find out what Luke remembered.'

'And that's why you killed him,' Horton said sympathe ically. He saw Gavin start but he quickly recovered himsel

'No. Of course not.'

Horton threw him a pitying look. 'We both know that not true, Gavin. Did you overhear Luke telling your fath on that Saturday afternoon that he'd begun to rememb certain things about Natalie's murder and that he believe he was innocent?'

Chawley said nothing.

Horton continued. 'Luke had been having hypnothera sessions while in prison, which were recorded. Is that why yc broke into the hypnotherapist's office on the Isle of Wight la Sunday? You stole the tapes to wipe out all traces of what Lul had remembered, just as you've wiped out all trace of Luke?'

Chawley returned to shaving the wood, frowning a litt as he did so.

Horton went on. 'The DNA on some of the hairs take from the therapist's office will match yours.'

The eyes that flicked up to Horton's were more wa now.

'You gave Luke a lift back to Portsmouth on th Saturday and told him you'd help him get to the truth. D Rookley see you pull up outside Crown House and overhe Luke saying goodbye to you?'

Still Chawley said nothing.

'Did you tell Luke to meet you on Tuesday at Portchest Castle, where it all began in 1997?'

The hands hesitated for a moment before resuming the careful motion on the wood.

'How did you kill Luke, Gavin? The same way yc killed Ronnie Rookley?' Horton kept his gaze steadily c Chawley. Would he continue to say nothing? Would he de it? Or would a desperate desire for approval or his ego mal him confess?

Chawley stopped planing and ran a critical eye over the wood while he said casually, 'Rookley thought he could blackmail me.'

Horton's heart jumped a beat. 'And that's why you met him in the cemetery at the committal of a lady called Margery Blanchester, who has left this organization a generous legacy. How did Rookley know how to get in contact with you?'

Chawley scowled. 'I gave Luke my mobile number. He didn't have a mobile phone but he scribbled the number down on a piece of paper. Rookley must have got it off him, or found the paper. And I told Luke that I could use someone like him at the sailing trust.'

And, Horton thought, when he and Cantelli had questioned Rookley in the café over Luke's disappearance, the little crook had seen his chance to make some money.

Picking up the piece of wood, Chawley turned to face Horton. 'Rookley telephoned me Friday morning. I was on my way to the funeral. I said I'd meet him in the cemetery. He said that unless I gave him money, he'd tell you about my meeting with Luke. I told him to meet me at the lock but half an hour before you were due to see him, only he wasn't getting any money. I knocked him out while he was leaning into the boot of my car to count it, or so he thought. I pushed him inside and slammed it shut.'

'And then you hit me.'

Chawley nodded. 'You'd think it was Rookley or one of his accomplices. And it would stop you following me if you were sharp enough to see me drive off.'

So the sound of the motorbike pulling away had nothing to do with Rookley or Luke's death. But Horton already knew who that was: their Georgian. And where was he now, Horton fleetingly wondered.

'What did you do with Luke's body, Gavin?'

'It's in the Solent, along with Rookley's,' Chawley said matter-of-factly.

'You took both of them out on a boat on separate occasions?'

'Yes. No one will miss them. One was a useless junki the other a violent thief. I couldn't allow them to ruin m father's reputation, and mine. My work is important her Lots of people depend on me.'

And they're going to have to manage without yc soon, thought Horton, and for a very long time. Angrily, l thought of Luke and his parents, destroyed by the Chawley He wanted one of them in court and convicted for it at leas He guessed that Gavin Chawley would deny what he'd sa later when Horton got him to the station, and he hadn charged and cautioned him, but Horton was confider they'd be able to assemble enough evidence to make hi think again. The gravedigger might even be able to identi Chawley talking to Rookley. There would be DNA in Ler Lockhart's office and they might be able to prove Gavin ha travelled across to the island by one of the ferries — unle he'd travelled by boat, but he didn't own a boat, accordir to his wife. Was that a lie?

Horton rapidly considered this, recalling that she sa he'd been sailing with friends. Had he taken time away fro them to slip up to Lena's office and steal the tapes? The would check. But if he didn't own a boat then how could l have disposed of Luke's body, and Rookley's, in the Solent, night? The dinghies and the small safety rib kept here weren up to such a task, but one boat was, and it certainly wasn this wreck of an old paddle steamer.

Gavin's fingers caressed the wood. 'Luke would hav been no use to society, and Rookley certainly wasn't. couldn't allow a man like that to blackmail me or my fathe He served the community all his life. He made one sma mistake.'

'I don't call what your father did small, and I don't mea covering up for Sean Lovell.'

Gavin Chawley's eyes narrowed.

Steadily, Horton continued. 'Sean Lovell didn't have a affair with Natalie and neither did your father. It was yo Gavin. You killed Natalie. Your father knew it. He covere up for you then and he's kept silent about it ever since. What did Natalie do to make you kill her, Gavin? Did she reject you? Laugh at you? Belittle you?'

Chawley's fingers tightened on the wood. Horton waited with bated breath, listening to the creaking and groaning of the old paddle steamer and praying Cantelli wouldn't burst in on him now and spoil this confession.

After a moment Chawley said, 'She told me the affair was over. She said she was bored, that I wasn't important enough. I was only a sales clerk then, working for Julia's father. He had a boat building company here. Well, I showed her. I knew Luke from the Castle Sailing Club. He should have been thrown out after that attack on a pensioner but the club secretary was too weak to do it.'

'So you tricked Luke onto your father's boat in 1997, where you drugged him. How did you get the heroin?'

Chawley smiled reminiscently. 'I've always done charity work. I think it's important to give something back.'

No, Horton thought, you need it to feed your overinflated ego and satisfy your craving for attention. Did Duncan Chawley know that his son had a serious personality disorder? He assumed so.

'I worked for a time helping drug addicts,' Gavin said. 'It was easy to get the stuff and know how much to use. Once I had Luke on my father's boat, I stripped him and put on his clothes and shoes. I was the same build then, and while I wasn't exactly the same shoe size, I could manage wearing his trainers for a while. It was perfect. I pressed his fingers on a water bottle, carefully preserving his prints, cut some of his hair and then drove to Hayling where I'd already arranged to meet Natalie. I strangled her and then hit her to make sure I got her blood on Luke's clothes, and I planted the evidence. Then I drove back to the boat. It was dark then. No one saw me.' He spoke as though it was a routine affair, something anyone might have done.

Horton said, 'When did your father know it was you?' He watched Chawley play with the wood in his hands, and

tensed in preparation for an attack that he knew must com
Chawley wouldn't let him live to tell this tale. He'd kill
three times; another death wouldn't matter to him. Nov
Horton thought, would be a good time for Cantelli to arriv

'Dad found Luke on the boat just as I returned fro
Hayling. I had to tell him. He said he'd take care of things c
condition that I marry Julia, though I didn't want to. He sa
she'd be a steadying influence on me. She was in love with n
of course but, well, she's not exactly my equal. You've seen he
she's a timid little thing and dull as dishwater. But it turne
out OK in the end because her father died soon afterwards ar
left her the house and the boat building business, which I so
to start this charity. So you see, some good came of it.'

As if that justified killing someone, Horton thoug
with anger. And not just three people, five if he count
Sonia and Neville Felton. Horton imagined what kind
life poor Julia had suffered, and those very quiet children. H
recognized a bully when he saw one, the kind that gradual
and relentlessly chips away at a person's self-esteem and co
fidence. He'd also like to know exactly how Julia's father ha
died. But that was for another time.

'Dad was pleased I'd made something of my life. H
could see it would have been a waste to sacrifice that for th
sake of Natalie Raymonds, a tart.'

Barely containing his contempt for the man in front
him, Horton said, 'Venetia Trotman wasn't a tart. How d
you justify killing her?'

'I don't know what you mean.'

'Oh, yes you do, Gavin. You needed her yacht to dispo
of the bodies.'

Chawley's lips tightened but he made no comment.

Relentlessly, Horton continued. 'I suppose you mu
have seen it on her slipway when you were walking along th
shore, or perhaps when you were out sailing with friend
When did you decide it would be useful for getting rid
Luke Felton and Ronnie Rookley?'

Still Chawley remained silent.

'Why didn't you just steal it in the early hours of Friday morning like you did on Tuesday night, when you took it out with Luke's body on board? Or did Venetia Trotman see you with Rookley's body on Friday night? Is that why you had to kill her?' Horton could see by Chawley's annoyed expression it was.

Chawley's hands gripped the wood and his face screwed up with anger. 'If she had been in bed like she had been on Tuesday night she would still be alive, but she was in the garden. She must have heard the engine of the safety rib where I'd put Rookley because she called out. Then she saw me and ran away. I had to kill her.'

And Horton's mind was now doing cartwheels putting together what he knew about Venetia, the Georgian and Jay Turner.

He said, 'Then you tied the safety rib to the yacht and took it out into the Solent, where you scuttled the yacht.'

But Chawley was shaking his head and looking shocked. 'No. I couldn't do that to such a lovely boat. It's a classic, made of wood, like this.' He indicated the wood his fingers were caressing. 'I dropped anchor in Southsea Bay, climbed into the rib and threw Rookley overboard. Then I took the yacht round to Chichester Harbour and picked up a buoy.'

But they hadn't found it. 'You changed the yacht's name,' Horton said.

'Yes, just as I did the first time, when I took Luke Felton's body out on it. Then I returned the yacht and removed the sticker.'

Horton had been right about that.

'With Rookley though I couldn't return the yacht, because the woman was dead,' Chawley was saying. 'I thought the police would assume boat thieves had killed her. So after ditching Rookley I motored to the Hayling shore in the safety rib, and walked home from there. It was a long walk but I didn't mind. I returned to the boatyard by car the next morning, Saturday, just before high tide and moved the yacht into the Hayling boatyard. It's there now.'

Horton should have known; in among other class boats in various states of renovation.

'I hitched the safety rib on to a trailer on my car ar brought it back here.'

Horton said, 'How did you know the yacht wouldn't l used on Tuesday night when you lured Luke Felton to it?'

'I'd seen the woman return on it, alone, some weeks ag at the end of February. It was a couple of hours before tl high tide. It was dark and windy and she was struggling r moor it up, so I gave her a hand. She didn't say much but thought it strange for her to be sailing on her own. She looke frightened. She told me she had been out sailing alone, h husband had died a while ago, and she'd got caught out l the bad weather. Then I saw the boat advertised for sale in tl newsagent's window in Portchester a week ago last Monday

That would have been on 9 March, thought Horto 'After Luke had visited your father.'

'Yes. I arranged to view it that day. I could see that tl hatch would be easy to break into. Just an ordinary padlo key, or a piece of metal and manipulation, would do it. I sa I would think about it and let her know my decision by tl end of the week. It was perfect for dealing with Luke.'

And if Venetia had told Horton this, would he ha been able to save her? He doubted it. He certainly wouldn have been able to save Luke Felton.

'So you arranged to meet Luke at Portchester Cast on Tuesday evening and walked with him around the sho towards the yacht. It was dark so no one would see you. Yc invited him on board, pretending it was your yacht, you just purchased it. You killed Luke, but not with a knife.'

Horton had been over that yacht viewing it on Thursda and he would swear there wasn't any evidence, and certain no blood.

'I strangled him. Took the yacht out, dumped his boc and brought the boat back again. It was so simple.'

And she'd said nothing to Horton about finding tl hatch open or the lock broken probably because she hadn noticed. And she hadn't gone on board with Horton when he'd viewed it. Neither had he noticed it. Even if he had, he couldn't see how it could have prevented what had happened.

The sound of a movement outside caught Horton's attention, but he didn't turn to investigate. He was more concerned about what Chawley might do with the piece of wood he was holding, and ducking out of its reach. But Cantelli had arrived. Good. Horton witnessed a flicker of surprise in Chawley's eyes and braced himself for Chawley to make a swing at him with the wood. Then suddenly a blow from behind struck Horton on the side of his head. For a split second he wondered why Cantelli had hit him, before the deck of the steamer rushed up to meet him and his world went dark.

CHAPTER TWENTY-SIX

His head hurt. That was a good sign. If he felt pain, h couldn't be dead. He tried opening his eyes but the pygm inside his skull was using it as a drum. He was vaguely awa of someone moving, and he could hear voices. They didn sound like Cantelli and neither did they sound very heavenl

He concentrated on opening his eyes and hoped h head wouldn't explode. This time he succeeded. Graduall the light filtered in. His eyes travelled up two pairs of leg one sitting and the other standing. His heart leapt into h throat as he found himself staring at Gavin Chawley's te rified face. Chawley was pressed onto a hard chair, his fe bound tightly with the chain that had stretched across th gangplank and his arms wrenched behind him and tie with something Horton couldn't see. But it was the ma beside him with a knife pressed to Chawley's throat th concerned and horrified Horton. He stared into the ho lowed, lined, dirty face and knew he was looking at the ma responsible for scratching the emblem on his Harley. It w also the hooded figure he'd glimpsed in the boatyard — th Georgian.

He staggered up. The Georgian shouted, 'One step ar I kill him, like he killed my Eliso.'

'Reason with him, for God's sake,' Chawley choked, his face contorted with terror.

Like you reasoned with Venetia, or rather Eliso, her real name, Horton felt like saying, but didn't. It wouldn't help matters. As he stared into the Georgian's deep-set dark eyes full of hatred and anger, he rapidly searched his brain to find a way of resolving this without anyone getting hurt or killed, which was looking increasingly unlikely. And where the hell was Cantelli? His heart somersaulted so violently that he felt sick. Surely the Georgian couldn't have killed him. But no, Cantelli wouldn't have come alone. But if he had . . . Horton went cold inside. He had to resolve this and rapidly. Cantelli might be hurt and in need of urgent help. Horton didn't even want to contemplate that he might be dead.

Urgently, Horton addressed the Georgian. 'I'll see that he is tried and convicted for Eliso's murder.'

The Georgian spat vehemently on the floor, making it perfectly clear what he thought of that. Chawley's eyes stared, wide and frightened. Speedily, Horton recalled his hostage negotiation training courses. Hostage takers fell into three categories: terrorists, criminals and the mentally disturbed, or the mad, bad and sad as they were generally referred to. Horton thought he was staring at all three in one man. OK, so . . . build rapport, keep an even temper, show empathy and self-assurance. Shit, how did he do all that before the Georgian plunged that knife into Chawley's neck?

Though his mouth was dry and his palms damp he said evenly, 'Was Eliso your girlfriend?'

'My sister.'

Chawley gave a strangled sob as the Georgian clasped a big rough hand around his throat, forcing his head back while the knife pricked at its side.

'You thought I'd killed Eliso at first, didn't you?' Horton quickly said. Get him talking, show patience, build a bond and hope to God Cantelli is still alive. 'You were inside Eliso's house when I arrived to look over her boat. Then while I was on the boat you waited for me somewhere out of sight along the lane and followed me to the police statior Horton hadn't seen him, but then he hadn't expected to l followed. 'You then followed me to the marina and scratch(that symbol on my Harley to warn me away from Eliso, b when you returned to her house in the early hours of tl morning you found her dead.'

Chawley stared at Horton, terrified.

Horton continued steadily, though his heart was racin 'You decided to follow me so that I could lead you to h killer.' And he'd been expert at that. Horton recalled seeing motorbike the day he and Cantelli had followed Rookley in the cemetery, and he'd heard one when he'd been pushed i the lock. He'd also seen one when with Cantelli a couple times, and with Uckfield, but he hadn't noticed anythir following him to Rowlands Castle or here, though two ha overtaken him and one, which must have been the Georgia had waited in a side street and watched him turn into tl industrial estate. Following him to the paddle steamer, he patiently waited and listened until he knew the whole trut

Chawley was pleading with Horton with his petrified eye

Horton pressed on. 'When you thought I wasn't doir my job in looking for Eliso's killer you left another messag this time on my yacht. You've waited a long time to fir your sister.'

'What's that to you?' he demanded roughly.

Chawley's eyes popped in his terrified face as the har squeezed tighter.

'I'd like to understand,' Horton said, praying that l sounded genuinely interested. He was, but not half as inte ested as he was in resolving this rapidly and without anyoı getting killed. 'Please tell me about Eliso,' he prompted, wil ing the Georgian to reply.

The man eyed Horton sceptically. There were sever seconds before he replied, but they seemed like minute Gruffly the Georgian said, 'I'm from the region of Shi(Kartli, part of South Ossetia.'

That explained the Kartli coat of arms, thought Horto

'I was captured by the Georgians two years ago in the fighting and escaped to Poti, where the captain of a container ship took me to Istanbul. He told me he had taken my sister out of the country some years ago and put her on board a cargo ship sailing to Naples. She told him she was going to live with an Englishman near a castle by the sea.'

Poor Eliso, thought Horton. She thought she was going to live a fairy tale existence. Some bloody fairy tale.

'I got the name of the cargo ship captain who had taken Eliso to Naples and waited in Istanbul for him to arrive. In January he came. He told me that Eliso had sailed from Naples with a man in a boat. He was taking her to a place called Portsmouth. I came with this captain to Southampton.' And Horton guessed he had stolen the motorbike there.

'I went in search of this castle by the sea, and there was Eliso walking down the street. I followed her.'

Eliso had been unlucky to the end. Fate, or sod's law, whatever you liked to call it, had played its card. But even if she hadn't been in the street that day, Horton knew that the Georgian wouldn't have given up his search until he found her. Locating that house by the sea and the castle would have been easy.

'Now I will kill him.'

Chawley squawked.

Hastily Horton recalled what Gaye Clayton had relayed to him about the symbol. He had an idea. He wasn't sure if it would work, but anything was worth trying. Quickly he said, 'The Lion on the Kartli coat of arms stands for courage and strength, and the Unicorn for purity and virtue. Surely killing this man must go against that.'

Hesitation flashed across the rough unshaven features. It was a start. 'You need courage to kill a man.'

'You need even more courage not to, especially when he has hurt you and someone you love,' responded Horton.

The Georgian's eyes narrowed.

Horton pressed home his advantage. 'You also need strength to let a man live to face his punishment, and to make sure that the truth is exposed. Isn't that what Eliso wou have wanted and what she'd expect from you?'

Horton held his breath as he saw the thoughts runnir through the Georgian's mind. Quickly he pressed on, speal ing earnestly. 'The man you are holding a knife to has ruin many lives, not only Eliso's. Killing him is too quick and ea a punishment for what he has done. He values his reputatio In prison he would lose that. He would feel the punishme and he would suffer.' Horton sincerely hoped that was tru 'Let him go,' he added gently, 'and he'll go to prison f what he's done, for a very long stretch.' Horton could see tl Georgian considering it. 'If you kill him now, he won't suff and you will go to prison, not him.'

Horton held the Georgian's steely gaze, trying not show any emotion. He took a deep breath and stepped fo ward, stretching out his hand.

'Give me the knife,' he said calmly, though his heart w in overdrive. He stood his ground with his hand outstretche He didn't look at Chawley but kept his eyes steadfastly c the Georgian, catching the flicker of hesitation behind tl exhausted eyes. He prayed now that no one would enter, n until he had the knife in his hand.

'Eliso wouldn't want him killed,' Horton said softly, ea ing another step forward. He could feel the sweat on his bac and the thumping in his head was matched by the poundir of his heart. 'She'd want you to tell her story. Don't yc think she deserves that?'

The Georgian's eyes held fatigue beyond weariness. H roughened hand came down a fraction. He paused. The flicking the knife round so that the hilt faced Horton, l stretched it across. Horton grasped it. But his relief w short-lived.

'I can still break his neck with my bare hand,' tl Georgian cried, squeezing Chawley's throat. Chawley's ey popped as the pressure increased.

'That would be too quick a death,' Horton cried hastil 'Better to let him suffer the humiliation of everyone knowir he's a murderer. He's not worth killing,' he urged, praying he wouldn't need to attack the Georgian. If he did, Chawley might be saved, but the knife in Horton's hand could be used against him, or end up in the Georgian.

Suddenly, with disgust the Georgian pushed Chawley so violently that the chair crashed over, leaving Chawley lying on his side trussed up tightly, his midriff exposed. The Georgian's leg came up and he kicked his boot hard into Chawley's stomach. Chawley screamed in pain. And again, as the boot struck out. Horton threw the knife out of reach and leapt into action, charging at the Georgian. He staggered, as his foot was raised in the act of striking Chawley again. They fell, and suddenly there were uniforms swarming all over the boat and the Georgian had his hands behind his back in cuffs. Chawley was howling with pain. A uniformed police officer bent over to release him.

'What kept you?' Horton said to Cantelli, heaving an enormous sigh of relief at the sight of the sergeant and in the rudest of health.

'We took the scenic route.'

'Next time try the motorway, it's quicker.'

'It's blocked in both directions, an accident. We couldn't get through and had to come over the hill.'

'Well, I'm glad you're here.'

Chawley was on his feet. Horton reached into his pocket and clapped his cuffs on him.

Chawley began to protest. 'You've got no right. I've been attacked. I need to go to hospital.'

'What's that noise?' Horton asked, waggling a finger in his ear.

'I think it's the wind,' answered Cantelli.

CHAPTER TWENTY-SEVEN

'Good result,' Uckfield said, swilling back his second whisk of the night, and helping himself to a third.

He didn't offer the bottle around because everyone el in the incident suite — Horton, Trueman, Dennings ar Marsden — were on coffee, except for Cantelli who was su ping a mug of tea and trying not to yawn. Uckfield adde 'Waverley's sulking so much they're thinking of making h lower lip a new railway platform at Portsmouth station.'

Horton managed a tired smile. It was almost eleven p.r It was a good result, and one that DCI Bliss had found diff cult to believe at first, until it occurred to her that she cou take the glory for it. Then she had hightailed it to Chi Superintendent Reine, her face the picture of triumph – two cases cleared up, one of national significance — th was if Uckfield would let her claim the Georgian's arrest, ar Horton doubted that. Although neither Bliss nor Uckfie had arrested Gavin Chawley or the Georgian, Horton kne they wouldn't let that small technicality stand in their wa Let battle commence, he thought. He was too tired and tc sickened by the case to really care who won.

Gavin Chawley had been only too keen to repeat h story, confident in the belief that a jury would see his side things. Horton thought otherwise. His father was in hospital, with an officer beside his bed. Duncan Chawley had slipped into unconsciousness not long after Horton had left him, knowing the truth would come out and that he could no longer protect his son. The Georgian was in a cell awaiting transportation to London.

Trueman said, 'Europol gave us a match on the fingerprints you found on the items in the derelict houseboat, Andy. Your Georgian's called Otia Gelashvili. He was a member of the South Ossetian Popular Front, captured by the Georgian army during the conflict in 2008 when the Georgian government tried to take the South Ossetian region by force, as they previously tried in 1991 and 2004. The Ossetian separatists and Russian troops gained control of the territory though. Russia recognizes it as an independent republic, but Georgia doesn't and considers most of its territory a part of the Shida Kartli region within Georgian sovereignty. Otia probably bribed his way out of captivity, given his background — he was big in the black market racket — had contacts and customers in South Ossetia, Russia and Georgia, and a lucrative black market trade between all three.'

'Was he involved with Jay Turner?' asked Horton.

'He says not,' answered Uckfield. 'But he could be lying to protect others. Waverley's team will check it, and his story about how he got here.'

And maybe, thought Horton, Otia Gelashvili had known all along where his sister was living and had only now decided to come to England because it was too hot for him in Georgia. 'And where does Jay Turner fit in?'

Uckfield nodded at Marsden, who said, 'The International Development Fund was established in Georgia in 1996 after British diplomatic relations were renewed with the country following the collapse of the Soviet Union. The International Development Fund has given hundreds of thousands of pounds in grants to help Georgia with its infrastructure and various government projects. It's overseen by several nationalities, including British nationals who are

experts in project management and accountancy. One o
them was Jay Turner.'

Uckfield broke in. 'Waverley's team, and Europol, hav been tracking disappearing money from Georgia for a yea They suspected Turner, although he'd obviously been at for longer than a year. They couldn't find out where tl money was going and who he was in league with. The con tents of the locker from Eliso's yacht might help them.'

Horton wondered if it would. It contained Eliso's sto and some jewellery, but no indication of where Jay Turn might have money stashed away. Gavin Chawley had ove looked it because he didn't know about the key in Eliso hand. Horton had read what she had written before Uckfie passed it to Waverley. Most of it he had already guessed.

Eliso had run away from her family and the troubles South Ossetia in 1993 and had ended up in Tbilisi, whe she became a dancer in a club. She had met Jay Turner 1997; she had been twenty. Jay had brought her to Englar illegally, promising her a better life. She got it too, Horto thought: a lovely house, yacht, designer clothes, but at price, which according to her notes she soon realized. Sl was virtually a prisoner, too terrified to go far except to wa along the shore, usually very early in the morning or at nigh and take a brief trip to the local shops, because Jay had to her she'd be arrested and deported if she spoke to anyon Horton recalled that shy smile. How lonely she must hav been without any friends or family, and how afraid. He kne how loneliness felt. Even throughout his marriage he reco nized his own solitariness and with a pang wondered if th had contributed to Catherine's infidelity, if indeed she ha been unfaithful.

Out sailing on 22 February, the wind had sprung u and Jay Turner had been struck by the boom as it swur round and had been swept overboard. Eliso claimed it wa an accident. She said that by the time she had turned tl boat round he was gone, and dead. Maybe, Horton though she had taken longer to turn it around than was necessar

Or perhaps he hadn't been on deck at all, his shoes had been missing from the body and he'd been dead when he entered the water. Perhaps she'd struck her husband and killed him, then dragged his body and hauled him overboard.

Horton pictured her returning to the house, struggling to moor up, because by then it was dark and windy. Gavin Chawley had decided to take a walk around the shore before heading home, a place that he was clearly reluctant to be according to what Julia Chawley had told the woman police officer. It had been bad luck for Eliso, as it turned out — but then she seemed to attract it, poor woman, much like Luke Felton. Chawley had helped her. She'd been grateful, not knowing how he was going to exploit and eventually kill her.

Not sure what to do next, she'd begun living off what she had in the house, and turning off the heating to conserve money. Then she must have decided to sell the boat; it would keep her alive until she could decide what to do. Otia had arrived almost at the same time as Horton had shown up to view the boat. That night Eliso had decided that escape was better than living with Otia on the run. She'd stashed her jewellery on the yacht, ready to set sail on the high tide, when Gavin Chawley had come alongside with Rookley's body and killed her.

Horton knew the Chief Constable was going to have to do some nifty footwork to prevent Duncan Chawley's corruption from being exposed. Maybe he was considering an even earlier retirement, like right now. It left a bitter taste in Horton's mouth, as it would with every honest copper.

He hauled himself up. 'I've got some paperwork to sort, this being my last case in CID.' He held Dennings' sullen glare before nodding at Uckfield, Trueman and Marsden. Cantelli followed him into the corridor. Falling into step beside him, he said, 'DCI Bliss might not be so keen to get rid of you now that we've got a result.'

Horton eyed him sceptically. 'I don't think she's that charitable.'

'You never know.'

'Well, if you see an empty chair at my desk tomorro morning, I've either overslept or my posting's come througl

'I hope it's the former. Better the devil you know Cantelli said with a tired smile.

Horton hoped so too. Bidding goodnight to Cantelli, l headed for his office where he flicked open the blinds in tin to see Tony Dennings' broad figure stride across the yard ar disappear from view. A taxi pulled in and Uckfield climbe into it. Then Marsden climbed onto his racing bike. Hortc watched his tail light flicker out of sight before turning awa

He was tired beyond belief, his head was pounding, ar every muscle in his body ached. Where would he end up? l Uckfield's major crime team, if Dennings transferred himse out of it? But why should he? He looked set for the duratio In a CID unit in another division? Possibly.

There was a knock on his door and he looked up to fir Trueman on the threshold. 'I'm just off home, Andy, and suggest you do the same.'

Horton stared at his paper-strewn desk. 'I guess you' right.' He could tackle this tomorrow, if he was still her And if he wasn't, then one of DCI Bliss's razor-sharp dete tives would clear it up.

'You asked me to find out if PC Adrian Stanley was st around.'

Horton had forgotten all about the PC who had fil the missing persons report on his mother.

'He's living in a retirement flat at Lee-on-the-Solent.'

Only eleven miles west along the coast.

'I've jotted down the address for you.' Trueman hand across a piece of paper.

'Thanks.' Horton stuffed it in his pocket without loo ing at it. He didn't see that it would get him far with h investigations into his mother's disappearance, whereas con paring his DNA against the database to find out if his moth was in cold storage might.

He shrugged on his leather jacket. Somewhere buri among the paper on his desk, or lurking on his compute could be a memo or email from Chief Superintendent Reine or DCI Bliss telling him about his new posting. He thought it far more likely to be a paper-pushing job or a training role at the college than something like CID or special investigations and he didn't relish that. Perhaps working with Detective Chief Superintendent Sawyer of the Intelligence Directorate to track down Zeus and get to the truth of his mother's disappearance wasn't such a bad idea after all, especially if Emma was safely away at school.

Closing his office door behind him he headed towards his Harley, considering the future. Whatever it held for him, though, and wherever he ended up, there was one thing he knew; that he'd survive. Which, he thought, breathing in the still night air, was more than Luke Felton and poor Eliso Gelashvili had ever been destined to do.

THE END

ALSO BY PAULINE ROWSON

THE SOLENT MURDER MYSTERIES

Book 1: THE PORTSMOUTH MURDERS
Book 2: THE LANGSTONE HARBOUR MURDERS
Book 3: THE HORSEA MARINA MURDERS
Book 4: THE ROYAL HOTEL MURDERS
Book 5: THE ISLE OF WIGHT MURDERS
Book 6: THE PORTCHESTER CASTLE MURDERS

Thank you for reading this book.

If you enjoyed it please leave feedback on Amazon or Goodreads, and if there is anything we missed or you have a question about, then please get in touch. We appreciate you choosing our book.

Founded in 2014 in Shoreditch, London, we at Joffe Books pride ourselves on our history of innovative publishing. We were thrilled to be shortlisted for Independent Publisher of the Year at the British Book Awards.

www.joffebooks.com

We're very grateful to eagle-eyed readers who take the time to contact us. Please send any errors you find to corrections@joffebooks.com. We'll get them fixed ASAP.

Printed in Great Britain
by Amazon

13369641R00155